PRAISE FOR
I NEVER CALLED HIM PA

"Diane Kane's compelling book *I Never Called Him Pa* follows the life of Ernest, a black veteran in the 1950s. The story takes readers on a journey with Ernest, from riding the rails in box cars to becoming homeless and near death. Ernest's travels eventually bring him to the farm of a grandmother raising her grandson. Here he finds miraculous healing of body and soul that leads him to become an instrument of change in other's lives through laughter and sometimes tears. This incredible story will strengthen your faith to hold on a little while longer."

~Catherine Reed, Author of Fire Goes Out Without Wood

"I would place *I Never Called Him Pa* in historical fiction, but its gentle nostalgia gives it an even broader appeal. Anyone who likes coming-of-age stories, heartfelt stories and a look at social changes might like this."

~Robin Shtulman, Assistant Director, Athol Public Library

"*I Never Called Him Pa* by Diane Kane spans time in a heartwarming Forest Gump style. I had to keep reminding myself that the characters weren't real. I felt as though I knew them—like we were old friends."

~Lynda Francoeur, Retired Educator

Set in the 1950s, *I Never Called Him Pa* by Diane Kane is a historical fiction novel that encourages readers to live their lives with love, devotion, and respect. Henry was barely five years old when his mother left him for a man or an adventure. His grandmother, whom he called Gram, began taking care of him. Henry never knew his father, so he couldn't quite miss the man. However, he missed his mother almost every single day. His life in the country was largely content, yet there was something missing. That missing piece of the puzzle came in the form of a man named Ernest. When he entered Henry and his Gram's house, he was a man on the verge of dying. Nevertheless, soon, not only did he defeat his illness, he even instilled a new joy and faith in the lives of everyone he met.

~Ankita Shukla, Readers' Favorite

I Never Called Him Pa

I Never Called Him Pa

A novel

Diane Kane

Live Well,
Diane Kane

Kane Publishing
Phillipston, MA

For Milo

Table of Contents

A life well lived—
the difference lies in the words, not the wealth.

Prologue

I always knew Henry was my given name, after Gramp. But up until that day, I had only been called "boy."

I sure hoped I didn't have to wear Gramp's shoes. At Old Man Larson's funeral, I heard someone say something about having big shoes to fill. Gramp's shoes were pretty big, and I wasn't sure I wanted to fill them.

We didn't bring any flowers to throw in Gramp's grave like they did at Old Man Larson's. Gramp wasn't really fond of flowers anyway, so I suspected that was why. After the pastor left, however, Gram pulled out a bundle of sage from her pocket and tossed it in the hole. It seemed an odd choice to me. Gramp did like it in the Thanksgiving stuffing, though.

The two men from town who had dug the hole waited on the edge of the family cemetery, leaning on their shovels and smoking Lucky Strikes. They straightened up when they saw Gram turn to leave. I wanted to stay and watch them fill the hole, but Gram told me to leave the men to their work. I thought it was a good job. People seemed to die a lot.

After Gramp died, it wasn't a whole lot different on the farm, just quieter. Gram said she had no way of getting in touch with Ma.

"She'll find out soon enough," Gram said.

1948

Chapter 1 - The Circus

Ma had left the year before Gramp died. I wasn't quite five when she ran off with a carny man from the traveling circus. I don't think it was the first time she left, but it was the first I remembered.

When the circus set up on the fairgrounds near our farm in Mendota, Illinois, in '48, Gram and Ma brought me to see the animals and the clowns. Gramp didn't come.

There was a big, colorful tent where a tall man in a fancy suit waved his hand and shouted into a megaphone. Ladies in sparkly underwear hung from ropes streaming from the top of the tent, and muscular men in leather skirts stood in cages with pacing lions and tigers. Repeating musical notes rolled and dipped magically in the air with a buzz of excitement. The deep voices of men and the high-pitched screams of babies swelled and faded as we made our way through the crowd. Gram held tight to my sweaty hand.

My eyes focused on the buttons running up the back of Ma's pretty flowered dress as Gram and I walked behind her. Men turned their heads toward her as she strutted through the crowd. Long low whistles followed by, "Hey, good-looking," floated in the air.

Gram stopped at a booth selling pink cotton candy while Ma disappeared into the fold of people. The cotton candy man took a paper tube and twisted the trails of pink clouds around it. My eyes got bigger as the bubble of candy grew. It looked like a beehive when he handed it to me. But it smelled like bubblegum and sugar. It melted in my mouth and stuck to my fingers.

We caught up with Ma in a long row of stalls, where men shouted for people to "step right up." She leaned over the counter of a game booth smiling at a man in a plaid cap—and he smiled back. Gram cleared her throat like she'd swallowed something she didn't care for. Ma turned and gave us a look as though she was surprised to see us there.

"Well, well," said the carny man. "Who do we have here?" His tin voice rang in my ears.

Ma's cheeks flushed red, and she didn't speak. I stretched my neck to see over the counter where white stone bottles stood lined up on posts. The carny held a bunch of small wooden hoops in his hand. He noticed me gazing up at a stuffed tiger on the top shelf.

"That's a beauty, ain't it?" he said, taking the point of his wooden stick to lift and drop it into his waiting hand.

He laughed and stroked the stuffed tiger cradled in his arm. "These are for the rubes—the paying customers," he said.

His dark eyes shifted, and he spoke out of the side of his mouth while reaching under the counter. "Because you're a friend of this pretty lady," he held up a small trinket, "I'll give you a genuine circus tiger keychain."

I stared at it, wondering what I'd do with a keychain. I didn't drive, and Gram didn't even own a car.

"She ain't my friend; she's my Ma—"

Ma interrupted. "Now, boy, you thank the kind man," she said with a tremor in her voice.

My lip quivered, but I stood my ground until Gram tapped me solidly on the back without saying a word.

"Thank you, sir," I said.

"You two don't need to wait for me. I'll catch up," Ma said.

The next day Ma was gone, and I rarely heard her name spoken.

1949

Chapter 2 - Feral No More

Gram took care of me the best she could. There was always something that needed her attention—cooking and laundry to be done, then animals to feed, and the garden needed tending.

But it was Gramp that claimed the most from her. They didn't talk much. Gramp was a man of few words. We ate our meals in silence at the kitchen table with the metal legs and dull gray-and-white Formica top. Gramp sat with his legs wide, boots solid on the linoleum floor. His body bulged over the sides of the worn, red-cushioned chair, cracked in places with white stuffing peeking out. After Gram cleared the plates, Gramp hunched over his glass of watery brown liquid he called his medicine and talked gibberish to himself mostly. At times, his voice got loud. I wasn't sure if he thought Gram couldn't hear him. About that time, Gram would ask me to fetch something for her from the root cellar.

From the outside, the root cellar looked like a hole to nowhere. A creaky wooden door opened to narrow steps leading underground to a dark, damp room smelling of earthworms and vegetables. The temperature dropped as I walked down the stairs. My best friend, Willie Larson, who lived next door, said you could dig a hole to China, and I wondered if this was where it began.

When my eyes adjusted to the dark, I saw the shelves with rows of canning jars and bins of potatoes, carrots, and winter squash—nothing loud and nothing angry like inside the farmhouse.

I never remember Gramp having a job, but I heard Mr. Larson say Gramp used to work with him at the sawmill. "He was a hard worker until the sadness took him over." Mr. Larson never said any more about it.

After Ma left, Gram took a job at the new Del Monte canning company in town to make ends meet, she said. Gramp was home, but I mostly fended for myself while she worked.

My best friend Willie Larson's gramp died in the spring of '49. My gramp said he wasn't going to Old Man Larson's service.

"I've got no use for the man," Gramp said.

I didn't think a dead man was much use to anyone, but Gram said we would go to pay our respects.

Gram ironed my best shirt and trousers for the occasion, and she wore a dress without an apron. There were a lot of prayers and people sobbing in cloth hankies. The pastor said a bunch of nice things about the old man. I never knew he was so important. To me, he was always the old man with yellow eyes who smelled like stale pipe tobacco. But he played checkers with Willie, and my gramp never played with me.

The church was full. Gram and I stood in the back with the other latecomers.

After the service, six strong men, including Willie's father, hoisted the coffin up to carry it to the church cemetery. I could see my reflection on the side of the big, shiny casket as it went by. The whole congregation followed behind.

A gaping hole lay waiting in the church cemetery like a hungry monster with its mouth ready to gobble up the old man. The men lowered the casket on ropes, and the pastor led more prayer. In the end, everyone said, "Amen."

After that, we walked back into the church where tables of food lined the back wall of the gathering room. Gram had brought banana bread in her basket. She took it out and handed it to the church ladies.

We waited in line for Gram to say, "Sorry for your loss," to Willie's pa. I told the same to Willie. He said, "Thanks." I tried to say something to his sister Laurel, but I lost my voice.

We went home without even a bite to eat. Maybe you had to be a regular churchgoer to get the treats.

Gramp died a few months later, in the late summer of '49, right after I turned six years old. I'd never known my gramp to set foot inside the church; maybe that's why he didn't get the full treatment when he died.

There was no church service. Instead, on Gramp's burial day, the pastor came to our family plot on the rise past the barn and recited a psalm.

"It's the twenty-third psalm," Gram said. "He asked for that particular one to be read."

I wondered when he asked and if I should be asking for one for myself.

Gram wore a dark-blue dress with white lace trim. I stood beside her, squirming in my black starched slacks. Gram gave me a nudge. Then, noticing my cowlick, she spat in her palm and ran her hand over my head.

Pastor Morgan looked like he had somewhere else to be. Gram didn't look exactly happy to be there, either. Of course, it was a funeral. I watched with Gram as some men from town lowered Gramp's dull pine coffin into the ground on that rainy August morning; Gram didn't cry, so neither did I.

When Pastor Morgan finished, he closed his Bible smartly and walked over to Gram. He shook Gram's hand and said, "Sorry for your loss." He tousled my hair but didn't say anything to me. Then he up and left.

Gram stood there a minute; then she turned to me. "Well, you're the man of the house now, Henry."

≈

At the end of the summer, when Gram brought me to see Doc Cunningham for my go-to-school check-up, Doc said he was concerned.

"Marg, you can't let the boy run wild like a feral cat," Doc said. "The work at the canning plant is too much for you with raising the boy."

Gram pulled out her crocheted handkerchief from her big blue purse. "We can't get along if I quit my job."

Doc took her hands in his. "Marg, you need to apply for government aid."

Gram looked like she'd taken a fright. "I'm too proud for that."

"Marg, pride goeth before the fall."

I didn't know Doc preached the Bible, but the words put Gram to thinking. Finally, she straightened her back and cleared her throat.

"You're right."

"My secretary, Ellie, is top-notch with paperwork," Doc said. "She can help you fill out the government forms."

The postman began to bring a check every first of the month. Gram stayed home on the farm, and I wasn't feral anymore.

1950

Chapter 3 - Right On Time

The winter of 1950 had been unusually cold and long in northern Illinois. Our house and barn nestled in a slight hollow between the road and the railroad tracks like a nesting bird taking shelter from the weather. By late March, the crocuses poked through the snow that still clung to the shady side of the farmhouse.

One day was like any other day on the farm—until everything changed.

"Henry! Breakfast will be ready soon," Gram shouted as the screen door slammed behind me. "Don't stay too long watching that train. It can get on without you."

I paused on the weathered wooden porch listening for the far-off whistle of the morning train approaching from the west toward our small town of Mendota on its way to the big cities beyond. Gram said Mendota meant "crossing of paths" to the Lakota Indians. I liked to imagine I was part Indian, although I had no reason to think it any more than to believe I was a cowboy. I was never sure what I was since I didn't really look like anyone in my family.

Ma had yellow hair like the wheat fields and just as straight. Gram kept her hair pinned in a bun while light-brown wisps often escaped. Even Gramp's hair, what he had of it, had been lighter than mine.

Thick black unruly hair covered my head and couldn't be tamed. Gram cut it often and short, only to have a stubborn cowlick sprout in the back. My brown eyes matched the dirt that seemed to grow from the ground, unlike their eyes, blue as the sky.

Many train tracks crossed in Mendota, so the name still held true. The fancy Depot Station lay to the north of town, where trains went east to Chicago or south to St. Louis. We never had reason to go there. It meant no mind to me; I preferred to watch the working freight trains that passed our farm.

Billowing puffs of smoke rose in the air like clouds trailing behind the engine. I greeted the seven a.m. train each morning, but that day I hesitated on the top step of the porch. Instead, my ears perked to the sound of a car rumbling to a stop at the head of Gram's long winding driveway. The exchange of voices drifted on the breeze. Finally, a heavy metal door slammed, and the car's tires tossed up rocks as it drove away.

A young woman walked down the driveway swinging a small brown suitcase in her hand. I hadn't seen her in some time, but I knew it was her. The cool breeze lifted thin strands of long straight hair, yellow as the sun. As she got closer, I saw the sun glint off the tiny clear buttons dotting the front of her sky-blue blouse. A bright, multi-colored skirt moved with the rhythm of her walk. I stood stock-still like the statue on the town common.

Ma was near the porch when she caught sight of me. She carefully set her suitcase down.

"Hey, boy, you just going to stand there like a bump on a log or you going to give your mama a hug?"

Her blue eyes sparkled like the fancy new bubbling lights Gram hung on the tree at Christmas. I ran so fast down the porch stairs I nearly fell. Ma caught me in her arms and twirled me around.

"That's my boy."

With my face buried in the crook of her neck, I got lost in the scent of her flowery perfume—all thoughts of the morning train gone from my mind.

Ma used to tell me, "It's French perfume, and the men love it." She bought the little bottle at the Five and Dime. I wasn't sure how it got from France to our Five and Dime in Mendota. And if the men loved it so much, why didn't they go to the Five and Dime and buy it themselves? I never asked.

Now I wondered if there was another Five and Dime where she'd been while she was away. Was there a farm, and a brown cow, I wondered. And was there a little boy who loved her where she stayed when she was gone? I didn't ask those questions, either.

She rummaged through her suitcase until she found a furry stuffed tiger. She dusted it off with her hand and gave it to me.

"I got you a prize from one of the game booths."

I recognized it from the circus the day before she left. I wanted it then, but the carny man thought the plastic keychain would do me fine. I tried to tell her I was too old for the stuffed animal now. But the truth was, I still wanted it.

The screen door slammed behind us. "Welcome home, Janie," Gram said without a stick of emotion. Ma gave me a wet kiss that I was sure left the telltale print of her cherry-red lipstick I wouldn't wash off.

"Run along now, boy."

I glanced at Gram, and she nodded her head. So, I dashed to the barn and hid behind the large swinging door with the wide slats.

I spied between the cracks as they talked, unable to hear their voices. Gram's plain linen dress hung past her knees, and green garden boots covered her feet. She wiped her hands on the corner of her worn apron as she spoke. Ma swayed and crumpled to the ground like a rag doll. Gram must have told her Gramp was gone. Finally, Gram raised her up and dug a hankie out of her pocket to wipe Ma's tears. She must have had memories that made her cry.

≈

The next morning after Ma returned, I smelled the air before opening my eyes. A hint of perfumed flowers and spice tickled my nose. Ma was still there.

All was right in my world as I pulled on my pants and grabbed my flannel shirt off the back of the chair. My bare feet banged on the wide pine boards of the stairs as I struggled to get my arms into my shirt sleeves. I ran through the kitchen, stopping only briefly at the door to shove my feet into my shoes.

The air in the kitchen was thick with the smell of bacon frying in the cast-iron skillet atop Gram's big ole wood-burning cookstove.

"Breakfast will be ready soon, Henry," she yelled.

Ma sat on the top step of the porch, still in her nightgown. I stopped to greet her.

She wore Gram's flannel robe, the white one with the handstitched pink flower on the pocket.

The morning air still had a chill until the sun was full in the sky. Ma pulled the robe snug around her neck with one hand while the other held a long white store-bought cigarette between her two fingers.

Ma's face was pale and her eyes puffy. She kept her fancy face in a small bag with a gold zipper that held bottles and tubes of different colors. She put the cigarette to her colorless lips and sucked in, long and hard. Holding her breath, she squinted her eyes, twisting her body around to look up at me from her seat on the step. She blew out a big cloud of smoke that floated to my nose. I coughed at the smell of dirt and burnt dead leaves.

"Where you off to in such a rush, boy?" Ma asked, picking a piece of tobacco from her tongue. "You look like you're on a mission."

Ma still called me "boy." It didn't bother me any. I called her Ma, but Gram was the one who took care of me. Ma seemed more like a sister to me but not exactly like my friend Willie Larson's sister.

The Larson family lived down the road, and Willie had been my best friend for as long as I could remember. His sister Laurel was the exact same age as him. They're what they called twins, although I could never figure out why.

They weren't the same at all, at least not to me. Willie was big and loud and full of things to say. Laurel was shy and much smaller, too. She looked like she might break if someone touched her too hard. Laurel had a hard time saying certain words, especially the ones with r's and s's. Willie told me she was something called tongue-tied. It sounded painful to me, although it didn't seem to bother Laurel much except when she was trying to speak at school.

Willie said his tongue was in the proper place when they were born; that's why he could talk so much. Laurel was born with her tongue stuck to the bottom of her mouth. So the doctor had to cut it. I covered my mouth to hold back a squeal when Willie told me this.

"The doctor didn't want to cut it too much," Willie said, ignoring my outburst. "You know, that could have made it worse." I could only imagine. "So, it's still a little stuck," Willie explained.

After Willie told the whole tale, I thought it sounded mighty funny, but I never laughed. Some of the kids at school did laugh. Well, that was if Willie wasn't around to set them straight. Willie was known to never back down from a fight. He was a protective brother.

Even though Ma wasn't really my sister, I felt that way about her, too. If anyone hurt her or laughed at her, I'd punch them. But I hadn't had to, so far.

I looked at Ma sitting on the porch step and thought to tell her about Willie and Laurel and tongues that are tied. Or I could have told her about the train, how the engineer blew the whistle and waved to me each morning, or even about the boxcar men. But I wondered if she would care. I didn't know if she remembered the Larsons. And as I recalled from the last time she was home, she never liked the trains much. They woke her up too early, and the coal smoke settled on her clothes hung out on the clothesline. And I didn't want to tell her about the men in boxcars.

It was then that I heard the call of the train whistle in the distance. The approaching sound brought me back to the task at hand. There was no time to sit and talk.

"The train," I said while running down the steps. I took my hat in my hand so as not to lose it in the breeze. I looked back and waved it at Ma. "I have to greet the train."

Pebbles pushed at the worn soles of my brown leather shoes as I ran across the dusty yard. On the rise above the railroad tracks stood the mighty oak tree.

Gram always admired it. "It looks like it's reaching out its limbs to give praise to the sun," she said.

The seven a.m. train was right on time as usual, and so was I. Puffs of smoke floated above the trees as it chugged around the bend into view. All other thoughts faded from my mind.

The long, sad whistle sang out when the train rounded the tracks snaking through the valley. The engineer stood proudly at the controls in his dark-blue cap.

I grabbed my hat and hailed him. Nearing my oak tree post, he gave two more quick pulls on the whistle cord. The men shoveling coal into the furnace knew this was their signal to back off.

Gramp used to say, "The coal men wear the color of their work smeared across their faces."

I well-liked them all, but it was the men in the boxcars I waited to see.

As the train slowed, I watched with butterflies in my stomach to see if the doors of the cars slid open. Men of all shapes, colors, and sizes shaded their eyes and peered into the light. Their clothes were ragged and dirty, and their faces unwashed. Hobos, Gram called them.

"They're hard men of hard times, making their way as best they can," she told me. Most had fought in the war and never went home. "War can change a man," she said. "Sometimes they can't bear to live in houses with mirrors anymore." I thought the big mirror in the hall would have given them a fright.

Gram sometimes left a box of vegetables from the garden down by the tracks, occasionally homemade bread or day-old muffins. She'd leave some tools by the garden gate and the ax near the woodpile. Gram said, "The last thing a good man loses is his pride, and I'm not going to be the one to take it from him."

At first, I wasn't sure what she meant until I saw them grab a hoe and make their way to the garden or lift the ax and head to the woodpile. They walked a bit lighter with a tool in their hands and stood a tad taller. They weeded and tilled the dirt or chopped and stacked wood. Only after they finished did they make their way to the food box. Gram never worried they would take anything not offered.

"Hobos have a code of honor," she said.

"Where do they go when they're not in the boxcars?"

Gram said, "They bed down in camps on the sides of the tracks—until their memories catch up with them. Then they take to the rails again. They know the safe places to exchange a little sweat for a bite of food."

I watched with interest as the men jumped down from the rail cars and headed to the woodpile that day. They took turns chopping and stacking—all except one man. He stayed back at the train sitting in the big sliding door with his back against the frame and his head hung down. But, even sitting, I could see he was mighty big, with bushy hair and ragged clothes. He caught me staring at him, and I raised my hand in greeting. I thought I saw the edges of his mouth lift slightly. He tipped his head. I slowly lowered my hand, never taking my eyes off him. I'd never seen a man that big—or black, for that matter.

I wondered where he came from and where he was going. I wanted to ask him. I had been my whole life on Gram's farm. We went to town and sometimes to church. Once I went to Joliet with Willie and his pa when he needed a tool Mr. Harlow didn't have at the General Store in town. The buildings in the city were tall and close together, and I was glad I didn't live there.

It put me in mind of Ma's travels. Gram said she had stars in her eyes and ants in her pants. The stars sounded nice; still, I didn't much care for the idea of ants in my trousers. I was never sure where Ma went when she was gone. I pictured her at the circus, just in different towns that all kind of looked the same as ours. And I wondered at the sense in it when she could just stay here without the ants in her pants.

After a time, the train whistle blew once, quick and loud, as a warning they were almost done taking on water and would be moving on soon. The men at the woodpile finished up and hurried over to the food box. The last man grabbed a couple of extra day-old biscuits and a small jar of fresh hand-churned butter Gram had thrown in. When he glanced at me, I noticed he was thin and gangly and looked younger than the others. His red hair blazed in the rising sun when he tipped his cap and nodded his head. I did the same in return.

Returning to the train car, he grabbed the ladder on the side and jumped up like a cat onto a shelf. He knelt beside the big, black man and handed him the biscuits and butter. They nodded to each other. The younger man took his hand and helped to hoist him up. The big man looked like it pained him. They stood with their hands together for a moment, saying words I couldn't hear. The train started to roll ever so slowly, and they moved to the inside of the railcar while the other men closed the big sliding door. I watched until the train disappeared around the bend.

I was happy on the farm with Gram, the chickens, the goats, the big sow and her litters, and Old Brown the cow. But if I was ever to leave, I thought I'd go on the train, in the boxcar, not the engine cab, because the men in the boxcars had a code of honor.

Chapter 4 - Louder Than Words

The next day, I stood outside the chicken coop tossing cornmeal to the busy birds, thinking about Ma being home, when the screen door slammed.

Ma slept in and missed breakfast. Gram had filled a plate, covered it, and set it on the shelf over the woodstove. Gram filled the stove every night to keep the chill away. The coals were still red in the morning when she added another log for cooking. Gram was partial to her white Montgomery Ward wood cookstove with two ovens and a shelf on top. She saw no good reason to trade it in for a modern gas one like the Larsons had. Gram used hers for cooking and heating the farmhouse.

"Can't do that with a gas stove," she said.

Gram was in the barn milking the cow. Ma must have found the plate of sausage and eggs because she was picking at her teeth when she came out the door. She sat in the rocking chair on the porch and lit a long white cigarette. She puffed on it, all the while staring in the direction of the family cemetery, her eyes narrowed and stone-cold.

"Morning, Ma," I called to her. She didn't seem to hear me. I followed her gaze and saw it set on Gramp's marker. There was no doubt which one was his because it was bigger than the others that had been there longer than I was alive.

Before he passed, Gramp bought it from the Stoneman. I supposed he knew he would need it someday. Everyone dies, after all. One time, when Gramp spoke loudly to Gram, it was about the stone. Gram mentioned the money might have been better spent on food for the growing boy. I took it that was me since there was no other boy.

Gramp took to talking in his loud voice, saying it was his money and he would spend it how he saw fit. Gram needed a jar of pickles from the root cellar, so she said, and I went to fetch it for her. Before I left, I heard Gram say in a soft voice, "A big stone won't get you a seat closer to the Lord."

I was at the bottom step of the porch when I heard the loud crack of a hand hitting against something soft. I ran to the root cellar and took my time finding the best jar of pickles.

I pushed the memory aside and focused back on Ma sitting in the rocker on the porch. She took one long last pull on her cigarette and walked down the porch stairs with her mind set on something I couldn't see. She tossed the cigarette butt in the dirt as she strutted across the yard.

I turned on my heels to follow her path. While the chickens squawked for more grain, I couldn't take my eyes off Ma. Her arms swung to and fro, cutting through the air like sickles cutting hay. She led with her forehead, her jaw tucked under and set. When she reached Gramp's stone, she stopped and stood a good long time as if she were a stone herself.

Then she lifted her dress and pulled down her drawers. She squatted facing the stone. The feed bowl fell from my hands. The chickens flew up in a flurry before settling back down to feast on the pile of scattered grain on the ground. Ma squatted in front of the stone. My knees buckled, and I went down to the ground like a person at prayer.

After a time, Ma stood and pulled her drawers back up, wiggling a little to set them right. Then she turned and walked back toward the house with a light step. Her dress swayed back and forth, and there was a hint of a smile on her face.

Still kneeling in the dirt and chicken droppings, I looked toward the barn and saw Gram standing with a full milk bucket in her hand. She looked pale, her mouth slightly open like she meant to say something, but her tongue stuck like Laurel's. Gram swayed like the birch trees in the evening breeze, and it crossed my mind she might lose her grip and drop the milk bucket. But her white knuckles proved she had a tight hold on it.

Ma paid no mind to Gram or me as she walked back through the yard and straight up the porch stairs. She was humming a happy tune that I couldn't quite place. I figured she must have had to relieve herself badly. The screen door slammed behind her.

I stood and shuffled among the chickens, searching for the feed bowl. I grabbed it and brushed the muck off. Glancing toward the barn, I saw Gram set the bucket on the ground, raise her head to the sky and fold her hands in prayer. And it wasn't even Sunday.

≈

Easter Sunday came early that April, and we all went to church together since Ma was home.

The Larsons were regular churchgoers. Gram and I were what my best friend Willie called occasional churchgoers. Willie said it didn't matter to him; we could still be best friends.

I heard Gram say her prayers every night, and she taught me to do the same. That Easter Sunday, Gram said she wanted to thank the Lord in his house. She didn't say what for. I thought it might have something to do with eggs.

The chickens had been slow to lay through the winter. That wasn't unusual, but spring had come, and they still weren't giving their full share. One Saturday morning, Gram took her basket and walked down the road to borrow a dozen eggs from Mrs. Larson. Her chickens were laying just fine. They seemed like a happy brood, and I wondered what made some chickens happier than others.

I tagged along with Gram, hoping to spend time with my friend Willie. He always had something to tell me about the way of the world and life in general. I didn't mind seeing his sister Laurel, either, even though she didn't have a lot to say. But that was probably because Willie talked so much.

Gram sure looked embarrassed standing on Mrs. Larson's doorstep with her empty egg basket. Mrs. Larson asked us in and said it was no bother; she had plenty of eggs to spare.

Willie came out of the parlor with Laurel right behind him. "Hey, Henry," he greeted me with a big smile. "*Puppet Playhouse* is on the television!" He grabbed my arm and led me into the big room. Last Christmas, the Larson family had bought a television with the money Mrs. Larson saved from selling eggs and vegetables at a roadside stand at the end of their driveway.

We didn't have a television or a roadside stand to sell things. Any eggs or vegetables we grew we ate, or Gram put up for winter. Willie's pa worked at the sawmill in town, so the money he brought home paid for all the necessities.

"That's why my ma's money is used for extras," Willie explained to me one time when we walked to school. He didn't say it to make me feel bad about not having a pa. Still, it did a little.

Mrs. Larson and Gram went out to the hen house, while I watched Buffalo Bob and Howdy Doody. Willie said Howdy Doody had forty-eight freckles on his face, one for each state in the union. I tried to count Laurel's freckles when she wasn't looking.

Pretty soon, Gram called for me from the yard to say it was time to leave. I said my goodbyes to Willie and Laurel and headed out. Gram thanked Mrs. Larson and told her she would return the favor. Mrs. Larson said, no hurry, and she would pray for our brood.

Mrs. Larson must have been in good standing with the Lord because the next week, our chickens took to laying eggs faster than we could gather them. Gram said it was an Easter miracle.

So, she hard-boiled a dozen eggs and put some food coloring in the water. She hid them around the house on Easter morning, although they weren't too hard to find.

I gathered them up in a bowl and took them to the table. When Ma came downstairs in her pretty Easter dress, we peeled the eggs and ate them with salt for our breakfast.

Then we washed up and got ready to walk to church. Gram checked her hair in the hall mirror on the way out. She gathered a few wispy light strands and re-pinned them in her bun.

When we got to church, I took a seat next to Ma. Gram stopped while making her way down the aisle and took Mrs. Larson's hand. She didn't say anything, but they exchanged a knowing smile.

≈

Gram took Mrs. Larson a dozen eggs and a loaf of her famous banana bread the next day. We stayed for coffee. Well, Gram and Mrs. Larson had coffee. Mrs. Larson served me, Willie, and Laurel tall glasses of milk, and we each had a slice of Gram's banana bread.

I took a big swig of milk and smiled at Laurel nibbling her bread. She cast her eyes down and peeked up at me, lightly wiping her hand across her mouth. I realized I must have been sporting a milk mustache. My face got warm. I glanced over at Willie, who had a white 'stache and a trail of banana breadcrumbs down his shirt. It didn't seem to bother him any. I wiped my mouth with the back of my sleeve and looked back at Laurel. Her big blue eyes twinkled, and she nodded her head in approval.

Chapter 5 - Planting Seeds

The sun warmed the air in May, and the ground thawed, although a chill remained inside the farmhouse.

Ma woke early to the sound of Gram clanging a pot to make the oatmeal. It seemed like a lot of rattling for one pot, but I was up already and happy for the hot bowl of grains topped with raw milk from the cow and honey from the Larsons' bees. It didn't look much to Ma's liking. She hunched over her bowl with her eyes barely open, stirring the sticky mixture around without taking a bite.

It was time to plant the garden. Ma rolled her eyes when Gram mentioned it.

"You know, there are such things as grocery stores in the city," Ma said with a wise twist in her voice. "People go there and buy vegetables, pasteurized milk, and all kinds of things."

"I'm well aware of that, Janie," Gram said, with the same sort of twist to her words. "While you were gone, I worked at the Del Monte plant, gluing covers on the vegetable cans, if you didn't know. Don't you know those vegetables are grown in places just like this farm?"

Ma turned her head away. Her mouth gathered up on one side, making a noise through her nose. She got up from the table, dumped her uneaten oatmeal in the pigs' swill bucket, and noisily put her bowl in the sink. The pigs would be pleased.

Her heavy footsteps echoed as she climbed the stairs to her room and slammed the door. Gram stood at the sink, looking out the window, and dried the dishes.

"Do you think she'll stay?" I asked, looking into my bowl like the fortune-teller I'd seen at the circus gazing into her crystal ball.

Gram put down the dishcloth and turned toward me. I raised my eyes, not my head, to meet her sharp look.

"I don't rightly know, Henry," Gram said. "Your Ma, she's a free spirit. We just have to love her while she's here and pray for her when she's away."

I looked back to my bowl, chasing the last grains onto my spoon. I guessed there was no crystal ball here.

"I can tell you two things for certain," Gram continued, and I raised my chin at this. "I'm not going anywhere, Henry." Her face was stern, yet I took comfort in her words. "And neither are your chores, so get to them."

At that, she turned back to the sink. I went over and hugged her waist, burying my face in the folds of her cotton dress. She didn't smell like fancy perfume that disappeared in the breeze. Instead, she smelled like bacon and soap and things that stayed put, and I knew everything would be all right.

I went to the barn to let Old Brown and her heifer out to pasture. She wasn't really old, but she was brown, and that's what Gram called her. I gave her a pat on the nose.

Her young one came over and stuck her tongue out, twisting it around to lick the remaining oatmeal from my hand. Her tongue was warm and wet and made me laugh.

We never named the heifers because they didn't stay. I thought Gram would sell this one soon, and she wouldn't see her ma again.

Out of the corner of my eye, I saw something move in the hay. I thought it was a mouse until I heard the mewing. I snuck into the pen past Old Brown, and to my surprise, I saw a mangy orange cat lying in the hay with a litter of four kittens stuck to her teats. She looked like she'd been through the wringer-washer and then rolled in the muck. She mewed again and began to pant like Willie Larson's hound dog on a hot July day.

I turned to Old Brown. "I know I ain't your usual milker, but I think that mama cat could sure use a sip of milk." I patted her side. "Do you think you can spare some?"

Old Brown mooed like she knew exactly what I was saying.

I grabbed the steel bucket off the stool and placed it under her udder. Squeezing her teats like I'd seen Gram do a hundred times, I jumped when milk shot out.

At first, my aim wasn't so good, and the white stream shot everywhere except in the bucket. Some drops even landed on the mama cat's face, and she lapped them up.

Finally, I got the stream going into the bucket and gathered a fair amount. "Thanks, Old Brown," I said.

Moving slowly so as not to spook the mother cat and her kittens, I inched closer. Tipping it so the milk puddled on the side, I held out the pail. She gently turned to crouch, her little ones detaching from her belly with sleepy yawns and landing in a pile in the hay. I held the pail still while the mama cat drank heartily.

She'd stop and cast her yellow eyes up to me every so often, and I made soft noises like I'd heard people make to babies needing comforting.

"You're a good mama," I told her, and she purred slowly at first, then faster. Finally, she let me touch her head. Her fur was coarse and stiff, and her eyes runny, but she looked beautiful to me, and I told her so. "We can't have you runnin' wild like some kind of feral cat now, can we?"

She went back and curled up with her litter and fell asleep. This mama wasn't going anywhere.

I could have named the cat Orange or even Cat, but I wanted her to have a special name. Ma said she looked like a drowned rat. Gram said she looked like she'd make a fine mouser. So, I named her Mickey, like the mouse in the cartoon I saw when I went with the Larsons to the matinee at the big theater in Bosen City. Laurel liked Mickey Mouse. I hoped she would like Mickey the cat too.

Mr. Larson said he could use a mouser around his farm, too. When the kittens got old enough to leave their mama, he took one home. Willie and Laurel named it Scooter since it scooted all over. The other kittens went to families around town. The mice in Mendota were in big trouble.

≈

Ma must have had a change of heart about the garden, or she figured she'd better lend a hand if she wanted to eat. Either way, she helped to turn the soil. We owned only two hoes, so Gram used the pitchfork. She usually used it in the barn for the hay, but it worked well in the dirt. In fact, she finished with her section way before Ma and me.

Gram went into the house and left us to it. Ma decided it was an excellent time to take a break and pulled a pack of cigarettes from the pocket of her worn sweater. The sweater was one she'd left behind when she took off with the carny man. I remembered seeing it hanging in her closet when I'd lie on her bed and daydream about where she might be. It looked a little snug on her now, and I wondered if she'd eaten a lot of cotton candy while with the circus. She lit a cigarette and asked if I wanted to try a puff. I blinked with wide eyes, and Ma laughed.

"You're so naïve, boy," she said. It sounded like a foreign word, and I wondered if it was French, like her perfume. "Someday, you'll get old enough to leave this run-down farm and see the world."

She took another puff of her cigarette and blew out the smoke. I didn't tell her I had no longing to see the world. I'd miss the farm if I ever left. I knew she wouldn't understand.

She sighed and looked down at her dirty hands, shaking her head. "Why the hell did I ever come back?"

I could think of a few answers to her question, but I didn't think she really wanted to hear them. I loved the farm, the animals, and the barn with the wooden ladder to the hayloft. I didn't think there was a better farmhouse or a prettier porch anywhere. I didn't understand why she didn't love it, too.

"There's a great big world out there, boy." She threw her cigarette butt in the dirt and took my hands in hers. I saw the stars in her eyes as she gazed over the top of my head, speaking to the sky. "There are buildings that reach the clouds and bright lights line the streets." The corners of her lips curled while she spoke of the memories. "There are clubs where the music is loud, and you can dance all night long."

She started humming a sad song and wrapped her arms around herself, standing and shuffling her feet in Gram's old rubber boots. Her eyes closed, with a soft smile on her face. I started swaying to her singing. I tried to hum along, and she opened her eyes, lips parted like she'd forgotten I was there. She took me into her arms, and we danced—well, she danced, and I hung on tight, stumbling across the tilled dirt. At that moment, I thought the whole world was right and things couldn't get any better.

≈

The garden came up real fine. We already had a good crop of spring asparagus by June, and the broccoli was almost ready. Gram said there were rumors of war beginning in some far-off place called Korea. But all seemed peaceful on the farm.

In late June, when the weather warmed, the man who sold brushes came around. I wondered where he went the rest of the year. Brushes seemed an odd thing to deal in, yet Gram always appeared to need some. He sat in the kitchen chair with his tattered suitcase open and a variety of wares strewn across the table. I stood in the doorway, leaning against the doorjamb, watching his greasy black mustache raise, wiggle, and puff out with the words he spoke.

"The kitchen brush I got last year broke," Gram said to the brush man. "You said they were guaranteed."

"Oh, yes, ma'am, that's right. I don't have that same one anymore, though. This one is bigger and better," he said, pulling a white plastic brush with black bristles from his case like a rabbit from a magician's hat. "Tell you what; I can sell you this one for half price."

Gram inspected the new brush with keen interest.

"That would be nice," she said.

"Well, all right, then. How about a fancy hairbrush for the pretty lady?" he said, winking at Ma.

He waved a brush with a pearl handle like a magic wand. "And it's got a mirror to match," he said, the mirror appearing in his other hand. He grinned out of one side of his mouth, and his gold tooth showed.

Ma looked in the mirror, tilted her head, and smiled.

"Add it in with mine," Gram said. "It's your birthday tomorrow, Janie. That will be your present."

"You ladies are surely good customers. I'll throw in this little fingernail brush for the boy."

He looked at me, and the corner of his greasy black mustache curled up on one side. "You can use it to get the manure out from under your nails," he said, handing me the brush.

I wanted to say I didn't need it; I liked the manure under my fingernails. Gram was watching me, so I said, "Thank you kindly."

I took it out back of the barn and threw it in the hog pen. The big old sow smelled it and snorted. "It's to get the manure out of your nails," I yelled. "You need it more than me."

The next day was June twenty-second, Ma's birthday. That morning I woke and smelled the air. No trace of fancy perfume; Ma was gone.

Gram never said a word about Ma leaving. After supper, she cut two big pieces of chocolate cake with cream frosting, and we ate them in silence. It wasn't as good as I remembered.

Gram put the new brush and mirror on Ma's dresser. She probably wouldn't need them. The brush man could give her another set.

Chapter 6 - It Takes a Man

That summer was hot and dusty. I turned seven years old on July 12. Gram said I was growing like a weed. Ma wasn't there to see it.

One morning Gram had come out on the front porch to call me in for breakfast when I saw one of the hobos—the younger one with red hair—hail her. Gram walked to meet him. He took his dusty cap off and held it in both his hands in front of him. He kicked a few rocks with his odd shoes; his head bowed toward the ground. I saw his lips move, and Gram listened silently. Finally, he turned and began to walk away.

Gram called out, "He can stay in the shed down by the tracks for now. I'll see to him."

I thought I saw a tear roll down the hobo's cheek. He quickly wiped it away. Perhaps it was just sweat; it was a warm day.

After supper, Gram packed up the leftovers in an old cardboard box. She put in some tattered blankets and a jug of water without saying a word. I watched her cross the yard and disappear through some trees toward the tracks.

The following morning after the train departed, I followed the path Gram had taken the evening before. I snuck down to the tracks and to the shed by the roundhouse. I heard heavy breathing and figured the person was sleeping.

I jumped up to peek in the window, hit my head, and said a curse word. Then I saw him, and I almost turned tail and ran.

"That's no way to greet the morning, son."

His voice was quiet and friendly, but his face was hard. I remembered seeing him from afar, sitting in the boxcar. Now that I could see him close up, I couldn't take my eyes away from the scar zigzagging like lightning across his cheek. I was too weak in the knees to run.

"I won't harm you, son." He had a voice that put me in mind of chocolate melting.

"That must have hurt," I said, staring at the scar.

He raised his large, dark hand to his face and touched the raised skin as though he'd forgotten it was there. "Not as much when it happened as it did later," he said. "It's funny how sometimes things don't hurt right away. It's when you think about it. It's the thinking that will kill you, son."

He called me son, and I liked it. I knew it was not his blood that ran through my body. I'd been on a farm long enough to know it took a ma and a pa. I'd never met the flesh-and-blood man I sprouted from, but I knew it wasn't this man. He was as brown as the dirt in Gram's garden and almost as big as Old Brown's two-year-old heifer. Tight curly knots of dusty black hair clung tightly to his head and glistened with tiny droplets of moisture.

He said his name was Ernest. I took to spending time with him, and I liked it. I got up a little earlier each morning to get a head start on my chores after the seven a.m. train came through.

To tell the truth, I missed the train a few times, and Gram was right; it got on without me.

For a big man, Ernest wasn't real strong. He had a hard time moving, and he slept a lot. Gram said he had a blood disease that people of color get. I didn't ask her why a person's color makes them sick. It didn't seem right.

Sometimes, I saw the red-headed hobo stop by the shed before returning to the boxcar. I wondered if he was related to Ernest, although he didn't look like him at all. His skin was fair, like the shell of a chicken egg. He was lean, and there was a skip to his step. His big toothy smile came easily, given like a gift you didn't know you needed.

≈

After supper, I cleaned up while Gram packed up a basket of leftovers for me to take to Ernest. Sometimes I'd hide my biscuit in my pocket to add to the basket on the way to the tracks.

Mickey, the orange cat, followed me. Sometimes she settled in Ernest's lap and purred while he petted her and told his tales. At first, he spoke about his travels across the country and his brothers in the boxcars. One of the travelers kept an opossum for a companion, Ernest told me.

"He kept that varmint on a leash with him all the time, and let me tell you, no one ever went near him, or his belongs."

I wouldn't have believed it if Willie had told me the story, but Ernest never lied.

He said the hobos found empty railcars and collected discarded items, hay bales, and old mattresses to sleep on.

"People toss away all sorts of things near the tracks," he said. "A man can collect most everything he needs to get by."

It didn't sound like a home to me, but Ernest said home is where you lay your head. I was glad I laid my head in my bedroom on Gram's farm.

I asked him if the red-haired man was his brother.

"Shamus?" he asked with surprise. "No, not by blood," he said. "But sometimes the bonds that connect us aren't in our veins but in our hearts."

Gram said Ernest's disease was called sickle cell. I asked Ernest what a sickle cell was. "It means my blood cells aren't exactly round like they should be. The Army doctors said mine are shaped like crescent moons. So, they get stuck on each other." He held his hand out, and it tremored. "It's gotten worse over the years; there are times it affects my whole body. I still have some better days, but they're numbered." He shrugged.

I wondered what number.

As the days went on, Ernest seemed to sleep less and slowly get a little stronger. One evening, Mickey curled up on my lap while we listened to Ernest's stories, and I fell asleep to Mickey's purring and the sound of Ernest's warm voice.

I felt him scoop me up to take me back to the farmhouse. His bones cracked and creaked. I felt bad letting him carry me home, but I loved the feel of his strong arms holding me.

"Pay no mind to those complaining bones of mine. It does me good to do some lifting," he whispered. "You're no burden, son."

He passed me into Gram's waiting arms and headed back to the shed.

I visited Ernest often, and Gram seemed to approve. He became the closest to a pa I'd ever known. I thought to call him just that. I came close, but the word never passed my lips.

"Someone needs to teach you how to be a man," Gram said. "God surely works in mysterious ways."

I wondered what Gram meant. I didn't ask her. Gram didn't talk much about God. That's not to say she didn't believe in God; she just didn't feel the need to make a fuss about Him.

Ernest spoke about God as though he knew the Bible as well as Pastor Morgan. And I liked Ernest's preaching a whole lot better. When Ernest told the Bible tales from memory, I felt like I was walking with a man called Moses across the deserts of Egypt.

After a while, Ernest began to tell me stories of the places he traveled to in the war. He said it was a world war and hoped it would be the last. I told him the news Gram had read about the Korean War. He shook his head. "Governments fight wars; men struggle to survive." He looked like he had struggled more than some.

Ernest said he went to the South Pacific in the World War and called the places he saw "exotic." I didn't know what that meant.

"The flowers were as big as my head and as colorful as a whole box of crayons," he said. "They smelled like perfume and honey."

"I wish I could smell them."

"I reckon you ain't missing much. Nothing smells as good as your Gram's warm apple pie on the evening breeze." He sniffed the air. "The sweetest things on earth aren't far from your doorstep, son."

I thought Ernest knew everything—everything important, that is.

One day, I brought along my Dick and Jane early reader from school to show him. I couldn't read all the words yet, but I thought he would like it. Ernest turned the pages just long enough to look at the pictures. He told me it was real fine.

"Don't you want to read it?" I asked.

He took a deep breath. "The truth is, son, I never learned to read very well. I'd probably make a lot of mistakes," he said with concern. "I'm a better storyteller."

"I can teach you."

He laughed, deep and echoing like the summer thunder in the distance. "I'm a might old to be learning new tricks."

"No, you aren't," I said. "Look here, see this word; 'run.'"

Ernest got close beside me, and our heads touched as we looked at the words on the page. His hair was bristly like one of those scrub brushes Gram bought from the brush man. But it wasn't like those brushes at all. Ernest's hair smelled like campfires, and hay, and things that made me feel safe.

Mickey rubbed her head against my arm as I put my finger to each word and read them out loud. Ernest read some of the sentences with me. I liked reading with Ernest. It became one of my favorite things to do. He seemed to like it, too.

As Ernest got stronger, we had work to do. Gram had nursed Ernest real well, and he looked a lot better than when his friend Shamus first left him in Gram's care. Ernest thanked the good Lord and Gram. Gram said it wasn't no miracle.

"A man needs to eat meat and fresh vegetables to feed his body and soul," she said.

"Amen, ma'am."

The nights got cooler, so Gram told Ernest to move up to the barn and make his bed in the tack room. It wasn't as comfy as my bedroom, but it was better than the railroad shed.

The tack room had four sturdy walls to keep the weather out. When Gramp was alive, he set it up as though he lived there, and sometimes I had the feeling he did. There was even a small cast-iron woodstove Gramp sat next to when smoking his stogies. Gram gave Ernest some extra warm blankets, and he said it was right homey.

"Better than the hard floor of the boxcars and not as breezy," Ernest said.

"A body ain't meant to sleep on wooden floors in cold train cars," Gram said. "A body needs a home."

Gram invited Ernest in to take his meals with us. I watched Ernest closely the first time he came into the farmhouse. He looked a little nervous and didn't look directly into the hall mirror.

I knew Ernest had a small mirror he shaved by. Maybe it was just house mirrors hobos didn't take to, as Gram said.

Gram told Ernest to sit in the chair Ma sat in when she was home. She wasn't there to know, anyway.

Sometimes Ernest still got up from his meal slow and stiff, and his bones cracked like branches in the wind. Gram gave him a look of concern, and he smiled a grin that looked a little sad and mostly grateful.

"It's just the Lord's way of telling me I've lived a good long life," Ernest said and went about his chores.

Chapter 7 - Amazing Grace

The white paint on the outside of the Congregational church in town curled and peeled. The big old bell in the steeple rang true and clear each day at noon and Sunday mornings.

Gram said we were Congregational because we didn't have time to be Catholic. I wondered why Catholics had to put so much work into it. Gram didn't say. I figured they wanted to be good at it.

On Sunday mornings, metal clanging on metal echoed across the town. "Calling all the sinners," Gram said when she heard it. We didn't always go. I guessed we didn't have many sins.

That didn't stop the preacher from coming to visit us. He usually stopped by on the first Sunday of the month, right around suppertime. It happened to be the same day each month that Gram killed a chicken and cooked it.

Usually, the unlucky chicken was the one laying the fewest eggs that month. I wondered if the other chickens knew. Luckily, we always had chicks growing to take their place. I think the chickens must have figured it out, though.

Gram gathered fresh vegetables from the garden in season. In the winter, she went to the root cellar and picked a couple of jars from the shelf. Then, she made thick greasy gravy, and we'd have a grand old feast.

Right around five o'clock, Gram said, "Go let the preacher in, Henry."

"Gram, no one knocked."

"Preachers don't knock; they just appear."

Sure enough, Gram was right. Every month Pastor Morgan turned up on our porch just like magic.

He took off his long, dark coat smelling of mothballs and his black bowler hat. "Good man," he said when I gathered them up and hung them on the coat pole. Of course, I always checked his hat for rabbits. I only found lint.

When the pastor came to the door on the first Sunday in September, he got a big surprise. Ernest opened the door, and Pastor Morgan nearly fainted. Ernest caught him before he hit the dusty porch boards. Gram hurried for a glass of cold water and a damp cloth. I helped Ernest settle the pastor in a sturdy chair in the kitchen.

No one said a word while the pastor took a long drink of water and put the cloth to his brow.

"God Almighty," he finally shouted and took another long drink. "What in blue blazes?" He paused for another sip. "This isn't proper, Marg."

"Well, Silas," Gram said. She always called the pastor by his first name, and I wasn't sure if that was proper. Gram didn't seem to care. "I don't recall anyone asking your opinion," she said.

"There will be talk."

"So be it." Gram stood over him with her hands on her hips. "Now, do you plan on staying for supper or not?"

The smell of juicy baked chicken and fresh squash floated in the air. Talk or no talk, the pastor wasn't going anywhere.

"Silas Morgan, this is the man who saved you from blood-staining the floorboards of my front porch," Gram said. "You can say your thanks to Ernest."

Ernest stood silent with his hands clasped behind his back, waiting while the preacher processed his thoughts.

"Are you a Christian man?"

"Yes, sir," Ernest answered. "Born and baptized."

The preacher shuffled his shoes on the wide pine boards. He raised his face to the ceiling, and I looked up, too.

"Thanks be to God, then," he said. "Now, I've worked up a mighty appetite."

Gram set four plates at the table. The preacher pulled out his usual chair and sat without a word. I'd never seen the preacher when he didn't have something to say. It was Ernest who broke the silence.

"Would it be all right if I say the grace?"

Pastor Morgan's eyebrows shot up, and his eyes near bugged out.

"That would be nice, Ernest," Gram said.

"When I was in Fiji in the war, it was the first time I'd ever seen a native Polynesian," Ernest said. "They looked different, and I didn't know what to make of them. My squad had been traveling with no rations for days, and we were hungry," Ernest continued. "The natives invited us to share their food, and we were thankful. This is the prayer they said in English so we could understand."

"Thank God for this food," he recited. "We share it with all who are hungry, even if they don't look like us. Amen."

The pastor nodded his head and said, "Amen."

The kitchen came to life with the clinking of utensils on the plates. The pastor asked Ernest about the South Pacific religions. Ernest told him about the missionaries and their work there.

After we emptied our plates and Gram got up to clear them, the pastor asked, "Is there a little more for a hungry man of God?"

"Now, Silas, I wouldn't want to be leading you into the sin of gluttony."

Gram had our food all planned out for the week, and it didn't include seconds for the pastor.

"Is that your famous apple pie I smell?" Pastor Morgan asked Gram.

"Flattery won't get you a bigger slice."

"Ain't no sin to speak the truth," Ernest said.

"Amen to that." The pastor smiled.

≈

Ernest kept improving; before long, he could chop wood for the stove and carry bales of hay to the barn. Gram was sure thankful. She didn't have to struggle with those chores anymore or hire the Harlow boys to help. And I liked working with Ernest.

It was good for everyone, except the Harlow boys. They weren't too pleased when they came around looking for work and saw Ernest hoisting up the ax to split a log.

They both stopped in their tracks and stood with their

mouths open. Butch Harlow hiked up his pants until the top of his white socks showed. His older brother Little Allan spat on the ground.

"Morning, gentlemen," Ernest said, setting down the ax. "What can I do for you this fine morning?"

Butch laughed out loud like something was real funny.

"You can't help us at all," Little Allan sneered. "We're here to see Mrs. Adams."

The screen door slammed, and Gram stood on the porch with her hands on her hips. "Morning, boys," she said, giving them a stern look. "I see you've met Ernest."

They both did a little shuffling and made noises that didn't sound like anything in particular.

Butch spoke up. "We came by to do some work for you, Mrs. Adams."

"That's right kind of you, boys. As you can see, Ernest is helping with the chores now." She paused a moment before she continued. "If you would like to give him a hand, I can pay you half what I usually give you."

The look on their faces put me in the mind of the raccoons that came by looking for scraps. Gram shooed those critters away with the broom, and they gave her a look that was a bit of fear and a pile of insult.

"We got other things to do," Little Allan said and turned his back to us. Butch stood with a blank look on his face until Little Allan reached back and grabbed his arm. "Come on. Let's get out of here."

Ernest glanced at Gram standing on the porch, watching the Harlow brothers leave. The boys mumbled, and I thought I heard some curse words. Smacking each other in the arms, they broke into a trot and raced up the driveway.

"Maybe the boys need the money, ma'am," Ernest said. "I hate to be the reason their family is burdened."

"Don't worry none, Ernest. They'll be fine," Gram said, still eyeing them. "Their daddy owns Harlow's General Store, and their ma sews on the side. Those boys spend all their money on smokes and beer when they can." She wiped her hands across her apron. "And they charge me more than they're worth."

"Well, I best earn my keep if I want to partake in whatever smells so good coming from your kitchen, ma'am."

Gram smiled more since Ernest came to stay with us. In fact, I couldn't remember her ever smiling before.

"Well, Henry, you could certainly learn some manners from Ernest and appreciate your old Gram's cooking a little more."

Ernest looked down at me in surprise. "Well, I declare, son," he said. "You don't know how lucky you are to have a Gram who cooks so fine until you eat Army rations for a couple of years." He paused. "I hope you never have to."

That was my hope as well. I didn't think I'd take to rations. The word put me in mind of last spring when I got a rash after playing in the milkweed near the swamp. Gram lathered me up with calamine lotion, but it still itched for weeks. But then, maybe rations were what made Ernest grow so big. Still, that was not a chance I wanted to take.

We didn't see the Harlow brothers again for a while, but we did get a visit from their ma the next day.

I was mixing the pig slop when Mrs. Harlow came tromping down the driveway. She paid no mind to me, marched up the porch steps, and pounded solidly on the screen door. I didn't see the need as she could have just shouted to Gram, who was in the kitchen making lunch.

"Afternoon, Marg," Mrs. Harlow greeted Gram with narrowed eyes through the screen door. "My husband sent me to deliver this invoice."

Gram opened the door and came out on the porch, not inviting Mrs. Harlow in for coffee. Mrs. Harlow held out a sheet of paper toward Gram.

"Good day to you, Edna," Gram said, although I think it would have sounded the same if she wished Mrs. Harlow ill health. "What's this about?" Gram said, taking the paper from Mrs. Harlow.

"Big Allan said your tab is a bit high, and he can't in good conscience let you add any more to it until you even it up."

"Good conscience, is it?" Gram pondered while looking over the invoice.

"Yes, he said he doesn't want to see you get yourself in too deep so as to struggle to pay your bills."

"Well," Gram took her sight from the paper in her hand and set her eyes on Mrs. Harlow. "That's right kind of Mr. Harlow. You tell him that I thank him for his concern."

"I will," Mrs. Harlow said curtly and didn't make a move.

Gram didn't seem in a hurry to leave her ground, either. That was when Ernest appeared from the barn carrying a full milk bucket and humming. I'd heard him sing the words to this particular tune on other occasions. It went something to the effect of being lost, then found. Ernest had a pleasant singing voice for such songs and knew many of them.

Then I noticed that I didn't hear a sound, not Ernest humming, not even the birds singing.

"This is Ernest," Gram said as a way of introduction. "Ernest, meet Mrs. Harlow. You met her fine sons yesterday." Gram threw that fact in at the end for good measure.

"Afternoon, ma'am," Ernest said, casting his gaze to the ground.

"Humph." Mrs. Harlow made a noise I might have thought came from a pig had I not seen her mouth move. "I heard you got a bum to do your side work."

"Well, that ain't entirely true," Gram said each word as though Mrs. Harlow needed a little time to understand. "Ernest is no bum."

"I meant homeless," Mrs. Harlow snapped back.

"Ernest isn't homeless, either," Gram said, like explaining to a child. "Ernest lives here on my property. This is his home."

Gram's words had the effect of a whip. Mrs. Harlow's head snapped around to face Gram. The color in her cheeks went as red as a cardinal but not as pleasing.

"You're looking for trouble," Mrs. Harlow said.

"If you don't have any more to say, Edna," Gram said between gritted teeth. "I'll ask you to take your leave."

Mrs. Harlow stepped back as if Gram had slapped her hard across the face.

"Ernest, your lunch is ready whenever you want to clean up and come inside," Gram said, turning around and never giving Mrs. Harlow another glance.

"Well, I never—!" Mrs. Harlow said and turned to leave, stumbling a bit down the porch steps in her haste. She stomped by Ernest, giving him a sideward glance, and another pig sound escaped her lips.

Ernest waited until she went by him and turned to watch her leave the way she came. I heard him singing some words to himself that spoke of amazing grace.

At lunch, Gram set Ernest's plate at the seat Gramp used to occupy. She didn't say it used to be Gramp's chair. Ernest seemed to know because I saw him hesitate. Gram pulled the chair out and, in no uncertain terms, told him to sit. And when Gram spoke in no uncertain terms, a person was inclined to listen.

So, Ernest sat and said, "Thank you kindly."

Gram poured us each a tall glass of lemonade with ice. We ate tomato sandwiches made from the second crop of tomatoes, still a little green on the edges and smelling like summer sunshine. I sunk my teeth into the soft bread and felt the juice flow over my tongue.

Ernest paused between bites and wiped his mouth on the napkin Gram had placed beside his plate. "I don't think that's the end of it," Ernest said without further explanation.

"No, I suppose it isn't," Gram said and took a sip of her lemonade. "We'll just cross that bridge when we get to it."

The only bridge close by was over the creek past Willie Larson's house. I made a note in my mind never to cross it. We finished our sandwiches and went about our afternoon chores.

Chapter 8 - O Christmas Tree

Autumn came and went without much ruckus. We harvested the garden, and Gram did a bunch of canning. Ernest cut the wood, and I helped to stack it.

"I think my muscles are getting bigger," I said, poking my upper arm.

"I do declare, I think you're right." Ernest squinted his brown eyes, and the corners of his mouth creased.

The first snow fell the second week in December, and I went with Ernest searching for a Christmas tree. Our neighbor, Mr. Larson, had a bunch of evergreens on his land. He cut one for us last year and brought it over. Willie had said his dad felt sorry for us since we had no man around to help.

Now Ernest was on the farm, and he was good at chopping wood. Mr. Larson said we were welcome to cut our own tree this year. As it turned out, Ernest wasn't good at picking Christmas trees. I got the feeling he didn't have much practice.

"How's this one look?" Ernest asked me.

I twisted my mouth and shook my head. "It's not the right kind of tree," I said. "We need the kind with short, hard needles."

"Oh." Ernest mulled this over.

"Didn't you ever have a Christmas tree before?" I asked.

"Well, yes." he rubbed the short bristly whiskers on his chin, and I noticed the scar on his cheek was pale pink from the cold. "As I recall, we weren't picky as to the type as long as it was green."

"Gram thinks it's kind of a big deal," I said, as though it was all that mattered—and it was.

"Well, maybe this one?" He pointed out a tree of the right kind, but something was off about it. I squinted my eyes and tilted my head. It still looked crooked. "I don't know, sir," I said. "We usually get a straight one."

"Huh," Ernest said, titled his head, and looked it over with puzzlement. "Maybe you should pick."

I thought that was a fine idea and searched for the perfect tree. "Aha, here it is!" I yelled to Ernest, who had fallen behind in the snow. He lumbered through the drifts with the saw in his hand, putting me in mind of my picture book, *The Legend of Paul Bunyan.* I put my hand over my mouth so I didn't laugh.

"What ails you, son?"

"Nothing," I said, swallowing my laugh. I couldn't wait to tell Willie Larson. He had the same book.

Ernest eyed my choice up and down and said, "That's a fine-looking tree, son. Shall I commence cutting?"

"Yes, sir!"

Ernest pushed away some snow with his hands and slipped under the tree on his back. I smelled the strong scent of sap as soon as he started sawing. The rhythm of the saw cutting through the tree's base sounded almost like the creaking of Gram's rocking chair on the porch.

"Oh, no," I shouted, remembering a rule of Christmas tree cutting.

"What is it, son?" Ernest stopped cutting and bumped his head on the bottom bough of the tree.

"You need to make sure the stump is long enough to fit in Gram's Christmas tree holder," I said. "It goes into the bowl at the bottom where we put the water."

Ernest peeked out from under the tree with big brown eyes. "I know that much, son."

"Good." I nodded once and stuck my chin out by way of letting him know to keep cutting—and he made short work of it.

The tree toppled over, exposing Ernest lying on the ground covered in snow with pine needles sticking out of the tight curls of his hair. He stood up, brushing his pants off and picking at his head. He caught me laughing at him and began laughing, too. I couldn't ever remember my gramp laughing, and I wondered why.

"Let's get this beauty back to the farm," Ernest said, with laughter still echoing in his barrel chest.

He picked up the tree's stump with one hand, which I could see was plenty long enough. His other hand held the saw, and I walked beside him with a warm feeling I thought might be from the hot oatmeal I'd had for breakfast.

Ernest started to sing "O Christmas Tree" in his deep, smooth voice. I joined in as best I could, not knowing the words as well as Ernest.

He didn't seem to mind.

Gram must have heard our voices coming through the woods. When we came into the yard, she was standing on the porch with a big smile, and her brown sweater pulled tight around her. She must have liked the looks of the tree.

"Well, look at the two of you," she said. I couldn't look at Ernest and myself at the same time, so I just let her do the looking. She took a handkerchief out of her pocket and put it to her face. She made a slight coughing noise and wiped her nose. I hoped she wasn't catching a cold. Who would cook our Christmas meal? I may have taught Ernest how to pick out a good Christmas tree, but I didn't know much about cooking, and I was willing to bet he didn't, either.

≈

On Christmas Eve, Gram seemed to feel fit. She worked in the kitchen all day humming Christmas tunes. After supper, she mixed up a crust, kneading the flour and butter until smooth and forming it into two equal balls. She took her heavy rolling pin off the shelf and sprinkled the cutting board with flour. Wisps of fine brown hair escaped her bun, and she wiped them from her face with the back of her hand, leaving a touch of flour on her cheek.

I rested my chin on the table, watching her roll the balls into flat circles, moving the rolling pin to keep the dough the perfect size and thickness. Ernest stood behind me and rested his hand on my back.

"The two of you look like a couple of hound dogs waiting for something to fall."

I lifted my head up and back to catch Ernest's eyes.

"Arh-ooo!" I howled like Willie Larson's hound dog.

"Arh-ooo!" Ernest echoed in a low deep reply.

Gram laughed, and it occurred to me she was doing that more often.

After she cut the crusts to fit the large deep-dish pie plate that used to be her grandma's, Gram took the extra dough, sprinkled it with sugar and cinnamon, and rolled it into little pinwheels.

My eyes got big as saucers. "Are those for us to eat tonight?"

She placed them on a cookie sheet, then stuck her hand inside the kitchen cookstove to test the temperature. She seemed satisfied and put the cookie sheet in the oven. "Yes, in about thirty minutes," she said. "After they cook and cool a little."

I was learning to tell time at school, so I kept my eye on the big old clock on the mantel and counted the minutes. The smell of melting sugar and cinnamon filled the farmhouse. When Gram pulled them from the oven, the smell was so powerful I couldn't even smell the Christmas tree anymore.

When I couldn't wait for them to cool any longer, I grabbed one and plopped one in my mouth. "You're going to burn your tongue, Henry," Gram warned.

The warm, flaky crust fell apart in my mouth, letting the sugar and cinnamon drip across my tongue. Its heat tingled my tongue slightly, but it was worth it. I closed my eyes, and a big smile spread across my face. Gram offered some to Ernest.

"I don't mind if I do, ma'am. They seemed to have passed the test."

We sat around the tree and sang Christmas carols. Ernest's deep, low voice mixed with Gram's sweet high notes like hot chocolate sauce on vanilla ice cream. Ernest knew them all, even "Here Comes Santa Claus" by a cowboy named Autry.

Ernest sounded just like Santa when he sang the chorus. After the last verse, about hanging stockings and saying prayers, Gram said that's exactly what time it was for me. I said goodnight to Ernest and hugged Gram.

≈

The next morning, I came downstairs early. Ernest was already stoking the wood cookstove in the kitchen.

There were presents under the tree, and I checked the tags. Ernest and Gram sat in the parlor, and I passed out the gifts, giving Ernest his first. He looked embarrassed.

"Ma'am, you shouldn't have. You've given me more than I deserve already."

"It's not much," Gram said, her blue eyes sparkling. "More of a necessity than an extravagance."

Ernest's lips parted as he opened it. "It's perfect, ma'am." He held up one of Gram's handmade quilts and put it to his cheek. "I ain't never had a blanket so fine."

Gram bowed her head and smiled.

Four more gifts sat under the tree; one from me to Gram, the other three were mine. I tore the paper off the first one. It was a set of Lincoln Logs, just like my friend Willie had.

"Thanks, Gram," I said, hugging her.

I told Gram to open her gift. She took the paper off slow and careful. I'm not sure why.

Her face lit up like Christmas lights when she saw what was inside.

"Henry," Gram said, "when did you make this?"

"Ernest helped me," I said. "Do you like it?"

"I love it!" She held up a hand-carved bird like the blue ones Gram loved to see. Ernest showed me how to stain it with crushed blueberries, which made it look almost real. "Henry, this is lovely," Gram said, and I thought she would cough again.

"Ernest carved the hard parts," I said.

"You did most of it, son."

"And we stained it together!"

"Well," Gram said, holding the bird to her chest. "You both did a fine job."

I looked at Ernest, and his skin looked a slightly redder shade of brown.

I opened my other two gifts, a checkerboard and some comic books. I liked them both and wondered if Ernest played checkers like Willie's gramp used to.

Gram cooked a big spread for supper. That's what Ernest called it. He said, "Ma'am, I've never seen a bigger spread of food except in the mess hall, and that didn't qualify as food."

Gram and I sat in our regular chairs, and Ernest sat at the head of the table.

While he said the grace, I peeked across the table to Ma's empty seat and missed her for a minute. I figured she was having a Christmas meal with her new friend—and I had mine with Ernest and Gram.

We were so stuffed after eating that we sat in the parlor for a while before having dessert. Mickey curled up under the tree, and I played on the floor with my Lincoln Logs while Ernest watched me.

Gram admired her carved bluebird and asked, "Ernest, what did you do for work before going to the war?"

I knew a big war ended around the time I was born. And Ernest had told me many stories about the places he went to during it. I never thought about where he lived or what he'd done before. Now I wondered if he would leave and go back there. I wished Gram hadn't brought it up.

"I'm from the South, ma'am. I'd say 'Bama if I had to be exact. At least that's where I was born."

I'd never heard of it, but Gram nodded her head as though she knew. I hoped it was far away.

"My family were migrant farm laborers. We traveled all over with the picking seasons." His eyes looked far away.

"That must have been a hard life, Ernest, not having one place to call home."

"I never thought much about it," he said. "We traveled together with a group of people; everyone was like family." He smiled a little. "Sort of like the train people. We came from all backgrounds, but in the boxcars, we were family." A slight noise escaped him. "Sometimes, people can test you. I had my share of anger." He paused. "I've learned to look for the good in most and try to stay clear of the rest."

I built my log house and tried to think about what was good in the Harlow brothers. I couldn't think of anything.

"You're a generous soul, Ernest," Gram said, rising to go cut the pie. "Better than me. There are some I can't forgive."

Ernest got up to help her. "I ain't no better at forgiving. Just don't have the strength to continue the fight anymore."

Gram took the blueberry pie down from the shelf over the cookstove, where she'd placed it to keep warm. We picked the berries in the summer, and she canned some to put on pancakes, toast, or in pie on special occasions like this. Ernest and I had borrowed some to make the bluebird blue. Gram hadn't missed them.

"Hmm, mmm, mmm," Ernest mumbled with a mouth full of pie. "Puts me in mind of my mama. Thank you for the memory."

"Do you think you'll ever go back to Alabama, Ernest?" Gram asked, and my stomach clenched. I suspected that was the 'Bama Ernest called his home. He paused for a good long time while he finished chewing, and I couldn't breathe.

"No, ma'am," he said, and I let out a long slow sigh. "There's nothing there for me now. My ma and pa died before the war. The Army seemed like a good place for me," Ernest said. "I would have stayed, too—a place to sleep and three meals a day—it wasn't all bad. But, after the war, the army didn't need us infantry grunts any longer. They were only letting the educated soldiers reenlist. Then my disease began to act up, so that was another reason to let me go."

"Their loss and our gain," Gram said.

I agreed.

Ernest asked me to play a game of checkers before I went to bed.

1951

Chapter 9 - Personal Property

The winter ended abruptly at the end of March in '51. Gram said the cold, windy weather of the first of the month came in like a lion, and that meant it should go out like a lamb.

"Lions have a big roar," Ernest explained. "But they can't keep it up for a whole month. Kind of like people. You just have to wait them out, and they usually blow over."

Early one morning, I lay in bed dreaming about lions and lambs, which brought my mind to thoughts of foxes and chickens. That led to my stomach rumbling, which put me in mind of Gram's chicken stew.

Gram took leftovers from the first-of-the-month Sunday supper, diced them up, and put them in the big iron pot on the stove. She started in the morning before gathering eggs and let them simmer on the stove until after she went out in the afternoon for the cow's second milking. The smell of sweet onions, fresh carrots, and broth thick with fat drifted in the air all day. It was hard to concentrate on anything. Even Mickey, the orange cat, sat on the porch and licked her lips.

I woke from my dream and wiped the drool from my mouth. Opening one eye, I smelled the air. There was no stew cooking, but there was a ruckus in the yard. I ran to my bedroom window and saw Gram and Ernest chasing chickens around the barn, trying to round them up.

They ducked and squatted while the chickens ran circles around them. I jumped into my pants and grabbed my shirt. Sliding my shoes on at the door, I paused on the front porch.

"Henry, get a broom!" Gram shouted.

I grabbed the broom leaning against the railing and made my way into the clucking mess. One of the chickens flew into Ernest's face. He spat out feathers and sneezed. I swept the bird down and chased it toward the coop.

We had managed to get all 'cept one stray hen back in the pen when a high-pitched screech rang out overhead. Ernest and I looked up to see a large red-tail hawk circling the yard. I watched as the bird hovered and set its sights on the lone chicken. It swooped down faster than a freight train and latched onto the chicken's neck.

As the hawk lifted the stunned chicken into the air, a deafening boom echoed over our heads. Redtail feathers littered the sky, and the hawk let out a screech, flying toward the trees. The chicken hurtled to the ground and landed with a sickening thud.

Ernest and I crouched together in the middle of the yard, bird-shot pellets raining down on us. We looked toward the porch where Gram stood, cradling her 12-gauge shotgun.

"Can the two of you pick your jaws up off the ground and fetch that bird?" she asked. "It looks like we're having first-Sunday supper early."

Ernest picked the chicken up by the neck and swung it around once, just in case. His eyes focused on something up the driveway, and I followed his gaze. A shiny black car with a round red bubble light on the roof came slowly down the driveway. Sheriff Fitzpatrick was at the wheel.

I stepped aside to get out of his way, and Gram came down from the porch. The sheriff got out of the car and spoke to Gram, never taking his eyes off Ernest.

"Some trouble going on here, Mrs. Adams?"

"No trouble, Fred," Gram answered politely. "How are May and the kids getting on?"

"Doing just fine," he said between tight lips.

"Give them my—"

"I'm here on official business, Marg." He put his hand to the gun on his right side.

"What business is that, Fred?"

His eyes were boring a hole straight at Ernest. "What was that gunshot?"

"I had to teach a red-tailed hawk a lesson in personal property, that's all," Gram answered in a light tone.

"What about you?" The sheriff challenged Ernest.

"No trouble, sir." Ernest dropped the chicken.

The sheriff undid the strap on his gun. My mouth was dry, and I realized I hadn't ate breakfast yet.

"You know why I'm here," the sheriff said to Ernest.

"No, sir, I rightly don't."

"You were with the boy who almost drowned yesterday—don't say you weren't."

Ernest stood silent. His mouth twitched, but no words came out. The sheriff grasped the handle of his gun. My stomach started to rumble.

"Are you going to come along with me easy?"

Gram clicked the 12-gauge shut. "What's the meaning of this, Fred?"

"Marg, stay out of this." The sheriff never took his eyes off Ernest. "Mr. Larson found his son out by the creek near Little Vermilion River yesterday afternoon," he said. "He was soaking wet and near drowned. He's in a stupor, only woke once to cry and rant about a black man."

Gram lowered the shotgun.

"Ernest doesn't have anything to do with that."

"He's the only black man in at least fifty miles."

Ernest walked toward the sheriff. "It's all right, Mrs. Adams. I'll just take a ride with the sheriff."

"But Ernest—" Gram said.

"Don't you fret now, ma'am."

The sheriff snapped the handcuffs on Ernest and closed them tight. Ernest had a hard time getting into the back seat, so the sheriff gave him a shove.

I always thought I wanted to ride in a police car. Now I decided I didn't.

Gram watched the shiny black car reach the top of the driveway and turn right toward town. The 12-gauge slowly slid from her arms, and the butt hit the ground with a thud. She walked toward me, dragging the shotgun, and bent to pick up the dead chicken.

"You best get to your chores," she said, looking me straight in the eyes. "Ain't nobody going to do them for you."

She marched into the house with the chicken dangling by her side.

Gram cooked the chicken just like she did every first Sunday of the month, with fresh vegetables and greasy gravy, but it didn't taste the same, maybe because it was Thursday.

≈

The next day, I walked to school by myself. Willie and I usually walked together. We'd meet at the top of Gram's driveway by the mailbox. If I got there first, I'd wait for him. His sister Laurel came, too, and she walked behind us. I looked back at her sometimes. She'd smile a little, and I'd smile back. Then Willie would smack me in the shoulder. "What do you think you're doing," Willie would say. "Don't be smiling at my sister. She ain't some kind of stray cat needing attention."

I knew Willie cared for his sister. He would pound anyone who troubled her. But sometimes I felt sorry for Laurel. Girls didn't get to roughhouse and play like boys. They didn't seem to have much fun at all. Maybe that's why Ma ran off.

With Willie in the hospital, Laurel didn't come to school, either. I waited a bit at the mailbox, but she didn't show up. I wondered if she was mad at me. No one talked to me when I got to school, which was fine because I didn't have anything to say.

The teacher, Miss Bishop, told everyone to hush up; she had something important to say. "You probably have all heard about what happened to Willie Larson," she said. "I want us to pray for him and his family and pray God will punish the terrible man who hurt poor Willie."

At supper that night, I told Gram what Miss Bishop said. Gram didn't say anything. I asked if Ernest was ever coming back. She didn't answer that, either.

I went to bed with an ache in my belly.

≈

On Sunday morning, we had eggs and griddle cakes for breakfast. When I finished and put my plate in the sink, Gram said, "Get your good shirt and pants on, Henry; we're going to church."

"Why?" I asked.

"Sometimes you need to talk to the Lord in person," she said. "This is one of those times."

Gram wore a dark-blue dress with white trim. I'd only seen her wear it at Gramp's funeral. When we got there, everyone was standing and singing "Rock of Ages."

Gram clutched her big blue purse, and we walked down the central aisle to the front pew. Each row of people we passed turned to watch us. Gram kept her head held high. When we reached the front row, she glanced at the people sitting there. There was a long pause before they scooted over to make room for us.

The singing stopped, and Preacher Morgan stepped up to the podium. He tipped his head to Gram. I didn't see her return the nod. Taking a deep breath, the pastor bowed his head and asked the Lord to look kindly on the Larson family and heal young Willie. Then he proceeded to give a rousing talk about the act of forgiveness and how the Lord forgives us all. There was a lot of squirming going on in the pews.

When the preacher finished, he called on the people to offer their prayers for people in need. It was slow to start. Finally, Mr. Harlow from the general store cleared his throat and asked we pray for good weather for the farmers to plant their crops. I figured he was really asking the Lord to see to it he sold lots of seeds and supplies at his store.

Widow Stone asked for prayers for her son, who lived in St. Louis and had the gout. She said St. Louis louder than she said gout, like that was the important part. Other people joined in with all sorts of needs. Finally, Gram stood, and everyone hushed up.

"Dear Lord," she began with her eyes straight ahead, focused on the cross hanging behind the altar. "I've come to your house so you can hear me loud and clear." There were some gasps in the crowd. "You know me to be an honest woman, and I know you to be a fair God. You don't judge people by the color of their skin but by the goodness of their hearts."

Gram turned to face the people in the pews. They all bowed their heads quickly. "I know Ernest to be a decent man of good morals. I pray that the righteous people of this town follow your lead, God, and reserve their judgment for the facts. Amen."

I heard a lot of mumbled, "Amens."

Gram held her hand for me, and we marched back down the center aisle and out the peeling white double doors. I didn't think the service was done, but Gram must have figured all the important stuff was over.

Chapter 10 - In the Eye of a Pig

The long, slow whistle of the seven a.m. train woke me. I hoped to meet up with Shamus, the red-headed hobo, and tell him about Ernest. I dressed quickly and went downstairs only to find a cold, empty kitchen—no smell of bacon cooking, no Gram.

From the porch, I surveyed the empty yard. Following soft squeaking noises coming from behind the barn, I rounded the corner and saw Gram sitting in the pigsty on a pile of straw, and all thoughts of the train and the traveler left my mind.

Wisps of hair, fallen from her pinned bun, hung around her face. Her tired eyes looked up at me, and she smiled. The fat sow lay next to her with a litter of shiny piglets latched onto her teats.

"I came out last night to check on the sow, and she was in labor," Gram said. "I could tell she was having a tough time of it."

The big mama lay still on her side with a rowdy bunch of piglets fighting for the best teats.

"Is she alright?" I asked.

"Yes, she's fine now," Gram said. "She sure had me worried, though. Usually, those little piglets shoot out like slippery bars of soap every few minutes. But instead, she was taking a good half hour between births."

I inspected the litter. There were twelve tiny pink babes.

"They've got black spots," I said.

"That damn sow must have gotten into it with the Hampshire boar down the road when she got loose four months ago."

Little squeaking noises came from Gram's lap. I moved closer to see a tiny ball of black tucked in the folds of her dirty apron.

I gently stroked the fine dark hair on its back, and it wiggled. "It's smaller than the others."

"It's the runt of the litter," Gram said. "I didn't think it would survive. It took so long to come out, it was near dead, and the sow doesn't have enough teats for it."

The little guy screeched for his mama. She didn't take notice.

"What will you do, Gram?"

"Sometimes nature takes a course that seems cruel."

I looked at her, and she drew a deep breath.

"God gives us choices," she sighed.

She untied her apron in the back and gathered up the pig in it. "This pig will die without a mama."

I sucked in my lower lip as she stood up.

"Sometimes it's not the ma you're born to that does the raising. It's a lot of work, mind you. But do you want to be this pig's mama, Henry?"

My eyes got big, and I sucked back the tears welling up.

"Yes, ma'am! I'm going to be the finest pig mama there ever was."

She gently set the apron in my arms, and the little pig peeked out of the folds. I unwrapped the squirming piglet and held him up.

"He's almost all black." I snuggled the shiny bundle to my cheek. He wasn't any heavier than a couple of freshly laid eggs.

"Well, if a pig is going to come live in our house, he'll need a name."

"I'm naming him Ernest," I said. "Ernest Pig, just so there's no—you know—so there's no confusion."

Gram thought it was a good name. We made a bed for Ernest Pig next to the woodstove to keep him warm.

Gram took a half-pint mason jar and filled it with milk fresh from the goat.

"We're lucky that Hope just gave birth. Her milk has all the important ingredients this little pig needs," Gram said. "Without it, he'd be sure to die."

Gram had named the old billy goat "Gruff." She told me the story about the troll under the bridge, and I was sure our Gruff could scare him off just as well. Our mama goat was named Hope. Whenever things seemed to be going wrong, Gram would say, "Well, we still have Hope."

Gram tied a clean cotton rag to the top of the mason jar. She showed me how to tip the jar slowly, letting milk soak into the rag, and Ernest Pig sucked it like a mama's teat. I was thankful for Hope.

≈

Since Sheriff Fitzpatrick took Ernest away, Gram wrung her hands a lot and made noises that came from deep in her chest.

They bubbled up and snuck out, sort of like Mr. Larson's farts, but they didn't smell.

I kept busy with chores and tending to Ernest Pig. Every time I went outside, I glanced up the driveway, hoping to see the sheriff's car enter with Ernest sitting in the front seat, smiling. At night I'd dream it, and in the morning, I pounded the pillow with my fist 'cause I knew it wasn't true.

When I fed Ernest Pig, I told him stories about his namesake. "It's a fine man you're named for," I said. Ernest Pig's little curling tail wiggled, and I knew he understood. "Everything is going to be okay," I promised him. "The judge will see the truth, and Ernest will come home." Of course, I didn't let on to Ernest Pig, but I wasn't all that sure it was true.

Gram said there would be a trial. "That's when a bunch of pious people sits in judgment of someone they don't know," she explained.

I wasn't sure what pious meant. I'd never seen the word in Dick and Jane. However, I had heard the word judgment at church. As I remember, it didn't work out too well for the man named Jesus. I hoped the pious people in Ernest's trial were kinder.

Gram visited Ernest in jail. She said it was no place for me, and I thought it was no place for her or Ernest, either. She brought him a bowl of stew and a thick slice of homemade oatmeal bread. "God knows what they are feeding that man," Gram said.

I heard tell of men in jail eating rats and bugs. Willie Larson had told me he saw it on television.

I wished Willie were here now so he could tell me more. Then I remembered that Ernest wouldn't be in jail if Willie were here.

I wished I could go to the hospital to see Willie. His sister Laurel came back to school. Her ma walked with her to school every morning, and they didn't stop at the mailbox for me.

Laurel didn't talk to me, but I'd catch her looking at me from the corner of her eye. She didn't look mad. Then I didn't think Laurel could ever have a nasty look on her face.

Our teacher, Miss Bishop, led us in prayer for Willie every morning. She quit saying anything about Ernest or "the black man," as she called him. She did make a point of giving me the stink eye from time to time. I heard her ask Laurel if there was any change in Willie. Laurel just shook her head.

Ernest Pig grew like a weed. After only a few days, Gram showed me how to mix the goat milk with some cornmeal. Ernest Pig licked it right up, and by three weeks old, he was as heavy as a basket of potatoes.

I wished I could see Ernest. I'd tell him all about Ernest Pig. I'd bring my reader so we could sit close and he could hear about Dick and Jane's latest adventures. No use dreaming. I wiped my sleeve across my nose and got on with my chores because I knew it was what Ernest would tell me to do.

Chapter 11 - Luck of the Irish

Each day I dressed and waited on the crest of the rise for the seven a.m. train, hoping the hobos were on it. The train stopped for water, and finally, the door of one of the freight cars opened. As they jumped off, I looked for the red-headed man.

Gram forgot to leave a food box with all that was going on, and they looked disappointed, but they still did some work. I approached them and called to the red-headed hobo.

"Is everything okay, lad?" he asked with concern. He spoke with an accent.

I bowed my head, and my tears wet the ground. He knelt beside me, and I told him the story.

"Bloody hell," he said. "Sorry, lad. I can't help myself when I get my Irish up. Shamus be my name. Now, let's see if I can help."

He gave me hope, and I brought Shamus to the house to give Gram hope. She met us on the porch.

"Good day, ma'am," he said with a serious look, and I could tell he didn't think it was a good day any more than we did. "I don't think we exchanged names when I last talked to you about helping Ernest. My name's Shamus, Shamus McGuire," he said, extending his hand to Gram.

"Welcome, Shamus," Gram said, shaking his hand. "You can call me Mrs. Adams. Any friend of Ernest is welcome here."

"Ernest is a special man, so he is, and I'm obliged for your hospitality, Mrs. Adams, I surely am," he said. "The young lad here told me of the troubles." He glanced down at me and back to Gram.

"It has been a sad time, indeed, Shamus."

"Yes, ma'am." He shook his head with sympathy. "Don't despair. I've brought a wee bit of the luck of the Irish with me, and it ain't failed me yet."

Gram smiled despite the circumstances. I found it hard not to smile when in the presence of Shamus McGuire. His luck, however, was yet to be proven.

Shamus was a man of many words, something like Willie; only he said his gift came from the Kiss of the Blarney Stone. I thought kissing rocks sounded dumb. Shamus said it was serious business in Ireland.

After discussing the problem over lunch, Shamus went to town. He didn't say what he intended to do but assured us he would return for Gram's generous offering of chicken stew and cornbread for supper.

Shamus came back at dusk, skipping down the driveway and whistling a tune. It crossed my mind he looked a lot like the leprechaun mascot of the basketball team from Boston. Willie Larson loved the sport, and he'd told me all about it. His pa built a hoop in the yard from a broken apple basket, and we played with an old ball, not quite the proper size or height, Willie informed me. But we made do. Willie told me with regret that the Celtics didn't have a bad record so far against our own Detroit Falcons. Maybe there was some truth to Irish luck after all. I sure hoped so.

At supper, Shamus didn't say where he'd been all day. But he did tell some grand stories about life in Ireland and coming to America on a big ship. He bunked in Ernest's room in the barn and turned in early.

The next day was the trial. Gram washed Shamus's old clothes overnight. Then she laid out my good clothes. In the morning, she put on her funeral dress. I hoped it wasn't bad luck.

≈

More people packed into the courthouse than at a holiday church service. I recognized some familiar faces. None looked back at me. My teacher, Miss Bishop, was a couple of rows in front of us, and over to my right, I saw the Harlows. They were all there, Butch and Little Allan wearing smug looks. I could barely make out Willie's ma and pa in the front row. Laurel sat beside them in her pink dress with the white ruffles. It was one of my favorites, although I probably wouldn't think as kindly of it anymore.

When the deputy brought Ernest into the room, everyone sat tall with their necks stretched. Some women gasped at the sight of him and held hankies to their mouths. Maybe they had never seen the scar on his face. It did set me back when I first saw it.

Above the crowd, I saw Ernest. His head was hanging down, but I could tell his face was thinner. He must not have eaten the rats and bugs.

Gram reached over and squeezed my hand. I wished she hadn't done that because it pushed water into my eyes. I blinked fast to make it go down.

Ernest raised his head and caught my eye. I smiled, and although he looked blurry through my tears, I could see him give me a little smile in return. Then, a gasp rolled through the room, taking both our smiles away.

In the silence, the sound of metal clinking and chains dragging across the floor filled the room as Ernest was escorted to his seat at the table in front of the judge.

Finally, the people in front settled in their seats, and I could see better. The sheriff never took his hand off Ernest's arm, while the deputy locked the handcuff on Ernest's wrist to the arm of the chair.

Gram took her hand off mine and clutched her big blue purse in front of her. It had handles that went over her arm when she carried it. The big silver clasp on the top put me in mind of the handcuffs on Ernest's wrist.

She only used it on our occasional church visits or shopping at Harlow's general store. I never saw inside it, and I was a little scared ever to look. Willie Larson told me women hide private things in their purses that men aren't supposed to see.

Hushed voices buzzed around the courtroom saying words like "ungodly" and "sinner."

I wondered if these were the pious people.

I heard some shuffling in the back of the courtroom and people whispering. Everyone turned to see what the commotion was.

Shamus squeezed through the crowd, tipping his cap to Gram and me. People moved away from him like he had something catchy. Finally, he found a spot against the wall and stood quietly with his cap held in front of him. Ernest turned in his chair, and Shamus tipped his head. Ernest's face seemed to relax a little, but he didn't smile.

Someone announced the judge, and the room got quiet as a church mouse. I got to thinking that I'd never seen a mouse in church. That's probably because they are so quiet.

The judge looked around at the assembled crowd as he sat and fixed his robes. Then, he looked directly at Pastor Morgan in the front row. "I bet you wish you could get a crowd like this for Sunday service." A nervous murmur sounded throughout the room as everyone sat again.

"Mr. and Mrs. Larson and Laurel," he addressed them solemnly, "you and your family have been in my prayers." He focused on Ernest. "We are here today to hear the case against Ernest Potts of attempted murder against William Larson IV."

A small gasp passed my lips.

"Do you understand the charges against you, Mr. Potts?"

Ernest rose slowly with the help of the deputy. "I do, sir."

"Good. And how do you plead?"

"Not guilty, sir."

This led to a rise in voices. The judge banged for order with his wooden hammer.

The trial didn't last long. The defense didn't call for any witnesses, so the jury left the courtroom before lunch to judge Ernest's fate.

The crowd exited out the big double doors in an unorderly fashion to get some fresh air while waiting for the jury to return. Gram and I stayed in our seats for the crowd to clear, and Shamus came to sit beside us. I looked at him and felt an emptiness in my gut.

"Don't give up hope, lad," he said, taking my chin in his long fingers.

"No disrespect to the Irish, Shamus," Gram said, "but I don't think luck can get Ernest out of this." She barely finished when her voice cracked, sobbing into her embroidered handkerchief.

"Ahh, I know it looks grim, ma'am." His green eyes twinkled like dew on the moss in the morning before the sun warmed it. "But never underestimate the Irish and the medical effects of a hot toddy." He winked at us and jumped up as the crowd flooded back into the courtroom.

The deputy announced that the jury had reached a verdict, and everyone was eager to hear it. Although it didn't seem like there would be any surprise to it, I was praying for one of those miracles like in the Bible.

The jury filed in as the judge entered and called for order, banging his gavel. When everyone settled in their seats, I noticed the Larson family was absent. Maybe they already knew the end of the story.

"Have you reached a verdict?" the judge asked the jury.

"We have, your honor," said the head pious man.

"Very well. Will the defendant, Ernest Potts, please stand." It didn't seem to be a question, and I heard the chains on Ernest's ankles clink against each other as he rose.

"How do you find Ernest Potts on the crime of attempted murder?" the judge asked.

Gram clutched my hand so hard it hurt, but not as much as my chest from the beating of my heart.

"We, the jury," the man answered as though reading a grocery list, "find Ernest Potts—guilty—"

I didn't hear the rest for the roar of the crowd, the banging of the judge's gavel, and the rushing of blood in my ears. The rest was not important.

Gram dragged me by the arm down the aisle, through the crowd, and toward the double doors. I glanced at Shamus, standing against the wall with a slight smile. My mouth was agape.

Coming toward us through the double doors was Sheriff Fitzpatrick, waving his arms. Gram pulled me aside so he didn't run us down.

"Judge! Judge!" Sheriff Fitzpatrick yelled. "Stop the trial! We have new evidence."

"It's a little late for that, Sheriff," the judge said. "The man's already been found guilty."

"You're going to want to see this," Sheriff Fitzpatrick insisted.

There was a rush of activity in the courtroom, and the deputy told everyone to go home.

"There won't be any more for you to see here today," he told the grumbling crowd.

Gram and I watched the jury file out, and the guard led Ernest back to jail. The judge disappeared into his chamber with the sheriff.

There was nothing more we could do, so we headed home. I looked around for Shamus. He was nowhere in sight.

When we got back to the farm, Gram paced back and forth in the kitchen. I was sitting on the porch with Ernest Pig beside me when I saw the bobbing red head of Shamus McGuire strolling down the driveway with a large, dark figure beside him.

Chapter 12 - No Beggars

Like someone turned on a faucet, tears poured out my eyes all over that little black pig. Shamus skipped up the stairs and into the house to get Gram. Ernest came slowly up the walkway toward me.

"That's a mighty fine pig you got there, son," Ernest said, standing in front of me like a vision.

"Yes, sir," I blubbered. "Gram said I could be its mama since its mama didn't have enough teats for it."

"Well, everyone needs a mama, and they can come in all shapes. I bet you're a good one." Ernest rubbed the pig's head. "He looks like he's good company to keep, too."

"Yes, sir, I talked to him a lot since you left. We didn't know if you were coming back."

"I wasn't sure, either," Ernest admitted. "But it wasn't because I didn't want to."

My thoughts carried for a moment to Ma, and I wondered where she was. Then I focused on Ernest in front of me.

"Does your pig have a name?" he asked.

"Yes, sir."

"Well, what is it, son?"

"It's Er—Ernest Pig," I stuttered.

Ernest's eyes got real big, and he threw his head back. A loud booming laugh poured out his mouth.

"Pig, not Potts," I assured him.

"Well, that's one fine name," he said and slapped his leg.

I wiped my nose on my sleeve and smiled.

"Yes, sir," I said. "He was a boar. Gram said he had to get fixed to live with us. So, the vet came round and made him a barrow."

"I see," Ernest said, raising his brow.

"So, I could change his name to Ernestine," I said. "Since he isn't really a 'he' anymore."

Ernest put his hand to his face and rubbed the whiskers.

"I reckon Ernest fits that pig just fine."

Right then, the screen door slammed, and Gram stood on the porch, a look of relief washing over her face with Shamus smiling behind her.

"Good afternoon, Ernest." Gram wiped her shaky hands on her apron.

"Afternoon, ma'am."

"Welcome home."

"That's right nice of you, Mrs. Adams." Ernest shuffled his shoes in the dirt. "My sentence got acquitted. The young Larson boy who near drowned finally wakened up. Like a miracle." He bowed his head while Shamus held his high. "He told his family he had to thank me for dragging him from the river after he fell in. He told them how I pumped the water out of him before he passed out. They called the sheriff right away, and they wrote up a statement to take to the judge."

"Thank God!" Gram said as though casting a heavy burden from her chest.

"The sheriff said I was one lucky nig—" Ernest looked at me and back to Gram. "Well, you know."

"It was luck all right, make no mistake," Shamus said. "The luck of the Irish." He proceeded to tell us what he was up to in town the previous day. We all sat down on the porch and listened intently, including Ernest Pig.

"When you told me the sheriff who arrested Ernest was named Fitzpatrick, I knew I could reason with the man."

"How?" Gram asked.

"Well, ma'am, here's the truth of it." Shamus began to tell us in his Irish accent, which Gram said was a brogue. I figured that must mean magic because that's how his stories sounded.

"In Ireland, we use the nectar of the gods to cure what's ailing, and the most potent one is called Jameson." He chuckled. "Aye, any good Irishman knows it cures all, and Fitzpatrick is full-blooded Irish," he confirmed with a tight nod. "His da's family came over during the great potato famine of the 1840s. His ma was a McCaffrey. When I heard him tell that, I knew we were on common ground since my great uncle was of the same name." He gave a wink.

"What does that have to do with the Larson boy awakening?" Gram was eager for Shamus to get to the point.

"Yes, ma'am. Well, here's the way of it." Shamus settled back into the porch chair to tell us a tale of whiskey and water.

"Fitzpatrick already had doubts that Ernest was to blame for the boy's condition. There were no marks of aggression on his body, and doctors said he must have had more water in his lungs to go into such a coma as he was.

Meaning something caused the bulk of the water to leave his lungs—or someone." Shamus rocked in a calming manner. "The good sheriff agreed the doctors had given up hope. When I proposed that the boy needed some Irish intervention to save his life, Fitzy was quick to approve. No matter to him whether Ernest was guilty or no, the boy needed saving." Shamus looked off toward the horizon. "We Irish are a blessed lot for saving others, even if we can't save ourselves," he reflected with a sad laugh.

"So, as luck would have it," Shamus continued, "Fitzy had a fine bottle of Jameson right there in his desk drawer, and we took to cooking up the brew on the single burner in the break room of the police station. The building was empty, so it was no trouble.

"The trick was to get it to the boy in the hospital, and to that end, Fitzy made the plan. It worked like a charm!" Shamus's smile lit in our eyes. "We snuck the jar of hot toddy into the boy's room, and with the assistance of an eyedropper, we dripped the contents slowly into his mouth." He lifted his brow. "We could see right quick that the boy was responding. We were confident of the results, but I hoped they would be more timely than after the reading of the verdict."

He eased back in the chair, crossing his arms over his chest. "Ah, the Lord God and Jameson work on their own accord. It's not for us to question." He tipped his head, and his red hair blazed in the last rays of the setting sun.

After Shamus finished, Gram looked at him and said, "Well, Shamus, I'm not sure if it was time or toddy that cured the boy.

I have a feeling it was a little of both."

She turned to Ernest. "I'm glad you're back."

Ernest turned toward me. "Son," he said, resting his massive hand on my shoulder, looking down at Ernest Pig glistening with my tears of joy. "You best go dry off that wet pig before it takes a chill out here, now that the sun's going down."

I stood looking into Ernest's eyes, not wanting to leave for fear he'd disappear.

"It's all right, Henry, get along. Ernest and I need to talk." Gram's voice didn't leave me any choice. I went around the house and crouched down with Ernest Pig. I put my finger to my lips and hoped he understood.

Ernest spoke to Shamus first. "Thank you for your help. You're like a younger brother to me." His voice lightened. "Well, a brother of another color."

"The color of our blood is the same, brother."

My heart skipped a beat when I heard Ernest say, "I'll be jumping the next train with you. It's time to move on." He took a deep breath and let it out real slow. "Ma'am," he said to Gram, "I just came back to thank you for your hospitality and set things right with you and Henry. I'll gather up my few personal belongings before I leave in the morning."

"Why would you be going?" There was a slight crack in Gram's voice.

"When you took me in, you thought I was in my final days, ma'am. I thought so, too, but I'm feeling right well now due to your good cooking and kindness. So, I'll hop the train in the morning with Shamus."

"You're too damned old to ride the trains." Gram's voice got loud, and she stomped her shoe on the porch boards.

Shamus's voice was low and sad. "Ernest, she's right. I know you're a proud man, but life on the rails is changing. The steam engines are almost at the end of their time." He paused. "And so is the life of the rail traveler. The new trains are faster, and they don't stop for water or take kindly to us."

Ernest seemed to mull this over, then he said, "I've been more trouble than you deserve, ma'am."

"You ain't no trouble to me," Gram said. "Besides," she paused, "the boy needs you."

I gasped and put my hand over my mouth.

"And so do I," she finished.

There was a long silence. My heart beat in my throat.

"Don't make me beg, Ernest," Gram said.

Ernest coughed, and I heard his large shoes shuffle in the dirt before speaking. "As long as I been on your farm, Mrs. Adams, I've never seen any beggars here." I held my breath, waiting for him to continue. "I best get to milking Old Brown and earning my keep because, if I'm not mistaken, that's some mighty fine stew I smell simmering for supper in yonder kitchen."

"Get to it, then, and clean up for supper after," Gram said. "That goes for you, too, Shamus McGuire."

"Yes, ma'am," he said, tipping his cap.

"Oh, Ernest," Gram called as he started to walk toward the barn. "I moved your personal items into Janie's room."

Ernest paused and turned back.

"But ma'am—"

"There'll be no buts about it. That's where you will rest your head until she returns," Gram said. "And only the Lord knows when that will be."

Ernest and Shamus continued to the barn, and I heard Shamus say, "Are you sure you're not part Irish, Ernest?" He laughed, and I peeked around the corner to see Shamus poke Ernest in the side with his elbow.

I sat silently with Ernest Pig, waiting for the screen door to slam.

"Henry," Gram yelled. "Get you and that pig cleaned up. We'll be having supper soon."

"Yes, ma'am," I yelled back. I rubbed the top of Ernest Pig's head with my knuckles, and he snorted.

We had chicken and dumplings for supper, and afterward, Shamus took a tall brown bottle from his backpack.

"Can I fix us all a wee hot toddy, ma'am?" he asked cautiously. "To ease our souls."

"Well," Gram replied, "I think it would be only fitting, Mr. McGuire."

Shamus mixed and boiled, like making a secret potion, and I suppose he was. I wonder if Willie liked it. I'd have to ask him, or maybe it was best to keep that part of the story a secret.

Shamus set the glasses on the table before us. Although mine was hot, it was missing the toddy part. I didn't mind. I held my glass high as Shamus spoke the toast.

"Here's to Ernest Potts, a man of honor, and to the luck of the Irish!"

I clinked my glass to theirs and yelled, "Cheers!" the loudest of all.

Shamus taught us to sing "O Danny Boy," tears and all. When I went to bed, they were still drinking and singing. Finally, I fell asleep to the line, *"And I shall sleep in peace until you come to me,"* and I felt safe again.

≈

Shamus and I ate a hearty breakfast. However, Ernest and Gram's faces looked greener than Shamus's eyes.

Shamus perked up to the sound of the seven a.m. train whistle.

"You are always welcome to stay here, Shamus," Gram said.

"Thank you kindly, ma'am. I'll keep that offer in my back pocket." He patted his trousers. "The whistle is calling me, and I need to leave while there are still boxcars to ride."

"Shamus, where will you go?" Ernest asked.

"I'll keep riding the rails as long as I can," he said. "Some of the men have already taken to the roads." He clenched his fist and held out his thumb. "There are many places to see that aren't near the tracks. I'll be fine."

"Stay safe, Shamus." Ernest clasped Shamus's hand. "And thank you for everything."

"You gave me more than you will ever know, Ernest."

"The Lord be with you."

"And with you, my dear brother," Shamus said and ran down to the tracks.

I watched Shamus McGuire jump the moving train and give us a final wave. I hoped I'd see him again.

Chapter 13 - The Bell Tolls No More

School let out for summer vacation, and I didn't have a care in the world besides finishing my chores so I could go over to Willie's house. Since Willie returned from the dead, I spent as much time with him as possible. Someone had to keep an eye on him.

I finished my breakfast. Rushing out to feed the chickens, I ran smack into Pastor Morgan standing on our porch.

"What the—" I said before determining what I had run into. "Oh, excuse me, sir. I didn't see you there."

"No harm done, Henry," he said while catching the breath I knocked out of him.

"Gram's doing the breakfast dishes," I said. "You can go on in." I thought it was awful strange for Pastor Morgan to be visiting when it wasn't the first Sunday of the month.

"Well, it's actually Ernest I've come to call on."

My stomach fluttered. The pastor didn't call on people without good reason, and since there was no chicken for supper, I wondered what trouble Ernest was in now.

My words burst from my mouth so fast that spit followed them. "Ernest ain't done nothing wrong, sir."

The pastor held his belly and made a jolly sound. "No trouble. I have a favor to ask. Do you know where I can find him?"

I pointed to the barn without saying a word, but my curiosity was doing a bunch of questioning.

Gram came out on the porch wiping her wet hands on her apron. We both watched the pastor make his way to the barn.

"What's the pastor up to?"

"He didn't say for certain. He's looking to ask Ernest a favor."

"Will wonders never cease?" Gram put her hands on her hips.

I was tossing grain to the chickens when I saw Ernest and Pastor Morgan emerge from the barn. They paused and clasped hands just like giving the peace at church.

The pastor made his way back up the driveway, his arms swinging to his walk.

I dumped the rest of the cornmeal on the ground and ran to Ernest. "What did the pastor want?"

Ernest grinned. "He needs help with a broken bell. And he thinks I'm the best man for the job."

Ernest said he'd need a helper and thought I was the best man for that job.

≈

The next morning, Gram made sure we ate a hearty breakfast before setting out for the church. Ernest said it was a big bell, and he hoped he could fix it.

"Well, eat up," Gram said. "You'll both need your strength."

I wondered if we needed spinach like Popeye the Sailor Man. I didn't bring it up since I wasn't too fond of spinach.

When we got to the church, Pastor Morgan greeted us.

"Thanks for coming, Ernest, and bringing your helper." He smiled at me with approval, and my chest felt like it had grown bigger. "As I told you yesterday, our steeple bell just stopped working. I went to ring it at noon like I do every day, and the ropes wouldn't move. It's been quiet ever since. The good folks of Mendota trust in hearing the bell every day, and it fills them with hope. I can't believe it's silent." He shook his head like he had water in his ears.

"Well, Henry and I will see what we can do. We certainly don't want anyone to lose hope," Ernest assured him. "Maybe it just needs a good tugging to jar it loose."

The pastor brightened. "That's what I'm hoping, Ernest. I figured a strong man could get it going again. And I immediately thought of you."

"Well, let's take a look and see if we can get it swinging for the noon ringing today!"

Pastor Morgan led us to the bell room and explained how he pulled the ropes. "There's a rhythm to it," he said. "But they won't go one way or the other."

Ernest took a firm hold on one of the ropes and pulled with great effort. Nothing. He tried the other rope with the same result. Ernest wiped the sweat from his brow and looked at a very disappointed pastor.

"Don't fret, Pastor Morgan," Ernest said. "Henry and I will climb the steeple and see what's stuck."

My eyes bugged out so far they hurt; I was going to climb the church steeple! As it turned out, it was not as exciting as I expected. We didn't climb up the outside of the church. Instead, the pastor opened an old creaky wooden door to a dark, web-filled stairway and bid us enter.

"Hmm." Ernest let his breath loose with a low vibration. I looked at the small door that put me in mind of the movie I had just seen with the Larson family about a tiny door and a big girl named Alice. Mr. and Mrs. Larson had invited me to their family outing to the big theater in Bosen City as a celebration after Willie woke up. But I didn't think Ernest wouldn't fit through this door, and we didn't have any magic mushrooms.

To my surprise, Ernest said, "Lead the way, son."

I peered into the doorway and blinked once or twice until my eyes adjusted to the dark. My nose took a little longer to adjust to the smell of musty air and mildewed bricks. I carefully tested the first wooden step of the spiral staircase, and it held me. I wondered if it would bear Ernest.

I felt Ernest's body wedged in behind mine; his arms stretched over my shoulders. He used his extended hands to wipe the cobwebs away as we climbed. I suspected his arms wouldn't fit at his side. Little windows let in light along the way, and when we rounded the last corner, I could see the cover of a trap door above me.

Ernest reached over my head and pushed it open. I'm not sure what hit me first, the god-awful smell or the oily wings of a million angry bats awakened from their daily slumber. Ernest covered me with his massive body, and we waited for what seemed an eternity for the bats to clear. I'm not sure how he managed it, but Ernest retrieved a handkerchief from his pocket and placed it over my nose and mouth.

I took hold of it and breathed in the scent of Ernest's sweat, which was a whole lot better than the alternative.

I peeked over my shoulder and saw Ernest pull his tee-shirt up to cover his lower face. "Well," he said in a muffled voice. "We're here, and the bats are gone, so let's see what the damage is." He gave me a gentle nudge, and I climbed through the hatch.

The bell steeple was quite an improvement from the stairway below. While there still wasn't a lot of extra room, it was open on all four sides, so it was light and airy. The sun warmed me from the stony chill, and the breeze took most of the stink away. We uncovered our noses and took deep breaths of fresh air, hanging our heads out the side. When we recovered our wits, we stood in stunned silence at the view spread out on all sides of us.

"I think I can see our farm through those trees," I said, pointing the way.

"This is surely a sight to behold," Ernest said in awe. He looked up toward the white puffy clouds that hung like cotton candy and appeared close enough to touch.

"And there's Pastor Morgan, way down there." I reached out and waved to him. Ernest took a firm hold of my shoulders with both hands.

"You can almost see Heaven from here," Ernest said.

I looked around, and I didn't see it.

Ernest moved to inspect the church bell. He walked around it, taking care to keep his feet on the wooden walkway where the bell frame was attached. The bell itself leaned to one side.

I got down on my hands and knees, peeked underneath it, and spied a giant metal clapper hanging down. Without thinking, I grabbed and swung it. It hit one side of the large bell, and the sound echoed louder than the sound of Gram's shotgun at close range.

Our hands shot to our ears, but it didn't stop the ringing. I could imagine Pastor Morgan below singing, "Hallelujah!" I was praying for it to stop. When it finally swung free, no longer hitting the sides, we lowered our hands.

"Sorry."

"Don't fret none, son," Ernest said. "At least we know that part works."

Ernest ran his big hand up the A-frame stand, across the yoke, and around the wheel.

I glanced over to where the ropes came up through the pine boards. "I think I see the problem, Ernest." I pointed to where the rope wheel was jammed into the floor.

"Good eye," Ernest said. "The wheel can't move, so the ropes are stuck."

Ernest finished walking around the bell like he was pacing it off. "Looks to be about twenty inches around." He rubbed his chin. "A nice cast bronze," he said, touching it. "It has to weigh near two hundred pounds or more." Ernest looked at me. "Are you feeling strong, son?"

I should have had spinach for breakfast, I thought.

Ernest tried to wedge his body under the bell. Only his head fit. It was enough for him to see a dead rat among piles of bat waste. "Humph," he said to the sight or the source of the smell,

I wasn't sure. "It looks like the bats in the belfry have made quite a mess."

"Look over there." I pointed to ropes coming through the floor, and Ernest turned his head, banging it on the bell's rim.

I cringed, but he recovered without a bad word.

"Ah, yes, I see," he said. "There's a broken brace; that's why the bell wheel is touching the floor."

Ernest rolled out from under the bell, stood, and gave me a hand up.

"I'm going to need your help, son," he said. "I can't fit down yonder under that bell, but you can. Are you willing?"

"Oh, yes, sir!"

"We're going to need some supplies. I'll wait here since I'm not sure how many times I can safely climb those stairs," Ernest explained. "Go tell Pastor Morgan we need two two-by-fours." Ernest wiped his brow with the back of his hand. "And some water would be much appreciated."

"Yes, sir!" I sat on the edge of the hatch, placing my feet carefully on the first stair.

"Oh, and Henry—"

I looked over to Ernest, who was surveying the arched openings.

"Tell him we could use some screen, a small hammer, and tacks if he can find some."

I nodded to Ernest and disappeared into the black hole, descending the stairs with much more confidence than I had on the trip up.

Pastor Morgan heard me coming and was standing at the bottom when I emerged in a flurry of excitement and excrement.

"Good Lord, boy," the pastor said, waving the air in front of his face to little avail. "What on earth have you rolled in?"

"Pastor Morgan," I stood tall. "You have bats in your belfry."

His head snapped back, and he looked like I had hit him in the face with a cream pie.

"Really!" I said. "And there is a broken brace causing the wheel to wedge against the ropes."

"I heard the bell ring."

My face got hot.

"Well, that was an accident. I swung the gong with my hand."

"I see, I see. It got my hopes up." His features drooped. "Well, no harm done. What's to do?"

"Ernest has a plan," I said with a confidence that the pastor seemed to grasp. I recited the list of supplies we needed, ending with water.

"I'll need to go to Harlow's store to get the items," he said. "You can fill a jug of water and bring it up to Ernest while waiting." He turned to leave and looked back. "And you might want to use some soap in the lavatory."

I didn't bother to tell him it wouldn't do any good. I was going to be working in the pile of dung—no sense explaining.

I didn't think his job called for him to be familiar with animal droppings.

I found an old milk jug with a cover in the church kitchen and filled it with water.

Then, I climbed the winding staircase two steps at a time. Ernest sat on the ledge of one of the arches with his feet securely on the inside floor. He had a look of nervousness and wonder on his face.

I handed him the jug of water, and he gulped it eagerly. He wiped his mouth with the back of his large hand and passed the jug to me.

"I've never been this high up before," he said, gazing at the view of trees and houses below. "Gives a man a different perspective."

I took a long swig of water and passed the bottle back to Ernest. "I climbed the big oak tree on the hill by the tracks once to see the train coming." I shook a little at the memory—not at the going up but the coming down. I looked at the ground to estimate. "It wasn't quite as high as this. Gram saw me out the kitchen window and came running with the broom in her hand. She told me to get my little behind down from that tree immediately before I fell and broke my neck." I looked at Ernest. "She was more concerned for my neck than my backside, which she beat with the broom all the way back to the farmhouse."

Ernest took another sip of water and chuckled. "Your Gram is a wise woman."

"Let's not tell her how high this is, okay?"

Ernest nodded with a smile.

"Oh!" I wiggled and held the front of my pants.

"What is it, son?"

I twisted my face. "I have to take a whiz, bad."

Ernest's face went blank as I stood on the ledge and let a

stream fall over the edge of the church steeple.

"Ahh," I breathed with relief.

Ernest's mouth froze open as he looked down and saw Pastor Morgan hurry into the church with full arms. Sprinkles landed on the top of his head, causing him to look up just as Ernest and I crouched down.

"Now that you've relieved yourself, I think you best go relieve the pastor of his load."

"Yes, sir," I said, quickly zipping my pants.

I descended the staircase and met Pastor Morgan at the door.

"Here are the supplies you asked for," he said. "There seems to be a passing shower. I hope it doesn't deter your work."

"Not a problem, pastor," I said with a cough. Putting the roll of screen under my arm, I stuffed the hammer and bag of tacks inside my shirt. Finally, I took a tight hold of the two-by-fours and headed up the stairs to avoid further talk about the weather.

The dragging wood clunked up each stair, and Ernest heard me coming. He reached down and grabbed the boards, hoisting them up. Then he relieved me of the roll of screen and reached down for my hand to pull me up.

I retrieved the hammer and tacks from my shirt, and Ernest nodded in approval. "Let's get to work," he said.

Ernest told me the plan.

He would use one of the boards as a lever to lift the bell while I wedged the other one into the place of the broken brace. The only trouble was I'd have to stand in the bat dung.

Ernest instructed me to crawl under the bell and ease myself into the chamber below. "I'd do it myself, son," he said in the way of apology. "But this big black body won't fit through that opening." He pointed to the bottom of the bell.

"It's okay, sir," I said. "This little white body can't lift that big bell."

Ernest chuckled.

I stuck my head under the bell, and the stink hit me anew. I couldn't hold my nose or cover my mouth because I needed both hands to lower myself to the landing. Ernest held my wrists while I hung down my entire length with still a ways to go.

"Let me drop. It's not far."

He did, and just like that, my shoes squished in dark gooey muck. It was nothing like cow muck or even chicken muck. I'd even take pig muck over this stuff. I lifted each foot one by one and grimaced at the sticky web of thick fluid connected to my shoes.

"Everything okay?" Ernest shouted down to me.

"Right as rain," I said. I'd heard Gram say that when it didn't look right at all to me. She said sometimes you just had to accept things, come what may—like the rain.

Ernest slid a board down to me, and I grabbed it. "Okay, son," Ernest said with a look of concern. "I'll wedge the other board under the bell and lift it. Hopefully, it will be enough for you to jam the board into the space." Then he changed his tone and said, "If I can't hold it, I'll yell out, and you drop the board and get out of the way as quickly as possible, you hear?"

"Yes, sir!" I nodded and kicked the rotted broken brace aside.

"Okay! Here goes!"

I heard Ernest jam the board under the A-frame and take a deep breath. I stood ready to do my part. Above me, Ernest huffed and grunted. Pretty soon, I saw the bell raise a little bit until I had a clear space. I lunged forward and slipped in the muck, barely catching myself.

"Get to it, son. I can't hold it long," Ernest said between gritted teeth.

I grasped the board and jammed it into the space. It fit perfectly.

"It's in," I yelled up to Ernest.

Down came the bell with a thud. The new brace held, and I said a quick thank-you to the Lord after hearing Ernest do the same.

Ernest stuck his head under the bell and reached his long arms down to me. I raised my hands as high as I could and jumped. He caught my wrists in his clamp-like hands and pulled me up. We both sat and leaned back on the bell frame, wiping the sweat from our faces while smearing dirt across them.

"Everything all right up there?" the pastor's voice echoed up the staircase.

"Right as rain," Ernest yelled down.

"Nice work, son," Ernest said and put his hand out. I shook it, and muck oozed out between our fingers.

"Gram is not going to like this," I said.

Ernest's laugh bellowed out the steeple and over the hills. It sounded better than a church bell.

"Grab that screen, and let's tack it up around the openings. The bats are going to have to find another home.

"Maybe they can go to the Catholic church," I offered. "Willie Larson said he heard they were looking for more members."

"That's a good idea, son," he said and patted me on the back.

I climbed up on the ledge and held the screen while Ernest secured it with the tacks. When we finished, it looked mighty fine.

Ernest took one more look out over the town.

"From up here, you can see what God intended," Ernest said with a faraway look in his eyes. "But we can't stay up here, can we?"

"I wouldn't mind, but I think the pastor wants to ring the bell, and I'd rather hear it from down below."

I pointed toward the opening, hearing Pastor Morgan calling to us again. So, we scrambled down the stairs. Well, I scrambled, and Ernest squeezed. We both made it to the bottom and securely closed the little door.

"Well?" the pastor asked with an anxious look.

"Ring the bell joyfully," Ernest instructed.

The pastor looked at his watch. "It's a little past noon. It looks like we're on the Lord's time today."

Pastor Morgan took a firm hold on the bell ropes and pulled. His face lit up as the first rope moved with ease, and the bell began to ring. He pulled the other, back and forth, twelve times. I hoped no one was setting their watch by the bell today.

Ernest and I left the pastor with a big grin on his face and made our way home. I skipped down the road to keep up with Ernest's long strides.

"You did good, son," he said, looking down at me.

"You, too." I beamed up at him. "You, too."

We went straight to the well and took turns dumping buckets of cold water over our heads. Gram stood on the porch watching us with her hands on her hips and a smile across her face. I didn't think she would be smiling if she could smell us. She must have sensed something stunk though because she brought us a bar of soap and towels.

We stripped down to our skivvies and put our clothes to soak. I wondered if Gram would burn them. I didn't care. It was the best day of my life.

Chapter 14 - A Glorious Day

The following Sunday was a glorious day. That's what Ernest called it. After breakfast, we went to Sunday service together and sang praises to the Lord for no particular reason. Ernest's voice ran like melted butter over mashed potatoes. It even made Pastor Morgan's off-key voice sound better.

Pastor Morgan thanked Ernest and me for fixing the steeple bell, right out loud in front of the whole congregation. And they all clapped with enthusiasm.

People came from four rows over to shake our hands when everyone said, "Peace be with you."

After the pastor said the final prayer, we all replied, "Amen." Then, everyone made their way downstairs to the fellowship hall. The last time I was there was after Old Man Larson's service when I didn't get to partake in the offerings.

I found Willie in the crowd, and we filled our plates to overflowing with cookies, cakes, and everything sweet. Later we would go back for sandwiches and salads. Willie said we had to keep our priorities straight.

"Willie," I said in between bites of brownie. "I'm glad you didn't die."

"Yeah, me, too," he said, wiping his mouth with the back of his hand. "I saw bright lights coming from the gates of heaven while I was in the coma."

"Really?" I almost choked.

"Yup," Willie said while chewing a chocolate chip cookie. "Then I saw an angel with flaming red hair. He dripped warm liquid down my throat and said, 'Drink the nectar of the gods and rise again, laddie.' I wasn't sure what it meant, but I woke up shortly after with a new burning for life in my chest!"

I spit out my punch in mid-gulp. "No kidding?" I stammered.

"Swear to God." Willie raised his right hand.

I stuffed a big cream puff in my mouth and didn't say another word.

Mr. and Mrs. Larson sat on the folding metal chairs talking with Ernest and Gram. I spotted Laurel standing with some girls from school, and she looked pretty as the punch bowl in her spring dress with a bow in her hair.

A few of the town's widows approached Ernest shyly. He stood to greet them. They each had tasks to be done that needed the help of a strong man. Ernest told them he would be honored to be of assistance.

They walked away, happily tittering to each other. Some of the men in the congregation stopped to thank Ernest for his generous nature and said he was a good citizen of the town. The Harlow family sat together at a table in the corner without a smile among them.

I glanced at the Harlows while Willie and I shoveled potato and macaroni salad into our mouths.

"What do you think makes them so cranky?" I asked Willie, tossing my head in their direction.

"Ah," Willie said with his mouth full of chips. "They're a complicated bunch, Pa says—Methodist, you know."

I didn't.

Willie saw my confusion. "Methodists are meth-od-i-cal," he sounded out the word slowly. I scrunched up my nose without understanding. "They don't know how to laugh!" he finally yelled, shooting crumbs in my face. We snorted, and I was thankful to have my friend back from the dead.

After most people left, Gram helped wrap up the leftovers and wipe the tables. Pastor Morgan supervised with big eyes.

"I covered a couple of plates of goodies for you to take home," Gram told him. "I left them on the counter in the back."

"You are an angel, Marg." The pastor hurried to retrieve the plates before someone else got them.

Ernest was folding tables and putting them in the storage closet when I saw the Harlow brothers go in after him. I snuck up and stood by the doorway, peeking in.

"Afternoon, gentlemen," Ernest said.

After the first time he met them I'd asked Ernest why he called them gentlemen when there was nothing gentle about them. Ernest had said you should address a person as to how you want them to act. But it didn't seem to be working with the Harlow brothers.

"You think you're some kind of hero, now?" Little Allan said and spat on the floor.

"Yeah," Butch echoed his brother. "Some kind of hero like Superman." He laughed and looked toward his brother. Little Allan ignored him.

Gram came out of the church kitchen and spied me peeking in the closet door. She strutted across the hall right into the storage closet without saying a word to me.

"What's going on here, Ernest?"

"I was just having a conversation with these fine young men about a man that knows how to save the day."

"Who would that be?" Gram asked.

"Why, Superman, of course," Ernest said. "Ain't that right?" he asked the Harlow brothers.

They mumbled some unfamiliar words and took their leave.

≈

The following week Ernest was busy. After we finished our chores on the farm, Ernest had a list of houses in town to call upon.

"Ready, son?"

"I'm going with you?"

"Every handyman needs a helper," Ernest smiled. "And you have experience."

First, we fixed the gate to Mrs. Hinckley's garden so the varmints wouldn't keep getting in and eating her radishes. Mr. Hinckley had a bum arm from getting kicked by the cow, and he couldn't swing a hammer.

"I'm sure thankful to you, Ernest," he said with a sorrowful look. "I feel like an invalid. I can't even take care of my own property anymore."

"Don't fret, Mr. Hinckley. You've done your share. I'm just paying back what the good Lord gave me." I looked sideways at Ernest, wondering what the good Lord had given him.

"Call me Edward," Mr. Hinckley said, taking Ernest's hand awkwardly with his good left hand. "And if you ever need your hair cut, my wife is handy with a pair of shears." Mr. Hinkley put his hand to his short gray hair. He paused and made a humming sound as he considered Ernest's tight-curled ringlets. "She can figure it out," he nodded. "Don't you worry."

Ernest said he had no doubt.

Leaving the Hinckleys, we stopped next at Widow Stone's house and hung a picture. She wanted to look at Mr. Stone's image when she sat in her rocker. She had tears in her eyes when we left. She said they were happy tears.

Ernest refused any pay. He said using his hands to help others was the work of the Lord. But we couldn't turn down some fine home-cooking. Before we left, Widow Stone served us grilled cheese sandwiches with tomato soup for lunch. She wrapped up a plate of fresh-made brownies to take with us.

After that, we made our way to Old Maid Morris's place. She asked if we could take some boxes down from a high shelf for her.

"I put them up there when I was a younger woman, and now I don't dare climb a ladder," she said sadly. "They're filled with old family mementos, and I've been thinking about them lately. It would sure do my heart good to see them again."

"Family is important," Ernest said, taking the boxes down carefully. He didn't even need a ladder. "Sometimes, all we have are the memories." He placed the boxes on the table.

Old Maid Morris's voice trembled as she said, "Ernest, you are a godsend."

I looked at Ernest with new regard. God surely had a plan when he sent Ernest to Mendota.

Old Maid Morris gave us oatmeal cookies with burnt edges, and I wondered about the color of the bottoms. Ernest told her they looked heavenly. However, they put me in mind of the opposite place. Ernest saw me studying them and gave me a gentle nudge, so I held my tongue.

On the way home, we ate Widow Stone's brownies, leaving Old Maid Morris's cookies for Gram.

Chapter 15 - A Burning Need

The sun was setting on a warm summer night as we walked home from the band concert on the town common. Gram and Ernest listened to the music while I played hide and seek with Willie and Laurel. The Larsons left for home before us. We walked along with other neighbors by the light of the full moon.

When we got to the end of the pavement and started onto our dirt road, Gram stumbled into a pothole and lost her balance. Ernest grabbed her elbow quickly so she didn't fall. Once she was stable, he pulled his hand away just as fast.

"Thank you, Ernest," Gram said in a whisper.

On the light breeze, we smelled the smoke first. Then Gram spotted the flickering light of fire coming from the direction of our farm. Ernest took to running. Gram and I followed close behind.

Mr. Larson must have spied it from his house. He and Willie met us at the head of our driveway with buckets in their hands. "I rang the fire department," he said. "We best get some water on it as quickly as possible until they get here." He headed for the well with Willie right behind him.

The blaze was coming from the back of the barn. Ernest grabbed the shovel leaning against the barn and headed toward the flames.

I followed Gram to get the animals out. She unlatched Old Brown's gate and led her out, a-mooing and a-fussing. The heifer didn't need any coaxing. I opened the door to let the goats and pigs loose.

More people ran into the yard with buckets. Mr. Larson shouted to form a water bucket line from the well to the barn. I crawled around in the hay calling for Mickey and her new litter of kittens.

"Hurry, Henry," Gram's voice called through the smoke. "The fire could take off any minute."

I heard Mickey mewing in the corner. She had her litter gathered close to her. They looked at me with scared eyes. I scooped the little ones into my shirt and told Mickey to follow me. I ran out the side door.

That's when I spotted the Harlow boys with a gas can—and I saw a shadow on the side of the barn looming like a monster. Little Allan and Butch Harlow looked like two cartoon characters. Their mouths froze in large O shapes, and the wind raised their hair to look affright.

On the side of the barn was the giant silhouette of a massive body with tight curly hair and a shovel held high. The fire surged, and the image wavered in the reflection of flames. The shovel appeared to come down with menacing speed and looked like it would hit the Harlow brothers over their heads.

Little Allan screamed, breaking the spell. The front of Butch's pants changed color with spreading wetness just before he stumbled into the fire.

Ernest had tossed the shovel in his hands aside and ran right into the flames. He grabbed Butch Harlow by the middle and hoisted him over his shoulder like a sack of potatoes. Except Butch was a flaming sack of potatoes. Ernest ran to the dirt driveway and threw Butch down none too gently. Although, I didn't think Butch felt a thing as he looked passed out. Ernest peeled Butch's shirt off and jumped on top of him—I thought he was sure to break him. Ernest held him tight and rolled around in the dirt. Mr. Larson ran over and poured his bucket of water on them for good measure.

Little Allan appeared out of the smoke bawling his eyes out, equal parts tears and snot running down his face. He was probably sobbing, too. I couldn't hear it over the fire trucks and ambulance sirens coming down the driveway.

The firemen went to work quickly to put out the flames. Gram hurried into the house and came out with an armful of blankets, handing one to Ernest.

The ambulance men jumped out and ran to Butch. He was beginning to stir. He should have stayed passed out because he looked like he was in a pile of pain.

I led Mickey, the mama cat, to the porch, and Gram put a blanket in the rocking chair. Mickey jumped upon it, and I settled her babies in with her. Laurel sat beside her, giving comfort while we watched the goings on.

Everyone's attention shifted away from the firemen when the Harlows' old delivery truck came bumping down the driveway, followed closely by the sheriff's car. Mrs. Harlow jumped from the truck before it came to a stop. I heard the gears grind as Mr. Harlow forced it into first gear.

The sheriff drove right up to where Butch lay, and Doc jumped out of the passenger seat with his black bag in hand. He pushed the screaming Mrs. Harlow aside and knelt down to check Butch over. Then he conferred with the ambulance men.

A few neighbors stood in the middle of the yard watching in awe. Mr. Harlow stood among them, looking like a lost sheep, with his head bobbing. He looked toward the sheriff and the other way toward Mrs. Harlow and Butch, then toward the barn as though he didn't know which way to go.

Gram was speaking to the sheriff when she turned her head toward the sound of Mrs. Harlow bellowing uncontrollably. Gram excused herself from Sheriff Fitzpatrick and went over to Mrs. Harlow. When Gram slipped her arm around the woman, she quit sobbing for a moment and looked startled.

Gram led her to the porch stairs to sit and said things like, "It will be all right, Edna." And I wondered if Gram was right.

Doc went over to where Ernest sat on a stump—burned skin shown on his chest and arms.

Ernest shook his head, "I'm okay, Doc. Tend to the boy."

"The medics are taking care of him. There's nothing more I can do for him here," he said. "The burns are bad where the boy spilled gasoline on his clothing, but he will heal."

Doc calmly spoke as he treated Ernest's burns.

"Butch would be a lot worse if not for you," he said. "Where did you learn to roll in the dirt to extinguish a person set aflame?"

"It's not a matter of learning, more of surviving under fire in a foxhole," Ernest said and winched as Doc applied suave. "You learn a lot of things in the Army. Some bad. Some good."

"I know what you mean," Doc said. "I was a medic in the Army during the war, myself. There are lots of things I'd like to forget."

Ernest rubbed his chin. "Maybe the Lord wants us to remember for a reason."

Doc looked at Ernest with sad eyes, "Hard times make good men." He shook Ernest's hand. "It's my honor to meet one."

"Same here, Doc."

Doc finished treating Ernest's injuries and wrapped gauze around his chest.

"Come by the office in the morning. I'll check the burns and reapply the salve," Doc said.

Seeing her son loaded into the back of the ambulance, Mrs. Larson cried out. Gram helped her over to Butch. The men helped Mrs. Harlow to get in the back, and I saw her holding Butch's hand as they closed the ambulance doors.

With the fire out, we stood at the back of the barn inspecting the damage.

"I'm surely beholden to all of you," Gram said to the small group of neighbors who had come out to lend a hand. "Especially you firemen. Thank you so much." She broke out in tears that she couldn't hold back any longer.

The firemen had broken down the back part of the barn, where Ernest had previously bedded down, to keep the fire from spreading to the loft.

The corner beam was still smoking. Ernest stood close beside Gram as the fire chief explained the repairs needed to make the barn whole again.

Gram cried into her hands. "I don't have the means to buy lumber and nails."

Behind her, Mr. Harlow cleared his throat nervously. "Mrs. Adams, I'll have those supplies delivered to you first thing tomorrow."

Gram turned to him and met his eyes. "I'm already in debt at your store. I can't afford it."

"The offer is without charge, if you will accept it." He bowed his head. "My boys are the cause, and the sheriff said you aren't pressing charges."

Little Allan stood beside his father, still wiping snot from his nose.

"That's right," Gram said and looked at Ernest. "We know what a trial is like, and I don't wish it on anyone, especially not wayward boys."

"Thank you, Mrs. Adams," he said and turned to Ernest. "I'm truly ashamed of judging you before taking the measure of your character. I'm forever beholden to you for saving my son, Butch."

Ernest looked more embarrassed than Mr. Harlow. "I accept your thanks, but you don't owe me anything for helping another human being," Ernest said, then turned toward Little Allan. "Everyone makes mistakes. I've made more than my share."

Little Allan looked taken aback.

"Mistakes are common; asking and giving forgiveness is divine," Ernest said. He paused and inhaled. "I can see the regret in your eyes."

Little Allan stammered, then found his words. "Yes … sir," he said. "I didn't think of the consequences to Mrs. Adams, my brother, or … to you." Little Allan's eyes started at Ernest's bandages as tears dripped from his eyes. "I'm mighty sorry, Mrs. Adams," he turned to Gram. "Can you forgive me?"

Gram nodded her head.

Glancing at Ernest, he said, "Thank you for saving my brother."

There was a hush in the surrounding group of people.

"I'm going to need some help fixing this barn," Ernest tilted his head like he was pondering a plan. "I've heard you're good with a hammer and nails. Is that so?"

"Yes, sir," Little Allan piped up. "I can come by tomorrow, and we can get right to it so the barn is secure." He turned to his father. "Would that be good, Pa?"

His father sprouted tears as well. "Yes, son. You can bring the supplies with you. But, of course, that's if it's to Mrs. Adams' liking."

"It sounds like a solid plan to me." Gram put her approval on it.

Mr. Harlow and Little Allan shook Ernest's hand in turn, like old friends making a pact.

"See to your boy, now," Ernest said. "We'll say a prayer for him."

Mr. Harlow and Little Allan left for the hospital.

The emergency vehicles had gone, and the neighbors dispersed down the long driveway. Silence fell around us. My eyes slowly adjusted to the darkness. The animals returned one by one, and we settled them in the sound part of the barn as best we could. Then we walked together toward the house.

"Well," Ernest said. "This was a glorious day."

A surprised laugh burst from Gram's mouth. "Ernest, your cup is always half full with optimism."

"Ma'am, my cup runneth over these days."

≈

Bright and early, the Harlows' delivery truck came bumping down the driveway filled with wood and supplies.

Ernest and I went out to greet Little Allan.

"How's your brother doing?" Ernest asked.

"Butch has some bad burns on his stomach. The doctor said there will be scars, but he's going to be all right." Little Allan was jittery. "I'm ashamed of what we done." He hung his head.

"Well, it's a good day for mending burnt wood and broken souls." Ernest put his arm around Little Allan's shoulders, and to my surprise, Little Allan didn't scoff.

"My brother was right, and we didn't even know it at the time," Little Allan said.

"How's that?" Ernest asked.

"You are a bit like Superman."

Ernest chuckled. "Let's keep that a secret, okay?"

"Like Clark Kent?" Little Allan smiled, and then he actually laughed. I couldn't wait to tell Willie; there was hope for the somber Methodists after all.

1952

Chapter 16 - Missing You

The following spring, the crocuses came up on the side of the barn, and I wondered if there were crocuses where Ma was. Sometimes I'd think about her—mostly, I didn't.

The trains weren't coming by as often, so I didn't need to hurry to finish my breakfast each morning. Gram said they laid new tracks on the other side of town for the diesel trains near the big Depot Station. They were faster and more efficient, she said. I didn't understand what was so great about them.

"The world is always changing, son," Ernest said. "Sometimes it goes too fast."

I hoped it didn't go so fast that I fell off. The old steam train went by every couple of weeks now. I saw a few travelers in the boxcars from time to time, but I hadn't seen Shamus. I wondered if he was in the same place as Ma. Probably not; I didn't think Shamus would like the brush man.

There was always so much to do. Ernest and I had a routine. We woke up at about the same time and ate our breakfast together.

Gram was up before the chickens, so she said, to prepare us a hearty meal. I never asked what time the chickens got up. The rooster crowed at dawn, but those old hens might be early risers. You never knew.

Gram and Ernest discussed interesting topics at the table. Sometimes they talked about the farm, and other times, they spoke of the world. I paid close attention between bites, hoping to learn something Willie Larson didn't already know. His parents must have done a lot of discussing at the table because he knew a little bit of everything.

Gram got the Sunday paper every week. She said staying in touch with the world was necessary even if we lived in a little town in the middle of Illinois. I liked to look at the comics. *The Lone Ranger* and *Roy Rogers* were my favorites. I thought the ma in *Li'l Abner* looked something like my ma, except she stayed to home.

Gram liked to read aloud to us as we ate our lunch. One day, she talked with Ernest about a golf story. I never knew Gram had an interest, and I couldn't imagine Ernest playing. Yet, that's what they talked about.

"That Joe Lewis the boxer really shook up the Professional Golfers' Association, didn't he?" Gram asked.

Ernest chuckled. "He's never been one to back down from a fight." He opened his mouth wide to take a bite of his sandwich made with Gram's homemade oatmeal bread, cut thick.

"They should have known Joe Lewis would call them to task when they let him play as a guest in the tournament but denied admission to Negro professional golfer Bill Spiller."

Ernest finished chewing and said, "He had them on the ropes when he said the PGA was the last major sport in America denying entry to Negroes."

"Things are changing, Ernest."

"Slowly," Ernest agreed. "Laws and rules can change, but it takes time to win the hearts and minds of the average man."

"Yes, some hearts and minds are harder than others."

Sometimes my teacher would say Willie was hard-headed. "I can't win with you, Willie Larson," she would say, red in the face.

So, I could understand how hard hearts and minds could be a problem.

≈

The Larsons asked us over for supper on the anniversary of Willie's return from the dead. They said it was a celebration of life and to give thanks to Ernest for saving Willie's.

Mrs. Larson cooked a pot roast with potatoes and carrots. In addition, she made biscuits and sweet potato pie. It was almost like Thanksgiving, except without the turkey.

I sat at the table between Laurel and Willie. Being left-handed, I kept bumping Laurel's arm by accident. She didn't seem to mind.

The sweet potato pie melted in my mouth and got me to thinking about Ma. Gram always did all the cooking at our house. Ma didn't take much interest in it. I wondered who was cooking for her now.

Sweet potato pie stuck in my throat as I hoped Ma wasn't going hungry.

Just then, Willie looked like he had something stuck in his throat when his pa asked him, "Willie, you never said what you were doing down by the creek when you fell in, scaring the daylights out of us all."

Willie chewed his roast beef like a cow with its cud, as if there was no end to it.

"Yes, Willie, we'd all like to hear that story," Mrs. Larson said.

That young Willie Larson was a natural-born storyteller, I'd heard my gram say. Sure enough, when Willie finally finished chewing, he took to spinning a tale.

"Well, it's quite a story," Willie began. "I was mucking out the horse stalls when I noticed Scooter the cat scootin' by the barn door like he was on a path to trouble."

Mr. Larson gave Willie a stern look. "Anything to get out of your chores," he said.

"I meant to come back to it," Willie said. "But I didn't want Scooter getting hurt."

Mrs. Larson smirked. "The cat is not the one we have to worry about."

Willie ignored his ma's comment and continued. "So, I followed Scooter to the creek, where he perched on a rock at the edge, peering into the water. Well, you remember how the creek was running high last spring from all the winter snow melt?"

Mr. Larson nodded, motioning Willie to get on with his story.

"I was running up to the water's edge when water sloshed over the rock, startling Scooter, who fell right in the creek." Willie's eyes grew big with the telling. "That cat was bobbing in the water and yowling its head off. I ran beside the creek trying to call Scooter over when all of a sudden, I fell in myself!"

"Well, that explains why the cat came home soaking wet," Mrs. Larson said. "But why didn't you get out?"

"That's a good question," Willie said. "And I almost did, until my head hit against a rock, and I got woozy, spinning around in the cold water. I was struggling to stay afloat when I saw something I'll never forget."

Willie looked at Ernest, who was turning a different shade of dark.

"Ernest," Gram said. "What were you doing down by the creek? You never did say."

"Yes, ma'am," Ernest said, repeatedly wiping his napkin to his mouth. "You see, it was a nice warm day—for early spring, that is. I had just finished slopping the pigs, and I thought—" Ernest paused, and we all leaned in to hear what was next.

"I thought it would be refreshing to go for a dip in the cool creek water." He finished and wiped his mouth again on his napkin.

"A skinny dip!" Willie yelled, and we all blinked our eyes like something was stinging them.

"Why, Ernest!" Gram said, and nothing more.

"I was just going in for a quick dip," Ernest explained, "when I heard young Willie here screaming." He took a drink from his glass of milk, and we all waited. "There was no time to put my clothes back on. I took off running toward the sound of Willie's screams."

"Yup, I saw Ernest running toward me as I took my last breath and slid under the current. You should have seen him!"

The image was swimming around in my mind, and by everyone else's looks, it was floating in their minds, too. I thought Gram's eyes were going to pop out of their sockets.

"I think we can just take your word for it," Gram said in a whisper.

"I saw Willie go down, and he didn't come back up," Ernest said. "I waded into the creek, and it took me some time to locate him in the current." He sounded breathless, like it was happening at that moment, and it felt like it was. "I finally latched onto him and pulled him to shore. He looked like a drowned rat, one that wasn't breathing. I rolled him on his back and pushed on his stomach as I've seen done before."

Willie held his stomach like he remembered.

"Water poured out of that boy like a fountain. But he still wasn't breathing." Ernest shook with the thought. "I put my mouth on his and filled his lungs with my air." His eyes brightened. "Willie took a deep breath." Ernest shook his head. "But he didn't come to."

We all seemed to exhale at once.

"That's when I heard you, Mr. Larson. You were calling for him." Ernest's eyes met Mr. Larson's. "I knew it wouldn't look good if you saw a naked black man beside your son with my lips on his mouth." Ernest looked down. "So, I ran, sir."

Willie looked taken aback at the part of the story he didn't remember. "Well, I'll be darned!" Willie said. Mr. Larson gave Willie a look for his language. "Maybe," Willie continued, a little softer, "could we keep that part between us?"

Mrs. Larson found her voice first. "Ernest, if your lips saved our boy, then yours are the best lips I've ever seen."

"Hey, hey!" Mr. Larson spoke up with a bit of a grin. "What about these lips?" And everybody laughed. "Ella's right, Ernest.

You risked your life to save our boy, and we are thankful to you!"

"I'm happy he lived to tell the tale," Ernest said.

"It's a miracle," Mrs. Larson said.

"More like the luck of the Irish," I blurted out. From the stern looks I got from Gram and Ernest, I guessed that part was meant to be kept a secret.

Everyone else at the table looked at me like I had gone plum crazy. Then Mr. Larson turned to Mrs. Larson.

"Well, Ella, you do have some Irish blood on your mother's side."

"Yes! My nana came from Belfast," said Mrs. Larson. "Let's give thanks to God and the Irish!"

A great cheer went up around the table. Gram and Ernest seemed to breathe out a sigh of relief.

"Let's make this a yearly tradition," Willie said. "Well, not the drowning part, but the eating!"

Everyone agreed. Mr. Larson helped Mrs. Larson clear the table. I went with Willie and Laurel to play a board game in the parlor.

"Can we play Candyland?" Laurel asked, running ahead.

Passing by the kitchen, I saw Mr. Larson put his arm around Mrs. Larson and kiss her on the lips.

Willie came up behind me, following my stare. "Do you ever miss having a pa?" he asked me.

I thought for a moment. "Nah, can't miss what you never had." I glanced back at Mrs. Larson and saw her sweet smile. I did miss my Ma, but I didn't say that.

When the grown-ups came into the parlor, Laurel shouted for them to come to play.

"Oh, I don't think I'd be very good at that game," Ernest said.

"I'm with you," said Mr. Larson. "Do you play checkers?" he asked, pointing to a board on a small table in the corner with two chairs.

Ernest raised his eyebrows. "That I do."

Gram and Mrs. Larson joined us while Ernest and Mr. Larson set up the checkers. Gram glanced over at Ernest a couple of times while we played our games. We had a good ole time with the candy drops and ice cream bar cards. Laurel won the game, and I was glad.

"This game is too girly. Next time we're playing Chutes and Ladders!" Willie said. He didn't like to lose.

Chapter 17 - Different Seasons

When school let out for the summer, Ernest said he needed my help with a bushel load of projects. First, we made the pigsty bigger to make room for another sow. Gram said we could make a good profit from a couple of new litters. Next, the dry troughs needed repairing. Ernest Pig watched us with interest, but I don't believe the area looked inviting to him after living in the farmhouse for so long.

I hardly had time to think about Ma until July, when I turned nine years old. I was out of sorts the whole day. I sat on the porch watching the driveway, jumping at every car I heard go by. I thought she would remember.

Gram tried to persuade me to help her make my birthday cake. She said I could lick the beaters, but I wasn't interested. Ernest must have walked by a dozen times while doing his chores, each time asking if I wanted to help. I just shook my head. Finally, after putting away his tools, he sat beside me on the porch step, watching the light fade from the sky.

"Are you thinking about your ma?" he asked.

"No," I said and crossed my arms over my chest.

"Sometimes, I think about my ma," Ernest said and looked toward the sunset.

"Really?"

"You bet," Ernest said. "I keep her memory right here." He tapped his chest. "Whenever I miss her, she's right here with me."

"Does it help?"

He nodded his head and put his arm around my shoulders. "It surely does."

I leaned my head against Ernest's chest and closed my eyes. He smelled like sweat and dirt, putting my mind adrift to when I danced in the garden with Ma. I felt a warm spot growing near my heart. But the memory of dancing in the garden didn't feel as good as resting my head on Ernest's chest.

Gram called us in for supper. Ernest squeezed my shoulder. "I think there's a special chocolate cake waiting for you after your meal, so we best get in there, don't you think?"

I smiled for the first time that day and nodded my head. Before I went inside, I glanced up the driveway one more time. Maybe Ma would make it home for my tenth birthday.

≈

The sun got warmer, but the season was no longer known as summer. It was polio season, and it was scary.

Gram held the Sunday newspaper open in both hands. I couldn't see her face, but her words were loud and clear.

"Tens of thousands of children are infected with the virus, with thousands paralyzed. Three thousand children have died." Gram lowered the newspaper. "Hospitals have special iron lungs that children have to live in." Her face was pale. "Polio is attacking rich kids and poor alike."

My head snapped to look at Ernest. His face looked a lighter shade of brown.

"I heard doctors are trying to develop a vaccine," Ernest said. "In the meantime, they are closing theaters and swimming areas where they think it's spread."

Iron lungs, paralyzed, vaccines—what did it all mean?

≈

"Willie, do you think we'll have to live in an iron lung?" I asked when I went over to his house that afternoon.

"I don't know about you, but I'm not moving." Willie had heard about them, too. "I'll live in the barn before I go to some iron house."

Laurel said, "If you get polio, you don't have a choice."

Willie kicked a rock. "Well, I ain't getting it."

We didn't, but Sandra Bolton did. When school began in September, she wasn't there.

"I heard, at first, they thought she had a cold," Willie said. "Then she got a fever and couldn't stand up."

"I hope I don't catch it," I said.

Laurel spoke up, "Ma says it's a virus that attacks nerves."

"Well, I want to attack it." Willie held up his chubby fists.

"Do you think Sandra is living in an iron lung?" I thought about the picture I saw of a boy in a giant metal tube with his head sticking out. It gave me goosebumps.

≈

"I heard Betsy Bolton is beside herself. The poor woman," Gram said over supper. "They had to take Sandra all the way to Detroit to get her in an iron lung."

Finally, word came that Sandra would be home before Christmas, but she didn't come back to school. Willie seemed to take it the worst. Willie wasn't real tall, but he outweighed all the other boys in our class by at least ten pounds. And he was known to pack a punch when given a reason. Willie acted like he could beat anything with his fists, but polio wasn't scared of Willie.

Chapter 18 - Righteous Rage

Just before school started in the fall, a new family moved to Mendota. They had a son the same age as Willie and me. Gram and Mrs. Larson put together a welcome basket, and we went over to deliver it.

A man opened the door, and a small boy with large brown eyes peered around him. Gram and Mrs. Larson introduced themselves, and me and Willie, too. They handed him the basket, and the man said thank you, but he didn't ask us in.

When he turned to close the door, I saw a little beanie on the back of his head. I figured his head must be cold, but I thought he could have found a bigger hat. I hoped he would get one for Christmas.

As we left, Willie and I saw the boy in the window watching us. We waved, and he waved back shyly. A strange-looking candle holder sat on the table near the window. It had a star and nine candles, four on each side with a taller one in the middle.

"What do you think those candles are for?" I asked Willie.

"They're Jewish," Gram said over her shoulder and nothing more. For once, Willie had nothing to add to the conversation.

"I'm not sure if the cheese was a proper gift," Mrs. Larson whispered to Gram. "I've heard they are partial to sweets, especially honey, on their holiday."

"We didn't know." Gram patted her arm. "I'm sure they appreciate the thought."

I felt bad for the boy if he couldn't eat cheese. It was one of my favorite foods. But sweets were even better, so I could probably learn to get along if I was Jewish.

Ernest was loading up the woodstove when we returned. "That was quick," he said.

"I think they were busy celebrating their new year's holiday," Gram told him.

"Oh, I see," Ernest said. "They're Jewish."

There was that word again. How come everyone knew what it meant except me? Well, and maybe Willie because he was awful quiet on the way home.

≈

On the first day of school, I walked with Willie and Laurel by the Feinstein's house when Isaac came out dressed in a suit. Willie and I did a double-take and then looked at each other.

"Do you think he is going to school like that?" I whispered to Willie.

Willie raised his eyebrows, and I glanced down at the hole in the knee of my overalls.

"It appears so," Willie said. "And I don't think that will go over too well. We need to watch out for him."

Isaac's ma sat in a chair on their porch with a blanket over her, even though it was a warm fall morning. His pa patted him on the back, and when Isaac looked up at him, I saw the beanie on the top of his head.

"Yup. That boy is going to need us," I said.

Isaac walked down his porch steps as if he was facing the lions at the circus.

"Nice suit," Willie said like he meant it.

Isaac looked down at his suit and back at his pa. "Thank you."

"I ain't one to make comment," Willie said, and that was as far from the truth as anything I'd ever heard.

As Willie continued, Mr. Feinstein came down the steps, "but you might want to save that fine jacket for a special occasion."

His pa helped Isaac slip out of the suit coat without a word, folded it neatly, and took it into the house. Isaac waved at his ma on the porch with a bit of a smile. She raised her hand like it took some effort.

"So," Willie said, (like he was going to ask, "how're you doing?"), "What's it like to be Jewish?"

I nearly choked, but Isaac looked relieved and started telling us about being Jewish.

It didn't sound all that bad. They had a lot of holidays. Not the same ones as we did, but they always included food.

"You don't have Christmas?" Willie asked with horror.

"No," Isaac explained. "But we have Hanukkah around the same time." The word sounded hard to say. "It's also known as the Festival of Lights," Isaac said. I knew that was what I would be calling it. "We even exchange gifts."

Willie looked relieved. Still, I wondered how Pastor Morgan would take this news.

When we got to school, me and Willie took desks on either side of Isaac, and Laurel sat behind him. It didn't stop the other kids from seeing the beanie, which caused a lot of talk. Finally, Mrs. Brooks banged her ruler against the desk just like a judge's gavel and told everyone to hush up.

Recess turned out to be a time for reckoning, as Pastor Morgan sometimes said in his sermons. As near as I recall, the pastor said reckoning is to help us understand what God thinks of us and what we think of ourselves. I was thinking I was pretty scared.

Willie, Laurel, Isaac, and I were the last to leave the classroom to the playground at the back of the school. Willie was talking a blue streak like usual when suddenly he stopped. We all glanced at him and then to where he was looking. Being a regular churchgoer, Willie had an even stronger understanding than I did of the situation.

"It looks like Judgement Day," he said.

A group of boys stood in a line before us, blocking our way. While we knew them all, the scowls on their faces made them look different. When I caught sight of Willie, he looked different, too.

I pulled at Isaac and Laurel's arms, huddling together as Willie stood in front of us. The group of about five boys hesitated for a second. Willie was a force to be reckoned with, God knew, and so did they.

"Why are you protecting this screwball, Willie?" Taylor asked with a sneer.

I could feel Isaac and Laurel shaking, and maybe me, too.

"So, Taylor." Willie got in his face. Willie's words were slow and soft, making them all the scarier. "You stand in judgment of my friends and me, do you?"

Taylor backed up a step, and Willie stepped up to him again, his face glistening in the sun, slick with sweat. "Come on, meet my righteous rage!"

Willie's voice rose, and he raised his arms like he was about to throw lightning bolts. He put me in mind of a story Ernest told me about Moses and the stone tablets. Taylor must have thought so, too, because he backed up, tripping on his own shoes. The other boys caught him, and they all took off in a hurry.

Willie stared them down, huffing and puffing. Finally, we all ran to him, patting him on the back, and he broke into a smile.

"That righteous rage is pretty powerful!" I said. "You could be a preacher!"

"Nah, I'd probably scare away the whole congregation."

We all agreed.

≈

On the way home, Isaac thanked Willie for protecting him.

"That's what friends are for," Willie said.

Isaac told us he never had close friends in the city where he came from.

"We moved to Mendota because my ma has a breathing disease." Isaac looked down. "Her doctor said it would be easier for her to breathe in the country."

I took a deep breath to check. It was pretty easy. It was another good reason for never wanting to move to the city.

Isaac's family had a big black car, and Willie whistled long and low every time it went by.

"Where do you go in your nice car on Saturday?" Willie asked.

"We go into Joliet for synagogue since there isn't one in Mendota."

"What's a synagogue?" I asked. The word didn't sound the same as when Isaac said it.

"It's like your church. We go there to worship on Saturday because that's our holy day."

"Oh, well, I could never be Jewish, then," Willie said. "I can't miss Howdy Doody on Saturday mornings."

Isaac laughed. "Our holy day starts on Friday night and goes all the way until Saturday night."

"That's a lot of praying," I said.

"Well, we don't pray the whole time, and there are some things we can't do."

"Like what?" I asked.

"Well, we can't do any work on the holy day." Isaac squinted his eyes in thought. "Like we can't do chores or homework."

"That doesn't sound bad," Willie said. "I wonder if we can talk Pastor Morgan into those rules for Sundays."

"So, what makes you Jewish?" I asked.

"I don't know." Isaac shrugged his shoulders. "What makes you what you are? What are you, anyway?"

Willie and I looked at each other and shrugged our shoulders. "We go to the Congregational church," I said. "Does that make me just a Congregational?"

"I'm named for my great-great-grandpa, and he was Swedish," Willie said.

"I'm named for the son of Abraham," Isaac said.

"Abraham Lincoln?" Willie looked at Isaac like he had two heads. "Why would you be named after his son?"

Isaac held his stomach while he laughed. "No, not Lincoln! Abraham in the Bible."

"Oh, that guy, yeah." Willie tried to look like he knew it all along.

"You see, we believe God made a covenant with Abraham."

"What's that?" I asked.

"It's an agreement, and God gave us a special job."

"You work for God?" Willie looked impressed.

"I guess we do," said Isaac. "We believe our job is to make the world a better place with more good in it."

"Wow, you are going to be busy!" I said.

"No wonder you have to rest on Saturdays." Willie looked tired just thinking about it.

≈

We all walked to school and home every day together. Isaac didn't hang around with us after school because he did his homework. Mrs. Larson said we ought to take a lesson from Isaac. Willie believed in a saying about all work and no play being bad for your health. Mrs. Larson said that wasn't quite how it went, but Willie was sticking to it.

The other kids in the class were still slow to be friends with Isaac; it could have been the beanie. Isaac told us it was called a *kippah*. Willie didn't think the name would help.

Then, it could also have been Isaac's brain that caused some bad feelings. Isaac was really smart. But it didn't prove to make him very popular. Especially with Walter Meuse, the smartest kid in our class—before Isaac came, that is. It didn't take the teacher long to figure out Isaac was smarter than all the other kids. So, she moved him up to the row with the smart kids. They didn't call it the smart row, but everyone knew it. None of the kids sitting there took kindly to anyone smarter than them. So, Isaac didn't get a warm welcome.

I hoped they thought twice about crossing Willie's righteous rage.

Chapter 19 - Abominable Snowman

Ever since Ernest and I fixed the bell, we were real church-going people. Gram seemed to enjoy the services, and everyone was happy to see Ernest. It didn't stop Pastor Morgan from visiting us every month for Gram's chicken supper on the first Sunday. Ernest and the pastor always had a conversation while eating. Last month they discussed the man just elected president, Dwight D. Eisenhower.

"He proved to be a smart commander in Northern Africa during the war," Ernest said.

"Let's hope he is a good commander-in-chief at home," the pastor said. "This country needs a forward-thinking leader."

"That we do," Ernest said. "That we surely do."

There were more important things to think about on the farm than a president far away in Washington, D.C. We harvested the last of the late vegetables from the garden before the first frost, and Gram was busy canning. Luckily, we got all the wood stacked before the first snow came early in December.

We were walking to Sunday service when the first flakes drifted down from heavy clouds. They stuck to Ernest's hair, turning it white like milkweed in the fall. I thought it might blow away if a breeze came by. Gram pulled her scarf over her head and tied it in a knot under her chin. I thought she almost looked like Ma and wondered if it was snowing where Ma was.

After the service, when we gathered in the fellowship hall, the lady folk always had some new handy work they needed doing. Ernest took to bringing a pencil and pad of paper with him to church to keep a list of projects for the coming week.

He said they were simple enough and didn't take too much time from his chores around the farm. The ladies said he was an angel sent from the Lord. Ernest laughed.

"Ain't no wings on this big old back," he said, "but my hands are always ready to do the Lord's work."

I thought the Lord was lucky to have Ernest on his team. By the time Ernest had a full list of new projects and Gram helped the ladies clean up, the snow was piling up outside.

Willie walked ahead, jumping through the snow, and I stayed in step with Laurel. Mr. and Mrs. Larson walked with Ernest and Gram, talking about the sermon.

We were almost to Isaac's house when we saw the group of boys tossing snowballs at the Feinstein's windows. I was close enough to see Isaac in the parlor window with tears in his eyes.

Willie took off running like a wild boar. He crashed right into the side of one of the boys, who turned out to be Walter Meuse. Walter never saw him coming and went flying in the air. Walter recovered and charged back. The other boys jumped on Willie and started to pound him. Laurel screamed, and I ran to try to help.

That's when the abominable snowman ran by with his big legs trudging through the snowdrifts. He was entirely white and extremely big, just like the Abominable Snowman I'd heard tell about.

Walter Meuse and his friends must have heard the same story because they let loose of Willie and turned tail to run.

The snow shook loose from Ernest, and now he just looked big and wet, but not abominable.

Willie took to laughing, holding his stomach where Walter Meuse had punched him. "Did you see their faces?" He laughed and cringed. "Ernest, you scared the bejeebers out of them!"

Ernest brushed more snow off his shoulders, then he reached out his hand to pull Willie up. The door of the Feinstein's house flew open, and Isaac came running down the walkway. He threw his arms around Ernest's legs. A look of surprise crossed Ernest's face.

He reached down and patted Isaac on the back. "It's okay," Ernest said. "I don't think those bullies will be back."

"Hey, what about me?" Willie asked. "I'm the one who took the beating."

Isaac hugged Willie, and Willie looked mighty proud.

Mr. Feinstein came out and shook Ernest's hand. "Thank you, sir," he said. "Can I offer you something hot to warm you up?" He looked around. "All of you? Please come in."

Isaac looked at his Pa with a big smile. We piled in the house, all talking at once and dripping with snow.

While stomping the snow off my feet, I noticed Isaac's ma lying in a bed in the parlor. I thought it was a funny place for a bed and kind of early in the day to be in one.

Mr. Feinstein saw me staring and put his hand on my shoulder, guiding me into the room. The others followed close behind.

Mr. Feinstein introduced us all to his wife. She looked fragile when she smiled and said, "Welcome. Thank you all for your friendship."

Willie and I said our howdies and went to the kitchen with Isaac. Ernest and Mr. Larson came into the room, followed by Mr. Feinstein. He heated some hot cocoa and put out a dish of some kind of sweets I'd never seen. Willie tried one and nodded in approval. I grabbed one, too. Gram, Mrs. Larson, and Laurel stayed in the room with Isaac's ma, speaking quietly. The men talked seriously at the table. We took our cocoa and sweets into the dining room.

"These are good," Willie said with his mouth full.

"They're Hanukkah Sufganiyot. Fried jelly donuts!" Isaac said, taking a bite of his.

I noticed that Isaac didn't have a television, so I wasn't the only one. Even though they had moved in about five months before, piles of boxes still leaned against the empty walls. There were a few decorations, if you could call them that. The big candleholder I had seen through the window sat on a fancy table with three of the nine candles lit.

"What's that?" Willie asked. I could always rely on Willie to ask.

"It's a menorah," Isaac said. He looked as though he liked to tell us more about being Jewish. "It's for Hanukkah, the Festival of Lights!" His eyes got big.

"Oh, the holiday you said is like Christmas, right?" I asked.

"Kind of." Isaac paused. "But not really."

Willie found some wooden tops and picked one up.

"Oh, that's the dreidel! Want to play?"

Laurel came into the parlor, and Isaac taught us the game. We were having a good time when Gram and Mrs. Larson came in and said we'd best get going.

Before we left, Mr. Feinstein offered us chocolate coins. "Gelt!" Isaac told us.

We each took a handful and ate them on the walk home.

"This Hanukkah stuff isn't so bad," Willie said with chocolate smeared across his lips.

"Poor woman," I heard Mrs. Larson say to Gram when we were well away from the house.

"Poor boy," Gram whispered.

They didn't look poor to me. But I soon learned that lack of money isn't the only thing that makes a person poor.

Chapter 20 - Joining Voices

Two days before Christmas, we all went to Mrs. Feinstein's funeral. Mr. Larson drove us to Joliet in his big Oldsmobile. Ernest sat in the front seat because he wouldn't fit in the back. Mrs. Larson sat in the middle between them. Gram, Willie, Laurel, and I sat close together in the back seat. I didn't mind because I was next to Laurel. We were the only ones at the service without beanies. Isaac said it was okay; he was just glad we came.

The next week was the *shiva* at Isaac's house. At first, I wondered why we wanted to go to their house and shiver. Gram explained it was part of the Jewish ceremony where everyone went to the house to pay their respects.

I did shiver when I saw Isaac wiping his tears. I thought about how much I missed my Ma. Still, I could hope she'd come home. Isaac's ma never would.

≈

At dusk on Christmas Eve, I went over to the Larsons with Ernest to help get the holiday hayride ready. First, Willie and I threw hay bales in the back of the flatbed wagon. Together we pitched one bale to Ernest's five. Next, Mr. Larson hooked up his two Belgian horses to the wagon.

Finally, Mrs. Larson came out of the house, and Mr. Larson lent her his hand to climb onto the front bench of the wagon. She settled in with a smile and draped a blanket over her lap.

Laurel stood in the doorway in a red-and-green plaid dress with a matching bow in her hair. She grabbed her red cape from the hook by the door and draped it over her shoulders. Clutching a warm woolen blanket, I watched her come across the yard. I held out my hand to help her into the back of the wagon. Luckily Willie didn't notice. Laurel slipped her tiny hand into mine, and when she looked at me, I thought I saw her blue eyes sparkle. It was probably the stars in the sky. Ernest climbed into the back of the wagon, and Mr. Larson headed for our house to pick up Gram. She stood at the end of our driveway, waiting with her own blanket and a basket of goodies. After Ernest helped Gram up, Mr. Larson clicked his tongue, and the horses' ears perked up.

Next, we stopped at Isaac's house. He and his pa came out on the porch.

"Will you join us?" Mr. Larson called out to them.

Isaac looked up at his pa with big eyes, and his pa held his stare. He nodded his head. "Can you wait while we get our coats?" Mr. Feinstein called back.

"We'll be right here," Gram said.

Isaac came running out with his pa close behind. Ernest gave them a hand up into the back. We continued picking up other families until the wagon was packed. I squished up against Laurel. She lifted the corner of her blanket and let me slide under it. Even Pastor Morgan came on the hayride.

We sang Christmas carols with Ernest's voice booming through the crisp air. Of course, Isaac and his pa didn't know them all, but they joined in on "Let it Snow" and "Silver Bells." Mr. Feinstein told us that fine Jewish men wrote those songs.

"Christmas songs?" Willie asked.

"Yes, that's right." Mr. Feinstein said with a smile. "Music is one place where we can all come together."

Gram passed around the goody basket of Christmas cookies, and we all took one—Willie took two. When snowflakes began to drift down from the sky, Pastor Morgan began singing "White Christmas."

After the singing finished, Mr. Feinstein said, "Irving Berlin wrote that song. He also wrote 'God Bless America.' "

"I read he was a Russian Jew who immigrated to America with his family," Pastor Morgan said. "He wrote both songs to give thanks to this country."

Mr. Feinstein and Isaac both looked proud.

"That's neato," Willie said. Laurel giggled. Willie liked to use that word to sound like the older boys. I thought I might take to saying it since it made Laurel smile.

That night, Mr. Feinstein mentioned moving back to the city, and I knew I'd really miss Isaac. I didn't think I'd be going to the city to visit.

I was happy a few days later when Isaac told us his father had changed his mind.

"He's going to open an accounting office in our house."

I didn't know on account of what, but I guessed others knew because it turned out that Mr. Feinstein had a lot of business.

1953

Chapter 21 - Piano Lessons

Mud season started in April and went clear to the end of May that year. School let out by the time the ground dried, and I was looking forward to the long hot summer days.

It was the week of the Fourth of July 1953. A big town social with food and music was planned on Sunday after church. Everyone was going, including the Larson family—and that included Laurel. I couldn't wait.

Gram filled her largest bowl with potato salad and brought two loaves of her famous banana bread. There was more food than I had ever seen in one place, but my stomach was too nervous to eat. All I could think of was my plan to ask Laurel to dance.

Willie, Isaac, and I stood near the punch table. "What's got you so worked up?" Willie asked. "You look like you need to take a whiz."

"Well, maybe I do," I said and stomped off.

I couldn't tell Willie what I was up to. He was very protective of Laurel, and he would clobber me. I knew he'd probably see us dancing, but the deed would be done by then, and I was willing to take the clobbering afterward.

I spotted Laurel standing by herself near the old stand-up piano.

"Um, hi, Laurel," I said, coming up beside her, and she jumped a little. "Oh, I'm sorry. I didn't mean to startle you."

A smile came across her face like the sunrise over the tracks. She wore a sky-blue dress to match her eyes. It tied at her tiny waist and puffed out at the bottom.

"Hi, Henrrry," she stuttered slightly. "You look ssso nice."

I brushed invisible lint from my jacket and shuffled my feet. "So do you," I said without meeting her eyes.

"Would you-ou like to dan-ancce?" she asked, and my chest felt as though it exploded like a pop rocket. Laurel had the same idea that I did!

"I sure would," I said and bumped her arm while trying to take her hand.

The music stopped, and my stomach sank. Fear spread through my chest. But then the band started playing a song called "That's Amore." I wasn't sure what the word meant, although Laurel said she liked it.

I wiped my sweaty hands down the legs of my pants. Turning to Laurel, I took both her hands in mine. Keeping at arm's distance, I tripped over her feet a couple of times.

Coach's son, Davey Kennedy, danced across the stage sporting his best suit and singing just like he was Dean Martin himself. He waved his arm through the air and sang about a big pizza pie.

By the time Davey sang the second chorus about "dancing down the street," Laurel and I were swaying in time to the music. I saw Ernest over by the dessert table, watching us. He gave me a nod.

When Davey sang the last line about walking in a dream, that was exactly how I felt. Looking around the room over Laurel's shoulder for Willie, I relaxed a little, not seeing him.

I wished the song would never end. Davey sang the word "Amore" over and over at the end like he was calling the pigs to supper.

Laurel and I didn't stop dancing until Davey sang the last long-drawn-out word.

I sighed and walked Laurel back toward her seat, still holding her hand. Then I didn't know what possessed me. I walked her right past the piano and around its back, where the wooden strapping crossed over the piano wires. And right there, I twirled Laurel around and kissed her on the lips like I had seen Mr. Larson do with Mrs. Larson.

She didn't jump back or even slap my face. She just smiled as we walked right around the other side of the piano as if we had just taken a wrong turn and nothing unusual had happened.

But if anyone looked at my face, they would surely know.

Without a word, we sat down next to each other on the folding metal chairs. I looked around for Willie to see if I was in big trouble.

Instead, I saw him coming in from outside with Isaac. They headed for the punch bowl at the other end of the hall.

"Would you like some punch, Laurel?" I asked.

"Ssure."

"I'll be right back." I hurried over and came up beside Willie as he ladled punch into a cup. "Hey," I said.

"Where the heck have you been?" he asked suspiciously. "I checked in the men's room, and you weren't there. Me and Isaac even went outside looking for you."

"Ah," I hadn't thought ahead and searched for a good answer. "I was checking out the old piano."

"What the heck for?"

"I'm thinking about taking lessons."

"Really?" Isaac asked, and Willie looked at me skeptically.

"That's when I saw your sister sitting there by herself." I motioned over toward Laurel. "I was afraid someone would bother her."

"They better not!" Willie got his dander up. "Let's bring her some punch and go sit with her."

"Great idea!"

We all sat and drank punch while talking and laughing— well, Willie did most of the talking while Laurel and I laughed— but we weren't listening to Willie at all. At least he had Isaac's full attention, which was enough for Willie.

Finally, Mr. Feinstein rounded up Isaac, and Mr. and Mrs. Larson came by and said it was time for them to head home. I excused myself with one last glance at Laurel and went to find Ernest and Gram. My lips were still burning.

Chapter 22 - Sleeping Arrangements

The summer days were long, and Ernest and I always had lots of work to do. First, we put manure in the garden and new hay in the animal pens. Then, the house and barn were in need of fixing up from the winter's storms, and the garden always needed tending. But Gram let me go to Willie's every Saturday morning to watch Puppet Playhouse. She said it was my reward for working hard during the week. I'd have done it all the same, even if I didn't get to go to Willie's on Saturday because I liked working with Ernest. But, of course, I didn't tell Gram that because I was curious about what Howdy Doody was up to.

I'm not sure what Ernest did to entertain himself while I was at Willie's. One time, when I came back, he was in the kitchen helping Gram can some peaches. He even wore one of Gram's aprons, even though it didn't cover much of him.

Another time I found them sitting in the parlor. Gram was knitting a blanket for the newborn baby down the road, and Ernest held the yarn.

After supper, Ernest sat in the old rocker on the porch with the worn cane seat and watched the sunset. He said it was good for his soul.

When Gram finished the dishes, she would bring out two cups of tea. She sat in the other chair beside Ernest, and they wouldn't say anything.

I felt sorry that Ernest was bored while I had fun spending time with my friend.

≈

It was July, a week after my tenth birthday when Ma came home again. I had stopped looking for her. I came out of the barn with Ernest when I heard the loud motor of the cab. At the slamming of the heavy metal door, we looked up; even Ernest Pig, walking beside us, turned his head.

None of us said a word as Ma sashayed down the long driveway with her brown suitcase in hand. I could feel Ernest's massive body stiffen beside me. My stomach clenched, but I wasn't sure why.

Ma smiled the way she did, with her mouth open in a soundless laugh, her chin up, head thrown back like one of those movie stars at the theater. Her eyes sparkled in the sun like the flecks of mica on the train tracks. I wanted to run and throw my arms around her, getting lost in the waves of her flowery perfume. I wanted to, but I didn't.

As she came closer, there was a flow of changes in her features. She lost her bubbly smile, and the sparkle left her eyes while she looked us over. I stood with my arms at my sides. There was a dull ache in my stomach where I used to feel excitement at seeing her. I saw a hurt in her eyes when she looked at me; still, I didn't move.

She glared at Ernest.

Ernest Pig broke the uncomfortable silence with a snort. Ma looked down at the brazen swine, and her face transformed into an uncertain smile.

"Well, who do we have here?" she asked.

"That's Ernest Pig." I found my voice and spoke up. "And this," I said, pointing to Ernest, "is the man he's named after."

Ma held her stare at the pig for another heartbeat before turning her gaze to Ernest. She lifted her chin up and then down, taking him all in.

"Ernest," she said and licked her cherry-red lips.

There was barely a sound as the trees stood stock-still. Even the leaves didn't move. I heard Ernest's intake of breath, and I wondered if he heard the beat of my heart pounding against my chest.

"You are a big man," she said in a way that made me want to hide.

"Yes, Miss," Ernest answered in his deep soft voice.

I realized I needed to use the facilities but couldn't move. I prayed my bladder would hold.

"Well, I'm sure you are a big help to the old woman," Ma said with a particular hike in her voice on the word "big."

She never touched me as she walked between us, although I saw her give Ernest a solid bump.

When the screen door slammed behind us, it was as though a trance was broken.

"Mama!" she called out.

Gram descended the porch stairs. Ma ran to her outstretched arms.

My arms ached at my side. I couldn't look at Ernest, even though he was so close I could feel his breath on the top of my head. A hundred questions ran through my mind—one kept coming back. *Where's she going to sleep?*

As though he read my mind, Ernest said, "I guess I'll be bunking up with you, son."

I nodded my head three times fast like a telegraph key. That question was answered—there were many more to solve.

Ma brought me a tin toy. She handed me the colorful merry-go-round and showed me how to wind it up. I told her I was too old for it. When I saw the hurt in her eyes, I was sorry I said it.

Ma looked the same, but she made special mention of how Gram had changed. "Your hair has gotten gray since I last saw you," she said.

"Must be something in the air," Gram said.

I looked at Ernest and noticed tiny flecks of gray in his tight black curls. I hurried to the big mirror in the entryway and checked my thick dark hair. I inspected Ernest Pig, too. He was black as ever. We were safe so far. Even so, I took to wearing a hat outside just in case.

Gram wasted no time stripping and washing the sheets from Ernest's bed. Well, it was Ma's bed, even though Ernest had occupied it for some time.

Ma and I watched from the hallway. She stood beside me with fists clenched at her waist as Ernest gathered his few belongings from her room.

"What on earth was that woman thinking?" Ma asked no one in particular.

She scrunched her nose and shook her head in a bothered way.

"Ernest couldn't sleep in the shed anymore," I spoke up, "because he's got moon blood."

Ma glanced down at me, although it wasn't as far down as the last time she was home. I looked at her feet to check her shoes. They didn't look any different, but she seemed to be shrinking.

"Look at me, boy," she said curtly, and I jumped. She almost sounded like a Ma.

Then her little girl's smile returned, like the sun rising after a stormy night. She gently took my chin in her soft hand and tilted my head up.

"Ain't you going to give your Ma a proper welcome?" she asked in a voice sweet as honey on toast. "You think you're too big, do you?" Her laugh had a little catch to it. "Well, you ain't."

The words were strong, and so was her grip as she pulled me into her arms. There it was, the smell of her flowery perfume, and I couldn't feel my legs anymore.

Ernest helped Gram drag a cot out of the closet I'd never seen before. Gram acted like it was something she did all the time.

"Now, this will do just fine," Gram said while dust-beating the thin mattress. She got a sheet and blanket and set it up in my room.

"Yes, ma'am," Ernest nodded, his head going up and down while his eyes stayed level on the bed.

I stood slightly behind him, looking up. Math was not my best subject in school but peering around him at the cot, I knew he wouldn't fit.

"Can I sleep on the cot, Gram?"

A noise came from Ernest that never had time to be a word. Ma appeared in the doorway, and she looked bigger than she did before. "Boy, you don't need to give up your bed for the likes of him," she bellowed.

I froze with uncertainty next to Ernest who stood like a tree about to be felled.

Gram continued to push the wrinkles out of the blanket and spoke each word as she meant them, "He ain't no boy anymore, and he can make up his own mind where he wants to sleep."

Ma seemed to shrink a bit, but she didn't move.

My shoulders came up and back as I raised my head. "I'll take the cot." And that was that.

Gram finished putting the sheets to rights and walked up to Ma, speaking between her gritted teeth. "That man has been here to help while you have not," she said, looking Ma straight in the eye. "Whether you choose to give him your friendship is up to you, but you will give him your respect." She paused. "Am I clear?"

Ma swallowed hard. "Yes, ma'am."

There wasn't much talking through supper. We all kept our mouths full and did extra chewing. After I helped clear the table, I went upstairs, punched the pillow a couple of times, and roughed up the blanket. It didn't make me feel any better.

Ernest didn't take up as much space as I thought he would. I stuffed my socks and skivvies in the same drawer as my pajamas and shirts so that Ernest could have the top drawer. I figured it would be a long way for him to bend down to the bottom one. He didn't have a lot of clothes, and they all fit in just fine. He placed the rest of his personal items on the shelf above my bed under the picture of Roy Roger's horse, Trigger. He said he was sorry to take up my space. I said it was okay.

Ernest snored a lot at night. I didn't mind. Ernest Pig slept on an old blanket on the floor and snored, too. The brush man never came back. I wondered where Ma had left him. Gram made do with the brushes she had.

Chapter 23 - A Four-Letter Word

In late July, the sun was hot, and there was barely a breeze. Gram went out to do errands. Ernest and I were digging potatoes in the patch near the house. Ma lazed on the top porch step with a long white cigarette to her red-colored lips. We had filled the basket, and Ernest was headed to the root cellar to dump it in the bin.

"I know you're fucking the old woman," Ma shouted loud enough like she wanted the Larsons next door to hear her.

My head whipped around, and I tensed like a doe at the snap of a twig. My knees ached from kneeling in the dirt, but I didn't get up to stretch. Instead, I crawled over to peek between the slates in the picket fence.

"Excuse me, Miss?" Ernest asked.

"You heard me."

I heard her, too, and goosebumps rose up on my arms. I tried to figure out what she meant by that word. It didn't sound like anything Ernest would be doing to Gram. Although, it seemed to be a word that got his attention.

Ernest tilted his head to the sky and took a deep breath. He let it out like a simmering pot on the stove.

Ma walked up to him real slow and put her finger on his chest. He looked down at it and then straight into her eyes. Ma walked around Ernest, dragging her finger across his brown arm and broad back. The muscles in Ernest's arm twitched while he held the basket of potatoes steady. Ma came around in front of Ernest and, taking a long drag from her smoke, blew into Ernest's face. He turned his head away.

"Now, you ain't scared of little ole me, are you?" Ma asked.

Ernest didn't answer, and Ma gave a little laugh.

Bile rose into my mouth. I didn't see anything funny.

"Why would you want some shriveled-up raisin when you can have a sweet juicy grape?"

Ma's eyes dulled, and I hardly recognized her anymore. Ernest looked like a turkey that just got peppered with birdshot. I knew Ernest wasn't too fond of grapes or raisins, but Ma didn't know him that well.

My nose started running snot before I even knew I was crying. My tears dropped in silence, but I couldn't keep my eyes from watching. It wasn't the words spoken that upset me. I hardly knew what Ma and Ernest were discussing. But I felt a tension like the smell in the air before a lightning strike.

Ernest carefully set the basket of potatoes on the ground and dusted off his hands. He tilted his head and cleared his throat.

"Miss—" he began.

"You can call me Janie," Ma interrupted him with a snicker that sent sharp pains to my stomach.

"Miss," Ernest continued. "You're a smart girl, so I ain't going to lie to you. Your Ma saw to me when I was ailing, and now I'm trying to return the favor. Ain't nothing more to it than that."

I held my breath.

Ma's eyes narrowed, and she looked confused. "Never had a man tell me I'm smart."

"You should have," Ernest said. "A man ought to see that real clear."

Ernest walked to the porch and sat on the top step where Ma had been. Ma stood in front of him, watching him with new interest.

"I noticed how you figure things out and help your ma with paperwork."

Ma's face softened.

"Why," he went on, "I reckon you have more brains in your little finger, Miss, than most men have in their whole head."

Ma smiled. "You think?"

"I know it, Miss." Ernest's face was sincere. "I know you've seen a bit of the world; I have, too. Sometimes it's not pretty. But there are new opportunities for smart young ladies like you. Work that has nothing to do with that four-letter word you mentioned."

"Like what?"

"You can go to school and have a proper career. Don't ever short-change yourself."

"Well, I always wanted to be a secretary." She bowed her head. "I didn't think I could learn all the sorting and filing." She paused. "And typing. That's hard."

"Miss, I don't believe you would have one bit of trouble learning all that."

Ma pursed her lips in thought.

"You know, I think you may have a point." Her face lit up, and the darkness was gone. "Yes, I am smart, aren't I?" she said.

"No doubt, Miss, no doubt," Ernest nodded his head solidly. "I think you're right."

Ma pranced up the porch steps and paused beside Ernest. "All that stuff I said," she stammered. "Pay it no mind."

"Done forgotten, Miss."

The screen door slammed behind Ma.

"Lord, watch over her," Ernest said under his breath as he rose and grabbed the basket of potatoes.

Ernest headed for the root cellar while I collapsed in the dirt, clutching my stomach and taking deep breaths. That's how Ernest found me when he returned with the empty basket.

"What ails you, son?"

I had a hard time meeting his eyes. None of the words running through my mind would cross my lips. I wanted to ask about what Ma said. What was the meaning of that word she used? And just like that, the question leaked out of my mind, and Ernest asked it.

"You heard what your Ma said to me? You're wondering what it means?"

"No, sir. I was just resting while you were gone." I got to digging potatoes as if my life depended on it.

Ernest twisted his jaw and started to speak, then stopped.

"Don't worry, sir." I quickly glanced at him. "I'm fine."

I felt Ernest continue to study me.

"Your Ma, she was just airing her thoughts," Ernest said. "No harm done."

I looked at him and nodded my head.

"But that word, it's still bothering you," he said, and it wasn't a question. "That's not a word you want to repeat, son."

"Yes, sir," I said, still unsure why. "Yes, sir." I continued digging like there was no tomorrow.

"Look at me, please," Ernest requested, and I put the spade down.

"I'll make you a deal," he offered. I eyed him sidelong, unable to look him straight on. "Promise me you won't say that word until you know for certain what it means." He paused. "And when you're old enough, I promise to tell you. Then you can decide if you want to speak it. I hope you don't."

He took a long look at me, and I nodded firmly.

"Deal," I said, wondering when I'd be old enough.

≈

After chores, I grabbed my fish pole and ran to meet Willie Larson.

"Where's your sister?" I asked, looking around for Laurel.

"Ma wanted her to stay home and keep her company. They're going to bake a pie." Willie rolled his eyes. "Ma still babies Laurel a bit, my pa says. That's okay 'cause she ain't going to have no more babies."

"How do you know?"

"When women get a certain age, they just can't anymore."

I wondered how Willie knew all these things. Willie commenced telling some other things about men and women. I asked him if he had ever heard the word that starts with F that wasn't proper for kids to say.

"Sure. It's a four-letter word for what men and women do," he explained. "Like the pigs and the cows," he said like I was stupid.

"I know *that* much, Willie," I said. "There has to be something different a man and woman do. Something special."

"Nah, it's the same," he said. "A lot of huffing and grunting. Well, the only difference is sometimes the woman screams, and the man starts to talk to the Lord."

The thought disturbed me a little. But before I could ponder any further, Willie interrupted my thoughts.

"What are you asking for?" Willie said with curiosity. I had never brought up the subject before, and he must have wondered what made me think of it now. But of course, I couldn't tell him what Ma said. Willie had a mouth bigger than the Great Lakes.

I thought quickly. "I heard some senior baseball players at a game talking about taking some girls behind the bleachers and doing that."

"Those guys think they're something in those uniforms," Willie said. "Coach Kennedy would have their hides if he caught them doing anything that doesn't have to do with baseball."

I thought Willie was right about that. Coach was really serious about sports.

But I still wasn't sure about the four-letter word.

Chapter 24 - Using Your Head

September snuck up on me like Brutus on Popeye. I didn't see it coming.

Ma and I were both going to school. I was in fifth grade, and she went to the Junior College to get a certificate to be a genuine secretary. Ma took a GED test in the summer to finish high school. She'd been nervous about it, but Ernest told her not to worry. She liked when Ernest said things like that. Ma said she passed the GED with flying colors. I didn't know it was a color test, but she got accepted into the secretary course.

Ma started to talk more to Ernest, and she asked him questions—nothing about grapes or raisins anymore. She must have figured out he didn't like them. And I didn't hear that other word again, either.

Gram handed me my Roy Rogers lunch box on the first day of school that September. It even had a real thermos for soup. Gram usually put a peanut butter and jelly sandwich beside it and sometimes a cookie. The silver latch snapped shut to hold it all in, and I carried it by the black plastic handle. Gram put Ma's lunch in a brown paper bag since she didn't have a lunch box. She packed the bag with a peanut butter sandwich, an apple, and a special square of cake that day. Ma kissed Gram on the cheek and gave me a big wet smack. I didn't even wipe the red lipstick off until later.

"See you all after school." Ma smiled and twirled around in her crisp yellow dress. The smell of sweet perfume floated through the air.

Gram looked pleased as Ma picked up her books and notepad from the old wooden hutch.

"Have a great day, Janie," Gram said.

Ma stopped uncertainly in front of Ernest. I never knew Ma to be at a loss for words, but she seemed to be struggling.

"You're going to be the best secretary ever," Ernest said.

Ma beamed. "Thank you, sir," she said and hurried out the door so she wouldn't miss the bus that went out to her school.

"Time for you to get going to school, too, Henry," Gram said.

I twisted my mouth in thought.

"What are you concentrating on, son?" Ernest asked.

"I'm wondering what I'm going to be when I get older," I said. "Ma knows she's going to be a secretary. Even Willie Larson knows what he wants to be."

"What's that?" Ernest asked with interest.

"He wants to be a brothel owner."

Gram tripped on her way to the woodstove, and Ernest caught her.

"Careful, ma'am," Ernest said with a lightness to his voice. "There seems to be something a little sticky around here this morning."

"Thank you, Ernest. I certainly don't want anything stuck to the bottom of my shoe." She grinned.

"So, Henry," Ernest wrinkled his brow. "What subjects does Willie think to be important for that line of work?"

"Willie said math is always needed for anyone in business," I said. "Geography is also helpful since brothels are in Europe."

"Oh, I see," Ernest said. "And what exactly do people do at these places?"

"Ernest, you know." I thought he must be joshing, but Ernest just looked at me with wondering eyes. "Ugh. I thought everyone knew." My bluff was quickly losing steam. "Well, you can ask Willie next time you see him. He'll be glad to tell you all about it," I said, quickly grabbing my lunch box and heading for the door. "See you after school."

I ran up the driveway like my pants were on fire. "Willie!" I yelled. He stood at the mailbox with Laurel waiting for me.

"What took you so long? We're going to be late for school."

"Ernest was asking me about brothels," I said, gasping for breath.

"He was? Well, I hope he isn't thinking about running one."

"Why?"

"I found out they're illegal."

"Oh no! Now, what are you going to be when you grow up?"

"I'm thinking about opening a speakeasy."

"That makes sense," I said. After all, Willie did have an easy time speaking.

≈

"Mr. Shoemaker," it said in big letters on the chalkboard in the fifth-grade classroom when we entered. He didn't look much like a shoemaker, and the name brought more than a few giggles from the other kids walking into the room.

Mr. Shoemaker had just moved to town over the summer

with his brother, whose last name was not Shoemaker. They rented a small house at the end of Willow Street with a white picket fence around the yard. Mr. Shoemaker's brother, Bob White, like the bird, worked as a nurse on the night shift at the hospital in Joliet. I thought a man being a nurse sounded odd, but I didn't mention it.

Mr. Shoemaker spoke with an English accent, thank you very much, he said when asked about it. It didn't sound like any English spoken in these parts. He said it was the Queen's English. The Queen seemed to look at things a little differently. When doing our spelling lessons, Mr. Shoemaker couldn't stop himself from telling us that we Americans had stolen all the s's in the proper English language and replaced them with z's. And he didn't look too pleased about the theft. If I could have found them, I'd gladly have given them back.

Not only was his brother, Mr. White, a nurse, but he was also a really nice man. On his way home from his overnight shift at the hospital every Friday morning, Mr. White stopped at the bakery in Joliet and picked up a couple of dozen special donuts for Mr. Shoemaker to bring into the class.

One Friday, Mr. Shoemaker didn't have the box of donuts. He didn't mention why but he looked a little sad.

"Is your brother sick?" I asked at the end of the day.

"My brother?" Mr. Shoemaker looked confused. "Oh, Mr. White."

I nodded and looked to the empty place on his desk where there was usually a box of donuts on Fridays.

"Yes, well, Mr. White is sick of heart," Mr. Shoemaker said.

He told me Mr. White had taken the day off to think about his future. "He wants to go back to Orleans." He paused. "He doesn't feel welcome here."

"Is Orleans in England?" I asked.

"No, New Orleans in Louisiana." Mr. Shoemaker smiled sadly. "England isn't very welcoming to our type these days, either."

I wasn't sure what type he meant, but it made me sad. I'd miss the donuts and, of course, Mr. White too, if he left.

≈

Thursday was gym day when everyone got to use the basketballs and hoops, not just the team players. We had gym class with the sixth and seventh-graders; many were on the team, including Nick Fowler. Willie and I were in the same group. We took turns throwing toward the hoop while someone ran after the balls we missed, which was all the time. My last shot not only fell short of the basket but also rolled clean across the gym. Willie ran after it.

"Your ma's a tramp," said Nick Fowler, dribbling a basketball by me with one hand. The ball hit the court with every word he spoke.

"Excuse me?" I asked. Ernest always said to give a person the benefit of the doubt. That meant having him repeat his words to be sure you heard him correctly.

"Your ma's a tramp," he said again, standing in front of me, bouncing the ball from one hand to the other in rhythm to his words.

Yup, I heard him right. And my ears burned.

"I don't like your words," I said. Always state your issue, Ernest had told me.

"Well, that's too bad for you, ain't it?"

I weighed my options. Nick had a couple of years on me and, being almost a foot taller, put my head at about his stomach level.

"Take it back," I said because Ernest says you should always give a person a chance to correct his wrong.

"I ain't taken back the truth. So, whatcha gonna do about it, shrimp?" Nick taunted me.

I braced myself and gave a running lunge of my head to his gut because Ernest said once you make up your mind to do something, use your head and put your whole self into it. I heard the wind leave Nick's body as he fell backward, sliding across the polished gym floor on his backside.

"What's going on here?" Coach yelled, running toward us.

Willie ran up beside me, breathless, his eyes as big as basketballs.

"I didn't think you had it in you, Henry."

Coach sent Nick Fowler to the showers, telling him, "I'll deal with you later." He took me into his office.

"What did Nick say to get you so worked up, Henry?"

I puffed like a bull focused on a red cape. Coach waited a few seconds for me to calm down.

"My ma ..." I said and stopped to wipe a tear from my eye with the back of my hand, hoping Coach wouldn't notice. I snapped my head to the side, trying to clear the remark from my memory. I certainly didn't want to repeat it.

"Ahh," Coach said with an understanding look. "I remember your ma in school not that long ago. As I recall, she was a great basketball player."

I narrowed my eyes. "Really?"

"It's true," he said. "Granted, your ma is shorter than most who play, but she was a spitfire on the court. She was the only girl who really played well."

Coach had my attention.

"She weaved in and out of the legs of the taller players and threw that ball with all her might. Whoosh!" Coach mimicked throwing the ball into the basket.

I kicked my heel against the chair, still letting out some steam.

"Maybe you could try out for the team," Coach suggested.

I scoffed at him.

"Your ma could help you with the fundamentals."

I felt butterflies in my stomach; I wasn't sure about fundamentals. "My ma's going to school. I don't think she has time." Then I remembered what Nick had said. "Besides, I don't want to play on a team with Nick Fowler."

"Nick's dad is a rigid man. I don't imagine he's easy to live with." Coach sucked in his bottom lip. "I'm going to have a word with Nick."

I didn't see the point. Nick was a bully; bullies just liked to make people feel bad. But I did like thinking about Ma on the basketball court.

≈

"No kidding?" Willie asked while we walked home from

school. "Coach said that?"

"Swear to God."

"That's really neato," Willie said. "We need to practice more to get good like your ma."

We ran the rest of the way right past my driveway and into Willie's yard. Mr. Larson was changing the oil in his '48 Ford pickup.

"Pa," Willie said, running up to him. "Can you raise the old apple basket to the proper height so we can practice for the school basketball team?"

He wiped the grease from his hands on an old rag and listened. He looked a little hesitant about Willie's request. Mr. Larson liked watching basketball. He knew regulation height was much higher than where he'd put the basket two years before. Even so, he got a ladder out and moved up the basket.

In the meantime, we found the old ball in the bushes where it had landed after our last attempt at shooting baskets. The ball was a little soft, but we didn't really care if it bounced as long as we could throw it into the basket.

With the hoop at the new height, our necks leaned back as we looked up at it. We wondered if Mr. Larson had made a mistake.

Laurel sat on the porch step, watching us take turns attempting to get the ball in the basket. Laurel tried to encourage us, but it didn't help.

"This isn't going to work," I said, kicking a rock, feeling sweaty and tired without a successful basket between us.

I looked up to see Ernest coming down Willie's driveway.

"You're Gram wondered where you got to after school today," he said to me, then turned to Willie. "That's a mighty fine hoop you got there, Willie."

Willie bent over with his hands on his knees, catching his breath. "Thanks, sir, but it doesn't seem to help us play any better."

With my back to the basket, I held the ball out in front of me and kicked it. It went up and over my shoulder and swished right into the basket without touching the edges. Our mouths stuck in the shape of O's.

Ernest looked from the basket to me. "Nice shot, son."

"Yeah, well, too bad I can't play with my feet."

On the way home from Willie's, I walked with my shoulders slumped.

"How was school today?" Ernest asked.

"Okay," I said without detail. Then a thought entered my head and came out of my mouth. "Are you a tramp, Ernest?"

"Humph," he said, stopping as if he'd run into an invisible stonewall. "Why do you ask?"

"Nick said my ma is a tramp," I spit out the words, and a tear escaped my eye, rolling down my cheek. "Ma likes to travel, like you, so I wondered if maybe it wasn't as bad as it sounded."

"Words have many different meanings, son," Ernest said. "It's more to do with the intent and less with the word."

He didn't answer my question. I didn't want to talk about it anyway. So, I went on to tell him about Mr. Shoemaker, the Queen's English, donuts, and Mr. White not feeling welcome. He listened with interest.

Chapter 25 - All You Can Hope For

Mr. Shoemaker asked, "Why the long face, Mister Adams?" on the following day when I came into his classroom before the bell rang. The other kids were still playing outside. I looked at him thinking he would never understand. Then, I noticed the box of donuts on his desk. Mr. White must not have left after all.

Mr. Shoemaker offered me one and smiled. "They do give a lift to the spirit."

"Mr. White decided to stay?" I asked while carefully picking up the donut with cream filling bulging out a tiny hole in the side.

"Mr. White is giving it a go for another month before making his final decision," Mr. Shoemaker said, reaching in for the jelly.

I sunk my teeth into the sugary dough, and the filling squirted out the side. While I chewed, my heart beat faster and I felt a little less sad.

"I saw you yesterday in the gym. You seemed to be having a heated discussion with Nick Fowler," he said.

I looked at him over my donut. "He called my ma a tramp," I blurted out and took another quick bite, looking for Mr. Shoemaker's reaction.

He tilted his head back, and his stiff English upper lip stuck out. "You don't say," he replied.

I did say, so I didn't know what else to say.

He licked some jelly from his fingers. "Nick has a way with words, and it's not necessarily a nice way," Mr. Shoemaker said. "I think he may have inherited it from his father."

"His father?"

"Yes, he's our neighbor and has a way with words as well."

I swallowed the last bite of my donut and licked my fingers clean just as the bell rang and the other kids filed into the classroom. I managed to avoid seeing Nick in the halls, but I couldn't forget his hurtful words. I wondered what his father had said to Mr. White and Mr. Shoemaker.

≈

The next day before school, I saw Coach in the gym when I walked by. That wasn't unusual. What was unusual was that Mr. Shoemaker and Ernest were there with him. I hid behind the door to hear what they were up to.

"Coach Kennedy," Mr. Shoemaker said. "I have a proposal for a new sport I think would be beneficial for younger boys who are not well-suited to the physical attributes of basketball. It could be a valuable resource to build self-confidence and boost their morale. I've asked Mr. Potts here to help implement the idea if you agree."

"What is it you have in mind, Mr. Shoemaker? I'm all ears."

I tried to follow Mr. Shoemaker's big words, and what I got out of the conversation was that Mr. Shoemaker wanted to teach us a new game, and he asked Ernest to help.

"Before Mr. White and I moved here to Mendota, we lived in New Orleans for a time. Some Scottish bloke introduced the game of soccer to the locals there. It was well-received. The younger boys who are late bloomers take well to the sport since the goal is on the ground."

"I've heard of soccer. This area had a go at it in the 1920s. The war ended that, and it didn't take root again. But I heard Chicago and St. Louis just started soccer leagues," Coach said. "I see your point, and I think it would be a great addition to our school. I just don't have time to organize another team."

"That is where Mr. Potts comes in," Mr. Shoemaker said. He turned to Ernest. "Would you help?"

"I don't know." Ernest sounded nervous. "I'm no athlete, sir."

"I've seen how the children take to you, Mr. Potts. I can coach them on the rules if you assist by offering support," Mr. Shoemaker said. "Can you give it a try?" he asked. "For Henry's sake."

Ernest rubbed the whiskers on his chin and nodded.

Me? Why me? I thought. I'm a failure at basketball; soccer would only give Nick Fowler another reason to laugh at me.

"Why don't you come by my house later," Mr. Shoemaker said, "and we can make a plan."

Ernest agreed.

≈

Gram stood at the stove cooking supper when Ernest returned from meeting with Mr. Shoemaker.

"How did it go?" she asked while stirring the spaghetti.

"Interesting," Ernest said.

Gram stopped stirring.

"Color ain't the only thing that can make a man feel like an outsider," Ernest said.

Ma sat at the table with her homework spread in front of her. She wrinkled her brow. "Being English?"

"No, they are ... well, there were men like them on the railcars. They prefer the company of other men."

"I see," said Gram. "Well, that does explain some things."

"Oh, for God's sake," Ma said, putting down her pencil. "I've met such men in the city. They're sometimes called 'queer' or 'gay.' It isn't catchy."

"No, it's not," Gram said.

"But the prejudices people hold can be," Ernest added.

Mr. Shoemaker didn't look very gay to me the last time I saw him. And Mr. White certainly wasn't gay if he was thinking about leaving Mendota. I wasn't sure what Ma was talking about.

Gram stirred the sauce and thought. "If people just got to know others for who they are inside, the world would be a better place."

≈

Mr. Shoemaker made a sign-up sheet for soccer and posted it on the wall. Willie and I were the first to sign. Then five more boys and four girls added their names to the list.

Mr. Shoemaker said, "Now we have a team!" And he didn't even mind having girls on the team. "Everyone is welcome," he said.

We practiced every afternoon in the field next to the school. Mr. Larson helped Ernest build a net for the goal, and Mr. Shoemaker told us the rules. Sometimes he had to remind us not to touch the ball with our hands. We were all getting the hang of it and having fun. I suspected it was what Ma meant when she said the word gay because we were having a gay time of it. Sometimes Nick Fowler stood over near the tree line and watched us. He didn't look so gay.

When other kids saw what fun we were having, more joined, and it was a good thing because there weren't many other teams to play. We mainly played against each other, which was fine with us. Mr. Shoemaker and Ernest were excellent coaches. Mr. Shoemaker kept us straight on the rules and did the scoring. Ernest was in charge of the equipment and keeping us all in our places. There was always a group of friends and family in the stands to cheer us.

≈

"All in all, it was a successful season," Mr. Shoemaker said, shaking Ernest's hand. Ernest said he couldn't agree more. Coach decided it was a cause for celebration. They planned an awards ceremony in the gym. Practically the whole town came. I wasn't sure if they came to see the awards or if most attended for the food. I got the feeling that's why Nick Fowler and his dad appeared.

Ma stood next to the beverage table talking to Coach, and people gathered around them. Nick Fowler edged over to the group like he wasn't really interested. I went up and stood beside Ma.

"This is little Janie Adams," Coach said to the group. "She's the best darn basketball player I ever coached!"

Some nodded their heads. "I remember," a man replied. "I always loved watching your games. You could run circles around the tall kids."

Ma blushed.

"What are you up to now?" Coach asked.

"I'm attending classes at the junior college," Ma said. "I'm going to be a professional secretary."

"Well, I know you can do anything you put your mind to," Coach Kennedy said.

At that, the buttons near busted off the front of my shirt.

I noticed Mr. Shoemaker come in with Mr. White close behind. I was happy to see that Mr. White had not left. Mr. Shoemaker looked pretty pleased about it too.

The Fowlers squeezed in ahead of Ma and me in the food line. Nick looked back at us once, but his pa kept his eyes on the food. They filled their plates and looked around for an empty seat. Finding all the tables full, they stood in the corner shoveling food into their mouths.

There was so much noise in the hall that no one heard Mr. Fowler hit the floor until Nick's screaming pierced the crowd. Nobody moved—except Mr. White, who almost flew to Mr. Fowler's side. Mr. Fowler's face turned red as a freshly washed beet, his hands clenched around his throat, and his mouth opened wide, but nothing came out.

Mr. White shouted to Nick to help him turn his pa on his side. Nick blinked. Mr. White repeated himself louder.

Nick looked straight into his eyes and nodded. They rolled Mr. Fowler on his side, and Mr. White made a fist and hit him in the middle of his back. Mr. Fowler jerked back and forth, and his eyes near popped out of his head, then he went limp. Nick helped readjust his pa. Mr. White hit him again harder. A bunch of spittle and unknown fluids, along with a big piece of Mrs. Larson's famous fried chicken, came out of Mr. Fowler's mouth, causing onlookers to turn away and scream.

"Holy cow," Willie said, standing next to me.

"I guess no one ever told Mr. Fowler to chew his food good before swallowing," I said.

Mr. Fowler recovered quickly and pushed Mr. White's arms away with a confused look. His head hung down, his eyes cast up and around the room at all the staring faces. He wiped the drool from his mouth with the back of his hand while hurrying out the back door. He probably didn't want to shake Mr. White's hand since he had spit on it. In any case, a big round of applause filled the room, and everyone else shook Mr. White's hand, even Nick.

Ma came over and stood beside me.

"Why do you think Mr. Fowler didn't thank Mr. White properly?" I asked.

"Mr. Fowler isn't fond of gay people," Ma said.

There was that word again, and it never seemed to fit right in the sentences I heard. Ernest came to stand on the other side of me. I noticed Mr. Shoemaker in the corner hugging Mr. White, not in a brotherly way. "Is that what it means to be gay?" I asked.

"Yes, son," Ernest put his arm around me.

"Do you think Mr. Fowler will ever be okay with that?"

"I'm not sure," Ernest said. "It takes some people a lot longer to stop seeing the ways we are different and accept the ways we are all the same. Sometimes they never do."

Willie kicked the soccer ball across the room, landing at my feet. I dribbled it with my feet across the floor and out the door, and others followed, even Nick Fowler. We had an exciting soccer game, and everyone who couldn't play cheered us on. Nick played on my team, and although he wasn't very good, I didn't judge him badly for it.

Afterward, Nick came up to me and said, "I'm sorry I judged your ma wrong. I hope you can forgive me." He took a deep breath and put his hand out to me. "And I judged you wrong, too." He held his other hand to his stomach. "You may be short, but you're pretty tough! And you are a great soccer player. No hard feelings?" he asked with a pained look.

I took his hand and pumped it like the pump handle on the old well. "No hard feelings!" I said.

"How do you kick a soccer ball up in the air and hit it with your head?" he asked, and I gave him some pointers.

Most people left after the game, and Gram helped the other women put up the leftover food while some men had smokes. The pastor supervised the food, and I helped Ernest fold the chairs.

"All in all, it was a good day," Ernest said. He didn't say it was a glorious day, just a good day. "Sometimes, that's all you can hope for," he said.

Chapter 26 - Merry and Bright

I couldn't remember the last time Ma was home for Christmas or the last time Ma was happy. In December of 1953, she was both, which was a reason to celebrate.

Ma came along with Ernest and me to pick out a Christmas tree on the Larson property. I walked beside her through the snowdrifts, and she put her hand on my shoulder to steady herself. She looked down at my feet and gave me a strange look.

"Henry, you're getting tall."

"Gram says if I grow into these feet, I'll be as big as Ernest someday." That gave Ernest a chuckle.

"We can only hope that you grow into as fine a person as Ernest."

The way Ma looked at Ernest made me think of Tonto and the Lone Ranger. He was her *Kemosabe*.

"Just don't let Ernest pick out the Christmas tree," I whispered to her.

"I heard that," Ernest's voice boomed with good nature.

As it turned out, Ma found the perfect tree, and Ernest cut it down. He was good at that. Snow began to fall, and white flakes stuck to Ma's eyelashes. She tilted her head to the sky and twirled around, catching wet flakes on her tongue. She looked like a Christmas fairy. I felt like I was floating on air until a wet snowball hit me solidly in the side.

"What the heck," I said, then turning toward the ball's direction, I saw Ernest trying to hide behind a tree.

I scooped up a big handful of snow and packed it tight while on the run. Ernest tried to duck, but he wasn't hard to hit. I got him right in the middle of the back. He laughed and made another snowball right quick.

We were exchanging hits when suddenly, a wet mess hit me from behind. I didn't even get to turn around when I heard Ma laughing like a hyena. She fell backward into the untouched snow and waved her arms and legs, leaving the imprint of a snow angel.

We trudged back home through the snow, with Ma leading the way. I walked beside Ernest dragging the best Christmas tree I ever saw.

"You've got a good throwing arm, son," Ernest said, still brushing snow from his head. "I think you might be a natural for baseball in addition to being a great soccer player."

"You think so?"

His eyebrows raised, and he nodded.

"Maybe I could play for the Chicago Cubs like Otto Vogel!"

"I hear tell he was raised right here in Mendota," Ernest said.

Ma began singing, "I'm dreaming of a white Christmas...."

Ernest joined in with a voice warm as hot cocoa. "... just like the ones I used to know."

I hummed along, listening to their voices mixing together. I raised my voice to the last line, *"May your days be merry and bright ...."*

"...and may all your Christmases be white!" we all sang.

189

≈

Christmas morning, we exchanged gifts. Gram gave Ma a Smith Corona typewriter she got at the secondhand store so that Ma could practice at home. Ma worked part-time in the college bookstore and bought me two Marvel comic books. I thought it was funny that comics were sold at college. Ma said they were all the rage on campus. Willie didn't have the same copies, so I couldn't wait to show him.

Gram cooked a big holiday meal, and it tasted better than any before. After, we drank hot cocoa and sang Christmas carols around the tree. I only hoped all our Christmas days could be as happy as this one.

1954

Chapter 27 - Homework

After the Christmas holiday, we returned to the regular school and homework routine. Ma laid her books on the kitchen table after we cleared the supper dishes. I watched her carefully as she opened her notebook and sharpened her pencil.

"Homework is an important part of education, Henry," she said. "You must take it very seriously."

I nodded my head.

I fetched my school bag, and she made room for my work across the table from her. Ma read and turned the pages of her school book with the tip of her pencil to her tongue. I tried it, but it tasted like ash and metal, and I couldn't say I liked it much. I figured it must be what Willie called an acquired taste, like whiskey. I hadn't acquired either taste yet.

We studied our books and wrote notes while Gram washed the dishes and Ernest dried them. It almost felt as though I had a real family, like Willie Larson's.

After putting away the dishes, Ernest sat down at the table beside me. "What are you fixin' to read?" he asked.

"It's my basic reader," I said, "called *New Times and Places*." I showed him the cover. Ernest's brow wrinkled.

"That's an interesting image," he said, looking at the drawing of a log cabin with tall city buildings looming behind.

He turned to the first page which showed a picture of a wagon train with a jet airplane in the sky. "It surely leaves an impression."

"I think they are trying to show how the world is moving forward," Gram said.

"Want me to read aloud the story the teacher assigned us this week?"

Ernest nodded, and Gram agreed. Ma even put her pencil down to listen.

"It's called 'Machines Are Fun,'" I began. The story told about Jill looking out the window while washing the breakfast dishes. Her brother Jack rode by on the farm tractor. "Then, Jill said, 'I wish I could do that!'" I read on with everyone listening closely. When I finished, it was quiet.

Ma frowned. "I know exactly how Jill feels. Boys always get to do the fun stuff, and girls do dishes."

I thought of Laurel and wondered if she ever wanted to drive her Pa's Farmall tractor. It was pretty big, and she was pretty small.

"Well, the story does tell how times are changing," Gram said. "Jill gets to drive the tractor in the end."

"I think she still has to finish the dishes after," I said.

"That's what I mean." Ma picked up her pencil and pointed it like dotting an i.

"Women are getting more rights," Ernest said, "Brave women like you are making a difference." Ma always shone when Ernest said things like that to her. "You're going to college and making something better of your life."

"That I am," she said proudly.

"You're setting an important example for other young women to dream big," Gram said, and she looked proud, too.

I decided that if I had a tractor, I'd let Laurel drive it because she could dream big, too.

"Someday, maybe there will be a woman president," I said. Everyone agreed.

"Or maybe a black president," Gram said, looking at Ernest.

"That would be something, wouldn't it?" Ernest looked at the cover of my reader again. "We can surely dream."

"The next story in my reader is my favorite." Everyone looked at me with interest. "It's about Nancy and the day her family gets a television."

"Now, that's a dream, Henry," Gram said, and everyone had a good laugh, except me.

Chapter 28 - Homerun

I tried out for the baseball team in the spring. Coach Kennedy said I was a natural-born athlete.

"You get it from your mother," he said. I wondered how he knew I didn't get it from my father, too. I never asked about the man because it didn't really matter.

"You're an outstanding soccer player," Coach said. "You can kick a ball like Fabri Salcedo."

Salcedo was one of my soccer heroes. He immigrated from Spain and was a fierce competitor. "People come from all over to America, don't they?" I said. "I read he was the top scorer in his league and won three titles in the '30s and '40s."

"You're right, Henry. And the way you swing a bat, equally as well with either arm, you're going to excel in baseball, too."

I listened to Coach's words and couldn't wait to get home to tell Ernest, Gram, and Ma what he said.

≈

"Coach thinks I'll be a switch hitter like the great Mickey Mantle. Coach says he's a Yankee, but he forgives him because he loves to watch him swing."

"That's my boy," Ma said.

"Baseball is an honorable sport," Ernest said. "Jackie Robinson was the first professional Negro baseball player in 1947." Ernest looked proud. "Willie Mays is another fine Negro player and an Army man. He played in '51 for the Giants until he went to fight in Korea. He just got back and has taken up his bat again. I hear he's better than ever, and I think he has a long career ahead of him."

When Gram cashed her check on the first of the month, she went straight to Harlow's General Store. Harlow's has just about everything a person needs. They carry all the tools and necessities to plant a proper garden and feed for farm animals. There's also a long meat counter with refrigerated compartments with sliding doors in the back and large windows in the front. Mr. Harlow has a big ole silver meat grinder to make fresh Hamburg every day and a shiny slicer to cut meat into roasts and steaks. He lines them all up neatly in the refrigerated display cases with square tags on each to tell how much they cost. The standup cooler holds milk and soft drinks. There are rows and rows of groceries, even canned goods from the Del Monte canning plant right here in Mendota, although Gram doesn't buy those. We grow all the vegetables we need. But sometimes she needs cloth and thread to mend my clothes or occasionally a new broom when the old one begins to look like a scarecrow's head.

This particular day she didn't go to buy any of those things. She went to buy me a baseball glove. Mr. Harlow said it was made in Missouri and was the best one he sold.

Gram game home carrying a large paper bag. She reached inside and pulled out a brown leather glove with the name Rawlings scrawled across the inside. She placed it in my hands, and I slipped my fingers in the holes.

Then, putting the mitt to my face, I breathed deep, filling my nostrils with the smells of animal and wood, like Old Brown's stall after I cleaned it.

The team practiced twice a week. Coach let me borrow a bat and ball to take home. Ernest coached me; he already knew the basics of sports from helping the soccer team. Ernest was a good pitcher, too. My hits would send the ball flying over the garden, practically to the train tracks. Gram and Ma sat on the porch, cheering me on.

Ma took to being my outfielder since we only had one ball, and it took a long time for me to retrieve it. Willie said he wasn't cut out for team sports. However, he liked watching boxing on television and hoped they might someday offer that sport at school.

"I'd be good at boxing," Willie said. "I like a one-on-one challenge."

Even so, Willie came with Laurel, Isaac, and Mr. and Mrs. Larson to all my games. I had the biggest group of fans there.

Chapter 29 - Happy Days

Ma finished school in May and became a full-fledged secretary. We waited for the bus at the end of the driveway in our go-to-funeral clothes to attend her graduation. When the bus driver in his blue uniform turned the lever, the door slid open like an accordion. Ernest helped Gram up the first step, and she took a dollar out of her big blue purse to pay the driver.

"It must be a special day," the driver said, looking at our fancy clothes.

"My daughter Janie is graduating today," Gram said with pride.

Ma's cheeks turned a little redder when the driver turned to the other passengers and shouted, "This young girl is graduating today!" Everyone cheered and clapped as we walked down the aisle to our seats.

Ma had a white robe with a square hat that looked silly to me. I wasn't sure I wanted to graduate if I had to wear a hat like that. But Ma seemed to like it. She wore it all day.

After getting her diploma, she ran over to show it to us. Her name stood out in big gold letters, Janie Adams, and under that, it said "Certificate of Graduation from the Professional Secretary Program."

Gram took out her handkerchief and dabbed her eyes. "I'm proud of you, Janie!"

Ma hugged Gram. I looked up at Ernest, and he had a big smile. He felt me looking at him and glanced down.

"Your ma and Gram are two smart ladies."

I'd never thought much about Gram being book-smart. She knew everything about cooking and cleaning; she was a fine gardener too. But I wasn't sure if she was good at school. My thoughts must have escaped into the air because Ernest caught them.

"Your Gram is one of the smartest ladies I've ever met." He nodded his head the way he did when making a point. "School is important, but life teaches many important things, too." I narrowed my eyes in thought. "So, pay attention, son."

"Yes, sir," I said.

Ernest was not *one* of the wisest men I ever knew; he was *the* wisest by far. He must have paid attention.

We rode back home on the big bus. It was a different driver, and he led another big cheer for Ma. It was probably the most excitement they ever had on the local bus.

Gram made a big sheet cake and wrote 'Congratulations Janie' in red frosting. Ma never looked happier. We sat at the kitchen table while Ma cut the pieces and handed them out. She even gave Ernest Pig a slice. We laughed at the red-and-white frosting all over his snout.

"That's one lucky pig," Ernest said.

I thought I was pretty lucky, too.

That summer, Ma got a job at Doc Cunningham's office in town, and everything was great for a while. Ma wore pretty dresses every day with red lipstick and a touch of perfume behind each ear, with a drop on each wrist for good measure. She had a new pair of cat's-eye glasses and a fancy white purse too.

Ma waited every day at the end of the driveway for the bus to town. She came home with the same big smile she left with in the morning. At supper she would tell us all about her important work.

"The patients love me," she said. "And so does Doc Cunningham."

≈

When Little League ended, I was unsure what to do next. Willie stayed busy planting a crop with his pa. He rode on the back of his pa's Farmall tractor with the tiller attached.

Mr. Larson decided to plant soybeans that season, while everyone in these parts planted corn.

"What are you doing with soybeans?" I asked Willie when he hopped down from the tractor to greet me.

"You will not believe this—they make cars out of them."

Willie had told some tall tales before, but this one had to be as tall as the Empire State Building in New York City.

"I'm not kidding you. Mr. Henry Ford hired scientists to figure out how to make plastic out of soybeans. He uses it for gearshift knobs, horn buttons, window frames, accelerator pedals, and light switches. My pa is a Ford man, so he wants to grow soybeans for Mr. Ford."

I sure hoped Mr. Ford was a fan of the Larsons' soybeans.

Laurel had a lot of time on her hands, as I did. So, I walked over in the afternoons to see if she wanted to play. Laurel always looked happy to see me. She said her ma got a part-time job at the town hall to keep busy. "Since the children are older now," Mrs. Larson had said.

Sometimes Laurel and I took a couple of fish poles down to the creek. We dug worms from the garden. I put them on the hook for her since she didn't like that part. Laurel talked a lot more when Willie wasn't around. She still had a hard time saying certain words, but I never hurried her. I had nowhere to go.

"Henrry, how come you'rre so nice to girrlss?"

This question stumped me.

"I didn't know I was nicer to girls."

"You'rre nice to everyone. But not all boys are nice to girrlss."

I thought this over. It was true; most boys in my class said girls were dumb. I thought about what Ernest said about Ma and Gram.

"Girls are smart, and any boy that doesn't think so is dumb."

Laurel's face sparkled like the sunlight reflecting off the creek.

"I like you, Henrry Adamss."

My face must have looked like tomato soup.

≈

On July 12, 1954, I turned eleven years old and Ma was there.

Gram made my favorite chocolate cake and invited the Larsons over like it was a real party. There were presents in fancy wrapping paper and even balloons. Ma said she'd never seen such a fine birthday party, and we pretended she never missed all my other birthdays.

Gram and Ernest gave me a secondhand bicycle they bought at Bosworth's Bike Shop. I didn't care it was used; it was shiny and red and went just as fast as Willie's. Laurel and Willie bought me a Mr. Potato Head.

Ma couldn't wait for me to open my gift from her.

"A globe of the world!" I twirled it around. Ma showed me some of the places she had traveled.

Gram lit eleven candles on my cake. Everyone sang "Happy Birthday" with enthusiasm. I blew out all the candles in one breath, and Gram served slices of cake with vanilla ice cream.

After we finished, Gram handed me three big spuds to play Mr. Potato Head with Willie and Laurel. We took them into the parlor, making funny potato people with plastic eyes, noses, and hats.

The grown-ups talked and laughed in the kitchen until after dark. I wished it would never end. Nineteen fifty-four was a good year to turn eleven.

Chapter 30 - Men and Dogs

As the summer got on, Ma looked less pleased with her job. Her smile was missing when she got home, and it disappeared in the morning as well. She didn't even talk about her job at supper anymore. One day, I saw Ernest stop to talk to her in the yard. I hedged up near to hear them without being seen.

"Morning, Ernest," Ma greeted him.

"Morning, Miss. How's your work going?"

Ma took a deep breath. She lifted her chin, and her lower lip trembled. "Why—?" she started and stopped. Then holding her head high, she asked, "Why are men such dogs, Ernest?"

Ernest raised his brow and nodded his head sadly. "Miss, that is surely a good question," he agreed. "I've asked the good Lord that myself on many occasions."

"What did he say?" Ma asked in a soft voice.

"Well, the good Lord doesn't always tell you answers straight out. Sometimes you have to figure them out like a puzzle."

"I've never been good at puzzles." Ma hung her head.

"Is Doc giving you some trouble?" Ernest inquired.

Ma nodded her head without speaking a word.

"Hmm." Ernest thought. "Has he hurt you, Miss?"

"No, nothing like that."

"Are you scared of him?"

"Not exactly."

"Oh," Ernest's face looked clear as the dawn sky. "Is he making unwanted advances?"

She nodded her head and paused. "You know the funny thing, Ernest?"

"What's that?"

"Last year, I would have been happy if Doc had come on to me."

"Now you're not?"

Ma shook her head.

Ernest pursed his lips together. "You're a smart girl, Janie," Ernest said, and I blinked. I had never heard him call Ma by her given name.

"You're getting smarter all the time," he continued. "Now you know the difference between a man and a dog." He looked Ma straight in the eyes. "I'm proud of you, Miss Janie."

I never saw Ma so pleased. I thought she was about to burst.

"You keep doing your work, and I think Doc will come to his senses."

"You really think so, Ernest?"

"He's got a good wife," Ernest said. "I think he just needs a little reminding of that."

"I'll ask him about her."

"That's a good idea. You're certainly becoming a fine young lady."

Ma blushed.

"Ernest, I'd be happy if you were fucking the old lady."

Ernest lowered his head. "Now that you are a proper young lady, I hoped you'd have second thoughts on using that four-letter word." He looked at her with his head tilted and raised one brow. "That's not love."

"You're right, Ernest. I'm sorry. I think I've learned the difference." She smirked. "I know now how a man looks at a woman he loves. I see it every morning right in this farmhouse kitchen." She turned to dance off toward the house and stopped.

"I won't use that word anymore," she said, turning back towards him. "Oh, and Ernest, I like when you call me Janie."

"Yes, Miss Janie," Ernest smiled and lowered his head.

She turned towards the house and stopped again. Pivoting on one foot, she looked over her shoulder at Ernest.

"Ernest," she said with a serious look. "I would be pleased if you made love to my ma." With a soft giggle, she turned quickly and skipped up the porch steps into the house.

Ernest stood with his mouth puffing in and out, looking like a stranded fish. Finally, he grunted and headed off to the barn shaking his head.

I kicked the rock at my feet with a fury. "When am I going to be old enough to know the meaning of it all!"

Chapter 31 - Like a Family

After Ernest finished his breakfast, he rose slowly from his chair. He made some noises as he used to when he first came to the farm when I visited him in the shack by the tracks. Gram took notice, too.

"What's ailing you, Ernest?" Gram asked.

"Oh, no need for alarm, ma'am," Ernest said. "Just some creaks in the back and knees."

"Is it your ailment acting up?" Gram reached out as if she would touch him, then she stopped.

I watched as Ma left to catch the bus with a determined look. Ernest told Gram he thought he'd pay a visit to Doc after tending to the animals. I finished breakfast and grabbed my school bag to meet Willie and Laurel.

"We had TV dinners last night," Willie couldn't wait to tell me.

"What?" Well, that takes the cake, I thought. The Larsons have a television, and now they have dinners to go with it. And I don't have either.

"Yeah, they come in a tin tray with meat, potatoes, vegetables, and a dessert!"

I wanted to spit.

Ernest returned from Doc that afternoon. He looked like it went well. At supper that night, Ernest asked Ma how her workday went.

"It was a trying morning with Doc," Ma said. "His mood changed after lunch, and he was quite pleasant." She looked at Ernest with a sly smile.

After supper, Ernest and I went outside. I brought a jar to catch fireflies. Ernest sat on the porch and watched me.

"I need to rest these weary bones, son," he said.

"Didn't Doc fix you up today?"

He laughed a little. "Ain't a whole lot Doc can do for me," Ernest said. "We just had a heart-to-heart talk, and I think it cleansed both our souls."

Ernest talked a lot about souls and cleaning them. I wondered if I should be cleaning mine. "What does a dirty soul look like?" I asked.

He chuckled. "It ain't how it looks," he said. "It's more how it feels. When your soul is unclean, there's no room in your heart for joy." He rested his hand on the top of my head, and his fingers touched the tops of my ears. "You need not fret about it, son. Your soul is as squeaky clean as your Gram's dishes."

"What about Doc's soul?" I asked. I surely didn't want him checking my tonsils with a dirty soul.

Ernest's bottom lip tightened, and he nodded his head slowly. "Doc just got a little off the path. He lost his way and needed a reminder of what's really important."

"What's that, sir?"

Ernest looked me straight in the face, and his eyes sparkled in the setting sun. "The people you love," he said, his face twisted with emotion.

Ernest took me into his large arms and held me close. I thought he didn't want me to see his tears. His talk with Doc seemed to make him sad in a happy way. I hugged him back tightly, and it felt good. I wanted to say I loved him, but I didn't know if it was proper.

He said, "The people who love you back are what's important."

I knew he must have read my mind because Ernest could do that sometimes.

I felt him wipe his hand across his face before letting me loose. "Now, go catch some of those fireflies so I can see them up close."

While I chased the flickering lights among the tall grass, I saw Ma come out on the porch and sit on the step near Ernest. They talked for a while, both smiling. I watched Ma put her hand up to touch Ernest but stop herself before she did.

I thought of the day in the yard when Ma first came to know Ernest, and my stomach clenched.

But it was okay this time. Ernest took her gently by the shoulders and hugged her. Not a hug like I had seen Butch Harlow give an older girl at school, full of moving hands and hips.

Instead, Ernest hugged Ma like Mr. Larson does Laurel when she needs some comfort. Ma reached her arms around, spanning Ernest's back, and patted him like burping a baby.

Gram came out on the porch taking in the scene. She dropped her dishcloth and wrapped her arms around them the best she could. I ran up to the porch, forgetting my jar of lightning bugs, and jumped into the mix. We were like a family that night.

≈

The next day Doc Cunningham's wife drove into our yard in her fancy little car. Willie would have gone crazy to see it.

Dressed in a pretty print dress with high heels and her hair teased up like a beehive, she looked out of place standing between the barn and the chicken coop. I continued to feed the chickens as Gram came out to welcome her.

"Mrs. Adams, it's good to see you," she said. "Janie has been a godsend to the business since Ellie retired. She's a quick learner and has taken much of the pressure off me. I had to do the books in the interim and didn't care for it." Despite her words, she didn't look relieved.

"Nice of you to say, Mrs. Cunningham. Janie loves her job." Gram looked pleased, but it seemed there was something both of them were holding back. Gram let it loose first. "Mrs. Cunningham, Janie is still a naïve girl for all her waywardness. She's not fully aware of her own devices."

Mrs. Cunningham interrupted her from going any further, "No. It's not her fault at all." She didn't say what *it* was exactly. "Men get to an age where they think the grass is greener. I should have seen it coming. I'm busy with engagements and clubs ..." Her voice drifted off, and she looked down at her fancy shoes.

"We never had children."

She glanced toward me, and I turned my back, tending to the chickens.

"I'm glad, to tell the truth; I'm not good with them. But maybe if he'd had his own, he wouldn't be so lonely for attention." She paused. "Maybe he would know when to be a man and when to be a father figure."

"Sometimes men do get confused about their place as a man." Gram seemed to think about someone else. "The good ones find their intended path."

I glanced over my shoulder to see Mrs. Cunningham pulling a handkerchief from her pretty little purse and pressing it to her eyes. "Donald promised he has seen the light and to alter his wanton ways." She gently wiped her nose. "I think I can trust him."

Gram nodded in silent support.

"Janie thinks the world of Doc—and you," Gram said. "I hope you don't think badly of her."

"No. I don't." Her voice cracked. "It's Donald who owes her an apology."

"I don't think there is a need for any apologies," Gram said. "Janie's old enough to know everyone makes mistakes."

"I don't truly know if Donald would have seen the errors of his ways if Ernest hadn't come to talk with him. Donald respects Ernest. He speaks about him often."

Gram smiled. "Ernest has a way of making wanton men good and good men better. Women, too, for that matter." She made a small laugh. "I believe everything is going to be okay."

"Me, too," Mrs. Cunningham said. "Me, too."

She got back into her sporty car and rolled down the window to take Gram's hand. "Please thank Ernest for me."

"I will," Gram promised. She watched Mrs. Cunningham drive away.

I finished tossing the feed, thinking there are all types of families—some more complicated than others. I was thankful for mine.

Chapter 32 - A Man in Uniform

In September, a stranger walked down the driveway wearing a smart-looking uniform, with a snap to his step and an odd sparkle in his blue eyes.

"United States Army, Sgt. Frank Wheeler, ma'am," he greeted Gram. "I'm on leave from the Army training base over at Joliet, and I'd be mighty grateful for a cold drink and a small bite to eat."

She nodded her head. "We get lost travelers here from time to time."

The two-lane road that came through Mendota was not well-marked. Cars sometimes got off in Mendota, thinking it was the main road. I looked to the road to see if he'd parked there and walked in, but I didn't see a car. He must have hitched a ride with his thumb like Shamus.

I stood next to Ernest. The stranger said howdy to me and messed my hair. He looked Ernest up and down with interest. Ernest stood tall with his hands behind his back, looking straight ahead.

"I can tell you're a military man by your stance, sir," the sergeant said and put his hand out. "What's your name, good man?"

"Ernest Potts, sir." He raised his right hand to his forehead.

"At ease, soldier," Frank smiled. "We're on neutral ground today."

Ma came out on the porch, and the sergeant's smile grew.

"This is my daughter, Janie," Gram said. "Now you've met everyone."

Ernest Pig came running from the back of the barn.

"Everyone except Ernest Pig," I said.

We all laughed and went in for cold drinks and toasted tomato sandwiches.

Frank's family must have wondered where he got off to because he stayed with us for his whole leave. He bunked in Ernest's old room in the barn and took his meals with us in the farmhouse.

Ma took a new liking to the garden, and Frank was pleased to help her. Ma weeded, and Frank did the picking. I never thought gardening particularly funny, but Ma sure laughed a lot while Frank helped her tend the crop. Ernest and I could have helped Ma, but Frank had to earn his keep. Ernest and I had plenty of other chores to keep us busy.

Gram asked Frank to help her get some cans from the root cellar one day.

I went to the pig sty to check on the mama pig and her new litter. They weren't nearly as good-looking as Ernest Pig, but they were cute enough. I crouched in the pen when I heard Ernest enter the barn with Ma.

"Miss Janie, I know you're a little mature to take advice from an old man like me." Ernest paused. "I just want you to be careful."

"Ernest, I been around a block or two, although I have to admit I've gotten a little lost at times. I was looking for love, but I just got fu—well, you know."

My ears perked up at what I thought was that word again. I stayed still, hoping I might catch the meaning.

Ernest cleared his throat. "The best kind of love finds you."

"You think so?"

"You're a fine woman, Janie, and you will be a wonderful wife for some lucky man."

Ma made a soft sound. "I hope I find someone as honorable as you, Ernest."

"Oh, no, Miss Janie," Ernest laughed. "You don't want someone like me."

"Well, younger and a little richer would be nice, too," she teased.

"And a lot lighter, I hope," Ernest added.

"None of that really matters." Ma sounded thoughtful. "The important thing is I find a kind man who loves me for me, not just the other thing."

"I'm happy you've learned that part." Ernest sounded proud. "And now that you're a professional secretary and a lady, I hope you've found another word for that particular business."

Ma laughed like a schoolgirl. "The f-word?"

"I try to speak the words I want people to follow," Ernest explained. "If you want a man to show you respect, you must let him know you deserve it. So, when you find the right man, find the words to fit how you want to be treated."

"Ernest, you are special, and we're lucky you came to live here."

"Miss Janie, I'm the lucky one."

They went along, and I was left to ponder this f-word further.

≈

It was nearly nine days since Frank had stopped for a drink and a bite to eat—it seemed longer. I didn't hate him. I wished I could. But there was something really likable about him. Frank helped Gram with the dishes after supper, and he played checkers with Ernest. He even played catch with me. It's hard to hate a man like that.

One evening after supper Frank sat on the porch with Ma having a glass of lemonade while I listened through the screen door. They talked about the places Frank had traveled.

When Frank told her about the big bridge in San Francisco, Ma's eyes lit up like stars. "I wish I could take you to all the beautiful places in the world." Frank took her hand.

"I'd love to see them." Ma sounded dreamy.

Frank told her about the many jobs for professional women like her in the army.

"There are offices in bases all over that need secretaries," Frank said.

"I have a good job here, and maybe it's time for me to settle down. You know, find a good man that deserves me."

"It'll be a lucky man who you settle with." That's when I heard the words. "You're a smart girl, Janie. You can do anything."

I knew there would be no more smell of fancy perfume at the farmhouse.

The following day, Frank said he had to get back to his post. He didn't mention visiting his family. Before he left, he thanked Gram for her hospitality. With his duffle bag hanging from one shoulder, he shook Ernest's hand firmly.

"You be a good boy, now," Frank said to me. I could see that sparkle in his eyes again. "Listen to your Gram and Ernest." He tousled my already messy hair, not quite looking me in the eye.

The next day Ma was gone. No one made mention of her until a couple of days later.

≈

I sat at the supper table with Gram and Ernest, eating gravy and biscuits.

"Move your things back to Janie's room," Gram said to Ernest. She looked at her plate, pushed her biscuit around in the gravy, and took another bite.

"There's no need—," Ernest began. "Maybe she'll be back."

Gram shook her head. "Henry needs his space."

I wanted to say I had enough space. Then I thought maybe Ernest Pig would appreciate the cot.

Ernest looked like he knew well enough not to argue with Gram by now. So after supper he gathered his things and put them back in Ma's room.

Gram left the cot up, and Ernest Pig liked it real well.

Doc Cunningham hired a new secretary, and the bus didn't stop at the end of the driveway to pick up Ma anymore.

The postman brought the first postcard a few weeks later. San-Fran-cis-co, I sounded out the name.

Ernest said he'd been there when he returned from overseas. "It overlooks the Pacific Ocean," he said.

Ma wrote that she and Frank got married. "He made an honest woman out of me!"

Frank's new assignment was at Fort Hunter Liggett in Jolon, California. Ma was working in an office for a general and said she was thrilled.

"As soon as we settle down in the perfect place, we'll come for you, Henry," she wrote on the back of the picture postcard she sent me.

I hoped they'd never find that place because I thought the farm was perfect for me.

Ma sent postcards to Gram telling of all her adventures. Gram sat in her rocker and read them over and over. Sometimes Ma would even send a postcard to Ernest. She told him to take good care of her boy.

"I'll pin them up on your ma's bedroom wall, so when she comes back, she can see them," Ernest said.

We never knew when that would be.

≈

Days passed, and it wasn't long before it seemed like Ma had never been there. Sometimes when I came downstairs in the morning, I'd see Ernest standing by the stove next to Gram, carefully placing strips of bacon in the old iron skillet while Gram dropped the eggs into the pot of boiling water.

The two of them put me in mind of the old clock in the parlor. Gram's hands passed over the tops of Ernest's in perfect timing, without a hitch, never quite touching.

If I paused before entering the room, I saw Gram turn her face up to Ernest and him look down at her; their eyes met just like they were sharing a secret. I wondered what it was.

I hardly thought of my gramp anymore, but sometimes he came to mind when I saw Ernest and Gram together; I don't know why. Gramp was nothing like Ernest. When he had talked to Gram, his voice was rough like sandpaper on metal, not smooth and soft like Ernest's. And his skin wasn't black, either, although sometimes it seemed like his heart was. I never remember seeing him smile at Gram the way Ernest did.

After a time, I began hearing soft voices from Gram's bedroom at night. At first, I thought they sounded like ghosts in the night. I wondered if Gramp had woken from the dead. Then I heard Gram's laugh like a whisper in the wind. I had never noticed it before, but there it was.

Each night, as I concentrated, I began to recognize the smooth, comforting sounds of Ernest's deep, warm voice. And I wondered what he and Gram discussed into all hours of the night. I always fell asleep before Ernest came upstairs.

Chapter 33 - Secrets

One night when I made my way to the toilet, the talk from Gram's room stopped suddenly. I did my business and went back to my room, closing the door soundly. Then I inched it open and squeezed back out without a sound. I snuck down the hall and sat on the top stair to listen.

"Ernest, I don't deserve someone as good and kind as you."

"Now, Margarette," Ernest said in a soft, low voice.

I scratched my head and wondered who he was talking to.

"I know you to be an honest woman," he continued, "and that statement has to be the most untrue words ever spoken."

My eyes bugged out as I realized he was speaking to Gram. I never knew her given name. Some people called her Marg. Ma called her Mama, and when Gramp was alive, he called her "Woman."

I listened, and Ernest repeated it. "Margarette." He pronounced each letter like my teacher reciting an important word.

Then I heard my gram weeping softly. "You don't know the terrible things I've done."

"We are none of us without sin, Margarette," he soothed her. "I can't imagine yours are so great. I've not always been a man of honor, and it is me who needs to ask your forgiveness."

"Hush," Gram said.

"No," Ernest continued. "You need to know something about my past."

"I don't care," Gram said with force.

"I do. And so does the Lord."

"So be it," Gram said. "Let us both cleanse our souls. I'm going first."

I held my breath as Gram spoke.

"It's my fault Janie left at such a young age," she began. "I knew. I knew what was going on, and I didn't stop it." She choked back a sob.

"You don't have to do this, Margarette."

"I do, and I'm going to," Gram insisted. "Henry had a hateful streak."

My ears perked up, and I realized she was talking about Gramp.

"I knew it from the day we married—not before. I thought he would mellow after the first babe was born. It didn't survive the beatings. I miscarried at seven months along. He buried the infant in the family plot without a word. It was a boy."

There was a shifting of bodies, and Gram continued her story. "Ten months later, Janie came along. She was a survivor from conception. I could feel it. Henry doted on Janie at first, and as she got older, he doted on her too much." She stopped to catch her breath. "I should have seen it coming—I just wanted it to be okay. Janie went to him and soothed him whenever he raised his hand to me. I didn't see then that she was saving me. Yet I didn't save her from his randy touches."

"You didn't know," Ernest tried to say.

"I should have," Gram shouted. "I should have seen it was more than fatherly affection."

Ernest made a humming sound like a person rocking a baby.

Gram spoke again. "When she ran off the first time, she was just fifteen; I was worried sick. Henry was fit to be tied. He beat me every day like it was my fault she left. And I felt like I deserved the punishment."

Gram continued. "I didn't go out in public. I didn't want people to see the bruises. That's when I stopped going to church, and I felt like the Lord deserted me, and Janie, too." She sighed deeply. "Yet, the good Lord must have been with her because she returned home unharmed a year later—with a babe in her arms. But I could see it then; she was broken. I tried to comfort her. She put on a tough act and took no sympathy.

"She loved the boy. I know she did, but she was just a child herself. I took him on as my own and let Janie be a child. The only saving grace was that Henry wanted nothing to do with her after she had the boy. "Tainted," he called her. The girl grew up without a proper pa, but he didn't touch her anymore. At least there was that.

"The odd thing was, Henry was good with the boy at first, and he stopped beating me for a while. It made me wonder if our boy had lived, would it have been different."

Gram paused for a moment. "Women never have it easy in this world. Janie struggled for the next few years. She did well in her studies when she put her mind to them. But she quit school just before graduation. Her mind wandered, and it wandered toward boys. Oh, Ernest, I didn't know how to stop it."

Ernest made a low humming sound like an idling motor with nowhere to go.

"When the circus came round, Janie was near twenty. She was searching for something, and it wasn't on this farm. I can't say I was surprised when the circus left town and Janie was gone, too. I told myself it was for the best. I said a prayer and let her go in God's hands."

There was silence, then Gram said, "The sadness took him over, and the year after Janie left, Henry carried the shotgun into the barn and took his own life." Gram gulped. "I was standing in the kitchen when I heard the shot. It was like it went right through me."

I sucked in my breath so fast that I almost choked. I stifled it and kept listening. I vaguely remembered the day as she was telling it to Ernest.

"I saw Henry grab the shotgun from the corner by the door. He stopped and put his hand on the boy's little shoulder. 'I never meant to hurt you, boy,' he said. I thought it odd for him to say, then I remembered a couple of days before the boy took a tumble while they gathered kindling wood, and Henry cuffed him before he thought.

" 'I know, Gramp,' the boy said to him. 'I wasn't watching my feet like you told me.' "

A chill ran through me as I remembered the day Gram was talking about.

"I didn't believe he'd ever meant to hurt the boy," Gram continued. "He didn't say a word to me. He didn't even look my way as he went out the door that day. I knew as soon as I heard the shot—one single shot. The boy was having his breakfast. He jumped up to see what his gramp was about. I stopped him from going out. I told him Gramp was taking care of some grown-up business. But, in truth, it wasn't grown up at all. It was the business of a guilty conscience. But I'm no better. I bear the guilt of hiding what was happening in my own family, and they all suffered for my lacking. How can God ever forgive me?"

"Hmm," Ernest said, with a low roll of the letters that made it sound like the start of a hymn. "Sometimes, our paths are not clear, Margarette. All we can do is the best with the circumstances we're given. There's no benefit in what-ifs. I can't speak for God, but I believe he sees all very clearly."

"That's rightly so. I think I'm better prepared for that meeting now that I've shared my burden with you. But the question in my mind still weighs heavy. While we're here on earth, how can you want to stay with me?"

"I'm certain the Lord knows your heart, Margarette. And so do I." Ernest seemed to be gathering his thoughts. "As for me, I thank the Lord for guiding me here to you. If you haven't noticed, and sometimes I think you don't, I'm a black man."

Gram gave a little laugh, and I heard a lightness in Ernest's voice. "You took me into your home without hesitation."

Gram stopped him. "I'm afraid I did hesitate a second or two when Shamus asked me to take you in."

"Okay, you took me into your home with only a couple of seconds of hesitation when anyone else would have let me die in a cold boxcar. Is that a fair statement?"

"Yes," Gram whispered.

"You fed me and nurtured me and kept me alive. And more than that, you trusted and protected me in the face of others who meant me harm." Ernest took a deep breath, "Now you've taken me into your bed. But even more unbelievable, you've taken me into your heart." Ernest's voice faltered. "I love you, Margarette. I love all of you, every hair on your head, every word from your mouth, everything you are, and everything you've ever been. I love you."

I stood quietly and tip-toed back to my room. I was unsure if there were more secrets to tell, but I was too tired to hear them.

≈

I awoke to the sound of a hammer on stone. Wiping the sleep from my eyes, I made my way to the window. I tried to place the relentless pounding and saw two figures in the distance in the family plot.

I squinted my eyes and watched Gram hoist up what looked like the big ole sledgehammer to shoulder height and let it fall. I blinked in shock as I determined what it fell on.

Gramp's headstone was the largest among the few stones inside the two parallel iron bars anchored in the corners to standing granite stones.

In the far corner of the plot stood the headstone of Gramp's parents. It was tall and thin, made of slate, unlike his.

His older brother Harold had a smaller granite stone with his name and dates. He never married and died before I was born. The only other stone was small and flat; it just said "Baby Boy Adams" with one date.

Gramp's stone was gray granite, thick, and sturdy. The Stoneman brought it sometime before Gramp passed. On the front, the name Adams stood out large and bold. Under that, near the bottom, read a quote from the Bible in a smaller script.

Yea, though I walk through the valley of the shadow of death, I will fear no evil.

Gram always said Gramp wanted it, and Gramp got things the way he wanted. The letters of his name carved deep on the back listed his birth date to the left and the date he passed to the right. Gram's name placed under it gave me a chill whenever I saw it.

The only time I looked at it up close was on Gramp's burial day. After that, I never went near it again. Sometimes I watched Gram pick daffodils in the spring or wild daisies in the summer and bring them to the cemetery. She didn't go to Gramp's grave, though. Instead, she placed them on the tiny flat stone and knelt to pray.

A loud crash of metal on stone brought me back to the scene outside my window. Now Ernest held the sledgehammer above his head. It came down on the stone with force, and a big corner dropped off. He handed the hammer back to Gram, and she took another whack.

Pieces of stone crumbled, and a brief cloud of dust rose, carried swiftly by the breeze.

I wondered if it was Gramp's spirit leaving for another place. I watched until they finished. It took some time, and Ernest did the brunt of the hammering. When they completed the task, I'd have thought there was never a headstone there if I didn't know better.

Winter came early and snow soon covered the family plot. Not a mention was made of Gramp's crumbled stone. Instead, we all seemed to be more concentrated on the living. Laughter and music filled the old farmhouse. It felt more like a home than ever, even if it didn't have a television like the Larsons.

1955

Chapter 34 - Just Visiting

Ma and Frank returned for a visit the following summer after I turned twelve.

Gram let them stay in her bedroom downstairs, and she slept on the cot in my room. Ernest Pig didn't mind too much. I told him it wouldn't be for long.

Ernest slept in Ma's room as though he always had been. Ma never went upstairs, so she didn't see the postcards on the wall. But, of course, she already knew what they looked like since she sent them.

They stayed for three days and told us all about their travels. Ma was busy seeing all the new places. I thought she'd forgotten my birthday again. But Ma said she would never forget my birthday. So I didn't bother to tell her about when I turned eight and nine and all the others she missed. They were a long time ago, and it wasn't important anyway.

She brought me a black *ViewMaster* in a case with circular slides of pictures.

"You look through the lenses, and it enlarges the little pictures," Ma said. "Just pull the lever on the side for the next slide."

There were pictures of California and even the new Disneyland Park with Mickey Mouse.

"Wow! Wait until Laurel and Willie see this," I said.

Ma smiled.

Later, I was coming out of the barn when I saw Ma stop to talk to Ernest. I stopped just inside the door. "I found a pair of your shoes under her bed," she said with a wink and smile. "She deserves some happiness. I'm glad she found you. Or maybe it was you who found us."

Ernest looked into her eyes. "You deserved some happiness, too, Miss Janie. I hope Frank treats you right, and if he doesn't, you let me know. You hear?"

"Frank is real good to me. I've never been happier," Ma said. "And you know what, Ernest?"

"What's that, Miss Janie?"

"It's all because of you."

"Miss Janie," he smiled at her. "Happiness is in here. You had it all along." He patted his heart with his hand. "When you open your heart, you find someone to share it. If you are ever looking for happiness again, that's where to find it. So don't forget it."

"Yes, Ernest. And you, too, okay?"

≈

When the time came for Ma and Frank to leave again, Ma took my hands, and I looked into her bottomless blue eyes.

"Henry, Frank and I are leaving for Boston. It might not be perfect, but you can come with us." She paused and looked up at Frank. "Frank approves."

Gram and Ernest watched us from the porch. I glanced down at the chicken droppings on Frank's shiny shoes that looked out of place on the farm.

"Gram and Ernest need me, Ma," I said. I had an itch on my back, but Ma had hold of both my hands. I was glad when Frank took Ma's hands in his.

"The boy's right, Janie," he said. "There will be other times."

Ernest Pig snorted and rolled in a puddle by the water pump. "Well, that pig will be glad you're staying," Ma said, and we all laughed. A tear rolled down Ma's cheek.

Ma sent postcards from Boston. She said I probably wouldn't like it because there were no chickens or pigs. If I had written back, I'd have told her there are no pigs anywhere like Ernest Pig, but I didn't have time. Ma and Frank lived in a different place every year. I figured they wouldn't make it back for my birthday next year, either.

Chapter 35 - Boy Talk

Willie and I sat at the bend where Mendota Creek flowed into the Vermilion River, throwing rocks in the water. A new eagle's nest spanned the top of a giant pine tree on the other side of the creek. The family of eagles had returned to the same tree every year for as long as I could remember. They added sticks and fixed up the old nest year after year until a blizzard took it down.

I looked up, admiring their new home. "Remember when the old nest fell?" I asked Willie.

He paused from throwing rocks in the creek. "Yeah, I think we were around nine," he said. "We didn't think they'd return." He looked up at the male eagle soaring in for a landing. "But they did."

The female eagle stretched her wings and took flight. "They take turns taking care of the young ones," I observed. "Like a real family." Two babies covered in gray-white downy feathers popped their heads up. "They sure look different when they are young," I said.

"Yeah, but they look exactly the same as each other, like twins."

"It's funny how your sister looks like you," I said. "Then she doesn't."

"What do you mean by that?" Willie asked.

"Well, you both have blue eyes and blonde hair." I paused. "You even have the same nose, but it all looks a whole lot better on her."

"You talk a lot about my sister," Willie said.

"I do not."

"Yes, you do—and the funny thing is, she talks a lot about you."

"She does?" I wanted to know more, but Willie never stayed on any particular subject for long. He had too much to say.

"I think Sandra Bolton likes me," Willie said. "She's always giving me that 'come-hither' look."

"Oh." I mulled this new phrase over in my head. "What's a hither?" I asked while Willie sat staring starry-eyed toward the sky.

"What?" he asked, jarred from his daydreaming. "Hither? Well, that's Bible talk for 'come here,' don't you know?"

Of course, I didn't, but Willie had attended more church than me.

"The pastor says it in the scripture." Willie puffed his chest and tucked his chin, giving his best Pastor Morgan impression. "Thou shall come hither, too, but no further!"

We both laughed.

"Besides," Willie said, "I heard my pa say it in conversation with Mr. Harlow in the back room at the General Store when they thought I wasn't listening."

I couldn't picture Mr. Larson or Mr. Harlow reciting scripture.

"Really?"

"Yeah, Mr. Harlow said Widow Stone gave him that 'come-hither' look when she came in the store to buy silk stockings. And my pa said he'd like to see a 'come-hither' look. But they both agreed it was best not to return the look."

In fourth grade, Willie and Sandra Bolton became good friends after she came down with polio. Willie always watched out for her, but this sounded like something more. "So, what are you going to do about Sandra Bolton?" I asked. "Are you going to 'come-hither' back at her?" I wondered about this look and whether Laurel knew.

"Nah, I'm going to play it cool." Willie squinted his eyes. "I don't want her to think she can get me to 'come-hither' that easy."

Willie was cool, so I decided to do the same. Besides, I didn't know exactly how it looked anyway.

≈

The next time I saw Laurel, I was a little scared. If she gave me one of those looks, I didn't know what to do.

She looked normal to me. But she thought I didn't look quite right.

"Is there something wrrong, Henrry? You sseem a little differrrent today."

"Me? Different? No."

She turned her head and looked at me sideways, maybe to see if I looked different from that direction. I passed.

"Hmm, well, Willie went to town with Pa."

I wasn't at all unhappy to hear that, but I didn't say it. Then, a dark cloud began to drop some summer showers.

"Do you want to come into the housse and watch television?"

There was nothing I wanted to do more. I said, "Yes."

I sat on the couch, and Laurel sat beside me. I glanced at her from time to time to see if she made any strange 'come-hither' looks at me—she didn't.

Mrs. Larson wasn't working at the town hall that day, so she baked some oatmeal cookies. She brought us some of them warm from the oven with milk. We watched a new show about a dog named Lassie, and we both thought the boy should be more careful.

"He's lucky to have that dog to save him," I said.

"That's a smarrt dog. When our old hound dog chasses after rraccoons, he'd never come back to ssave uss."

Laurel was right about that. Lassie came to live on the farm with the boy, his ma, and his grandfather. It wasn't a regular family like the Larsons. It was more of an irregular family like mine. But they didn't have an Ernest like we did.

Chapter 36 - Less Fortunate

We formed a line in the school hall that reached all the way from the gym to the front door. Voices blended together to sound like the chatter of chipmunks. Girls with bows tied in the back of their dresses and patent leather shoes stood with their hands folded while boys pushed and shoved each other with smiles on their faces. We waited to walk over to the town hall to get our polio vaccinations. Gram said it was the new vaccine a doctor named Salk developed. She said it was a miracle.

"They're going to stab us in the arm," Willie said.

"It's better than going in an iron lung," I said.

"Orrr having to walk with brracess on your legss," said Laurel. She didn't say "like Sandra Bolton," but we all thought it.

When the line started to move, we filed past our classroom door. Willie peeked in at Sandra Bolton. She sat alone at her desk, a metal brace with nuts and bolts wrapped around her withered leg and a small metal cane lying on the floor next to her.

I turned and whispered to Laurel, "Why isn't Sandra getting the shot?"

Laurel shook her head. "It's too late for herrr."

Too late? Didn't they have a shot to make her better? It didn't seem fair. But Ernest always said fair is a matter of view. Looking at Sandra Bolton, I didn't think the view looked very good.

Willie bolted out of line and ran to the front when we got near the town hall. I looked at Laurel, and she shrugged her shoulders.

The teachers talking with each other didn't notice Willie cut the line. The kids in the front didn't care because no one wanted to be the first to be stabbed except Willie.

"Maybe he just wants to get it over with," I said.

The line snaked through the school halls, down the sidewalk, and into the town hall auditorium. Doctors in white coats and nurses in uniforms with stiff folded hats stood armed with needles.

We didn't even sit. They just stabbed us as we walked by. Laurel looked back at me with big eyes as the nurse jammed the needle into her upper arm and pushed in the liquid. Laurel's eyes filled with tears, but she sniffed them back. I was still watching her when I felt the jab in my arm. I wanted to cry out, but I couldn't let Laurel think I was a baby. There was a lot of crying, though, and no one seemed to care.

We walked through the building, out the back door, and back to the school like nothing had happened.

When we returned to our classroom, Willie was sitting beside Sandra Bolton. She must have given him that 'come-hither' look, I thought. They played tic-tac-toe on a sheet of paper.

I saw Sandra mark a third x that won the game, and Willie smiled. Willie seldom lost, and if he did, he never smiled.

Willie seemed unusually quiet the rest of the day and whistled a happy tune on the way home.

≈

"Ernest, why do some kids get polio and some don't?" I asked when I got home.

"Doesn't seem fair, does it?"

I shook my head.

"Why do you think some people appear more fortunate than others?" Ernest asked.

It seemed to me to be a lot more questions than answers.

"Well, Willie is more fortunate because he has a television," I answered.

Ernest considered this. "You think you are less fortunate because you don't?"

I did, but I didn't think saying so would help, so I didn't say anything.

"So, little Sandra Bolton is less fortunate than you?"

I couldn't deny that. I nodded my head.

"Do you think there are children less fortunate than her?"

I hadn't considered that there were kids still in iron lungs and other kids that never came home at all. Still, that didn't answer my question of why and Ernest knew it.

"I can't tell you why, son," Ernest put his hand on my shoulder. "I can only tell you that we have to do the best with what we're given—even if it doesn't seem fair."

Chapter 37 - Old Enough

That fall, Old Brown got a visitor. The bull had fierce red eyes as the handler led him down the ramp from the trailer. Ernest said the bull would give us a calf to sell next year to help us through the following winter. But the handler didn't bring a calf with him.

Old Brown made a slight throaty sound when she saw the bull. She didn't make a move. The bull mounted her right quick. I knew exactly where the calf was coming from. I had seen the pigs doing the same thing, although these animals were much bigger, and the act much more violent. Ernest stood close beside me like he wanted to shield me but didn't.

"Is that f-ing?" I asked cautiously.

Ernest stretched his neck, and it creaked. "How old are you?" he asked with a slight grin.

I smiled. "You know I'm twelve. You had a big piece of Gram's homemade chocolate cake on my birthday in July."

"That's right," he said. "I remember." He rubbed his large hand across his whiskered chin. "I suppose you're old enough now."

Butterflies stirred in my stomach.

"Let's take a walk," he said.

We went down by the river, never saying a word. The birds chirped in the trees, and squirrels scampered in the woods.

Ernest sat on a large rock by the water, and I settled beside him. He picked some small stones up from the ground and skipped them across the standing pool of water caught in the rocks to the side of the river flow.

I waited.

"There are two parts to this talk," he started like he was telling me a bedtime story.

I relaxed, leaning back against the smooth rock.

"The word that brings us here today isn't the important part."

I never knew Ernest to lie, but I wanted to tell him it was the important part to me.

He glanced down like he was reading my mind again. "You've grown up on a farm. You know how babes are made, where they come from."

I nodded and didn't interrupt.

"That is technically what the f-word means," he uttered quickly, like telling a tale out of school.

My mouth dropped open, and I sat up.

"You mean there isn't any more to it?" I had been waiting for years, and it turned out it wasn't a secret at all. I was annoyed. "But Willie said—"

Ernest gave me a look, and I shut up.

"The thing with words," Ernest continued, "is they are just words, and sometimes people throw them around carelessly. They may use them in anger."

I thought of the first time Ma said it.

"Other times, they may use the same word in jest."

And I thought of the last time Ma said it in a teasing voice.

"Mind you, there is nothing funny about the reference when used in such a manner, but some—" Ernest paused long, "—some may use the term because they have heard others use it, so they think it's okay." He looked me in the eye. "It's not. But we can forgive them because everyone makes mistakes."

I nodded, knowing he was referring to Ma.

"The saddest part is," Ernest said, and goose bumps popped up on my arms. I didn't know there would be a sad part. "Some people say it because they don't know what it's truly called."

Okay, I thought, now we are getting to the good part.

"Many people never find out because they keep looking for the definition of that word, and they miss the real thing."

I nodded fast, hoping we were getting close to the secret.

"Words are fast, thoughtless, hollow. Actions mean much more," Ernest said.

I thought about the action with Old Brown and the bull, but Ernest pulled my thoughts right away from that.

"When two adults love each other, there is a bond between them."

I wondered if we were getting into the screaming and talking to the Lord part now.

Ernest paused, and I thought he was waiting for me to ask a question. Nothing came to my mind that I wanted to say aloud. He took a deep breath and went on.

"The consummation of that love eventually happens when they come together in sexual intercourse."

I held my breath so I didn't make any usual sounds.

"And that act is what some use that unfortunate word to describe. That word gives it no justice at all. Now that you know what the word refers to, I'll ask you never to use it." He looked me in the eye again. "Do you understand, son?"

I nodded.

"That's the part about the word." He let out a long breath of air. "Now, I'll tell you the important part."

There's more? I thought.

"It's the best part," he said with promise. "It makes your heart beat faster, and it fills you with feelings of hope and joy. It's slow and meaningful and never rushed. It's the bond between two adults that grows stronger with time and trust." He put his large hand on my shoulder. "It's called true love. And that is what all men should be searching for, not the other."

I thought about the feelings I got when I sat next to Laurel or held her hand and how it felt that time when I kissed her behind the piano. I grinned and nodded. I thought I understood. Or at least I looked forward to the search for understanding. It sounded much more interesting than that f-word.

"Do you think Ma found true love with Frank?"

Ernest looked at me a long moment, then cast his gaze across the creek. "I think she has. I truly think she has."

I was glad.

We strolled back to the barn, where the handler loaded the bull back into the truck. Old Brown munched on some hay as though she didn't care a hoot for the bull, and the bull looked a little disappointed.

Foolish bull, I thought; *he'd never know true love.*

Ernest turned to me. "Son, what we talked about, it's just between you and me. Okay?"

"Sure." Darn, I wanted to tell Willie.

"Mr. Larson and other pas will do the telling in their own way and time."

Something in Ernest's words made my heart skip a beat, and I didn't know why. One thing I knew for sure was that no one's pa could explain it as well as Ernest.

Chapter 38 - Tongue-Tied

L aurel was excited to tell us about her visit to the doctor in Joliet. And for once, Willie let her talk. She missed school the day before to go with her parents to see what she called a specialist. She had a hard time saying the words, but Willie and I waited patiently while she got it out.

"He ssaid he can fix my tongue with an operration," she said carefully. "Then I'll be able to talk norrmally."

An operation on her tongue sounded scary to me. I wanted to tell her I didn't care how she talked, but she was so happy I told her I was pleased.

"I hope your operation goes well," I said.

"Thhanks. I thhink it will." She smiled and looked perfect to me.

Willie stayed with us while Mr. and Mrs. Larson drove Laurel to the hospital for her operation. At the supper table, Willie talked even more than usual. I think he was nervous for Laurel. I was, too, but it made me quieter. I hardly heard what Willie said, but Gram and Ernest looked like their heads were spinning, so I thought I better pay attention.

"Red Bud, Illinois," Willie was saying. "It's south, near Missouri." His eyes were big, and he nearly jumped out of his chair. "I saw a picture of it in *Flying Saucer Magazine* on the magazine rack at Harlow's store."

I'd never heard of the story, and by the looks of Gram and Ernest, they were equally stunned.

"It happened in April of 1950!" Willie continued. "It could come again. Who knows when!" Now he had my attention.

"A UFO?" I asked to make sure I had heard right.

"Yes!" Willie practically shouted. "A flying saucer! The man who took the picture said it was suspended about twenty feet over his head. It was round and looked to be made of metal. He said it was enormous!"

Ernest began to speak. I was glad because I couldn't think of anything to say. "Willie, that is an amazing tale," Ernest said.

"It's no tale, sir. Boy Scouts' honor." Willie raised his right hand, clenched with two fingers extended straight up.

"I wasn't doubting the telling," Ernest assured him. "I've seen some incredible things with my own eyes."

Willie's mouth snapped shut like a bear trap. It was the first time I ever saw him speechless.

I asked, "Ernest, have you seen a UFO?"

"If you mean, have I ever seen something I couldn't explain, then yes, I have."

Willie gazed at Ernest like he was the second coming of the Lord. "What did you see?" he asked breathlessly.

Gram cleared her throat and rose to pick up the supper plates from the table. Maybe she had already heard the story.

"It happened in the war," Ernest began. "My platoon deployed to the island of Kiribati to help the British forces. The fighting was fierce, but do you know what strange occurrence happened in Kiribati just before the war?"

"No! What?" Willie and I said at the same time.

"Someone found a skull, a bottle, and a woman's shoe," Ernest leaned in. "Now, those might not seem like odd items to find on a South Pacific Island, and maybe they would have gone unnoticed except for one small coincidence."

"What's that?" Willie totally forgot about the Red Bud UFO.

"Amelia Earhart," Ernest said the name and let it sit.

"She's the pilot lady, right?" I asked.

"That's right," Gram came over and took her seat. "She was the first woman to fly solo across the Atlantic," Gram said. "In 1937, she attempted to circumnavigate the globe when her plane disappeared in the South Pacific."

Willie took all this information in, then asked, "What did you see on the island, Ernest?"

"Well, they could never definitely identify the skull as Earhart's and never found the rest of the skeleton. However, that didn't stop people from seeing her ghost walking around in the jungle from time to time."

Willie clenched the seat of his chair, white-knuckled. "Did you see it?"

"I won't say I did, but I can't say I didn't. That's the way with unexplainable things."

"Whoa!" Willie exclaimed. "Ghosts are even better than UFOs because they are real."

I wasn't sure what Willie based his judgment on. Even so, I agreed ghosts were scarier.

"Boys, I think that's enough strange stories for tonight. Why don't you go to the parlor and play? Willie, maybe your parents will call soon with some news about Laurel," Gram said.

Willie ran to the parlor. I knew he wanted to discuss the ghost thing some more. I hesitated just outside the kitchen and heard Gram scold Ernest. "You're going to be giving those boys nightmares about ghosts."

"Well, at least they won't be thinking about getting abducted by aliens."

Gram gave him a look. "Ghosts are better?"

"Yes, you heard Willie. Ghosts are better."

Gram gave Ernest a playful smack, and they both laughed. "Well, it did get them thinking about real history."

The phone rang, and we all ran to it. Gram picked it up first. "Hello?"

We could hear the loud voice of the operator. "Please deposit thirty-five cents."

We heard the metal clinking of coins deposited in the payphone slot and finally the murmur of Mrs. Larson's soft voice. "Hello, Marg."

"Oh, Ella, it's good to hear your voice. How is Laurel?"

I held my breath while Gram listened, commenting with ohs and ahs, which got me nervous.

"Well, Willie is fine here for the night," Gram reported. "You stay there as long as you need to."

Gram hung up and turned around to all our stares.

She took a deep breath. "There's no need for worry," she said, looking like there was plenty of need. "The operation went well. Laurel just had a reaction to the anesthesia." Gram wrung the dishcloth in her hand and her eyes teared up.

"She hasn't woken yet." Gram's voice broke.

Even Willie didn't know what to say.

≈

Willie and I stayed awake, talking for a while. But we didn't talk about UFOs or ghosts.

"It must be nice to have a sister," I said.

"I never thought about it much before," Willie spoke in a hushed voice. "She's like part of me, you know."

I did, and I didn't.

"We've always been together," he continued, "even before we were born."

I tried to imagine how that must feel. "I wish I had a sister or a brother."

Willie looked at me, and his eyes glistened. "Henry, you're just like a brother to me."

We both hushed up for a minute. We must have fallen asleep in that moment because the next thing I knew, it was morning.

Willie and I woke at the same time to the sound of Gram downstairs making joyful noises. We looked at each other and ran downstairs to see what was going on. Ernest stood beside Gram while she held the phone receiver to her ear.

"The boys are here now, and I'll tell them the good news, Ella. Praise the Lord!"

Gram hung up and scooped us both into a hug. "Laurel awoke this morning. She's going to be all right."

Gram started to cry like she had been holding back all her tears like a dam to water. Ernest put his arm around her, and she cried on his shirt. I knew Ernest wouldn't mind. He wasn't partial to that shirt, and Gram washed it for him, anyway. Willie and I jumped up and down like a couple of fools or a pair of brothers.

Laurel came home, but she still had some healing to do. She wasn't to talk at all for two weeks. I went to visit her every day. I read to Laurel, and we played games that didn't require talking. Mrs. Larson said I was a good friend.

Willie would stay in the room for a while, but he was never one to sit for long. I didn't mind.

The days went by, and I lost count until the day Laurel met me at the door. "Hello, Henry," she said, as clear as a bell. "I'm happy to see you."

"She's been waiting for you, Henry," Mrs. Larson said. "She wanted you to be the first to hear her new voice."

Her new voice sounded just as beautiful as her old voice to me. But Laurel was happy she could now clearly say r's and s's. I told her how wonderful she sounded.

1956

Chapter 39 - As the World Turns

The following spring, Willie's celebration of returning from the dead was extra special. After supper, we watched *The Wizard of Oz* on television in the parlor. Mrs. Larson said the Ford Star Jubilee Theater was right in their home. Gram and Ernest sat on the couch while Mr. and Mrs. Larson sat in their usual stuffed chairs. Willie, Laurel, and I lay on the floor on our stomachs, chins in our hands. Before the show started, a big lion came on the screen and roared loud, causing Laurel to jump.

Mr. Larson made popcorn, and I shared my bowl with Laurel. When our hands touched, I got that tingling sensation I thought was the making of true love. I hoped she felt it, too, because I wasn't sure what happened if only one person felt it.

Dorothy lived on a farm with her Auntie Em in the movie, just like Gram and me. I wondered if her ma was off with some fella, but it never said. The wizard reminded me of Willie because he was a great showman. I laughed, thinking of Willie with a white mustache when he got older. The wicked witch was scary, and the flying monkeys were scarier. The lion, the scarecrow, and the tinman all searched for something they already had right at home. Maybe they should have just been looking for true love.

The thaw came early in April. Ernest and I got a head start on tilling the garden.

"President Eisenhower signed the Federal Aid Highway Act," Gram announced at breakfast one spring morning.

I chewed my sausage, wondering what the heck the big title meant.

"I heard tell," Ernest said. "Over 40,000 miles of new highways will cross America!"

"That's a lot of roads," Gram said. "And our little road to Joliet will be a real highway."

I pictured Shamus with his thumb out, hitching rides across the country. He would have lots of new roads to travel. I hoped he would travel our new road when they finished it. Maybe he could stop for his supper.

In June, the roadmen began working on the interstate highway near the farm with large new equipment, making it bigger for tourist traffic.

Ernest said the tourist might wander off the highway looking for country treasures in Mendota.

Boy, will they be disappointed, I thought.

"We could set up a stand at the head of the driveway and sell things just like Ella Larson," Gram said.

With Ernest's help tending the farm, we had some things to spare.

"We won't put our eggs for sale," Gram said. "That's Ella's stock and trade, and I won't be stepping on her toes."

"We can plant some extra corn. The city folks will buy it," Ernest said.

"I think you're right, Ernest. And tomatoes, too." Gram tapped her finger to her cheek. "I could offer some of my hand-knitted washcloths for sale."

"Good thinking. I bet city folks don't knit," Ernest said.

I felt sorry for city folk; they seemed a little backward. On the other hand, it got me to thinking.

"I bet they don't know how to carve, either. I could make some wooden birds and sell them!"

"That's a great idea, Henry," Gram said.

I was so busy that summer I hardly went to play with Willie. Gram said I caught the fever, making carved birds by the dozens. If making things to sell was a fever, Willie caught it, too.

"I'm making birdhouses to sell at our roadside stand," Willie said. "My ma says the city folk will love them."

I hoped the city folks had lots of money. Maybe we would make enough money to get a television like the Larsons. Willie and I couldn't watch his television after school anymore because Mrs. Larson claimed it was her television time. She watched a new show called *As the World Turns*. It seemed like a foolish story; everyone knew the world turns. I couldn't figure out why she needed to watch a show about it every day. Willie and I were not allowed in the house while she watched. I thought there must be something else to it.

Willie said it was about a bunch of people fighting, crying, and kissing. I thought the kissing sounded interesting. Willie said it was dumb. I was glad Mrs. Larson liked it because that meant Willie and Laurel started coming to my house every afternoon instead. We sat at the kitchen table while Gram made us peanut butter and crackers with big glasses of milk. We'd go outside to play hide and seek, or if it was raining, we played board games in the parlor.

"This is more fun than having a television," Willie said. Of course, I couldn't say for sure myself, but I was glad he thought so.

≈

Ma's birthday had come and gone in June, and I hadn't even thought about her for months. I felt a little guilty when I remembered. I hoped she hadn't forgotten about me. But she wasn't there when I turned thirteen years old in July. Maybe I was on her mind, though.

At supper, Gram brought up Alabama. I hated when she said the word. It reminded Ernest of where he came from, and I was still afraid he would leave us to go back there. Gram said there was a fight about buses going on. Ernest didn't like to fight, so I figured he would stay with us.

"The Civil Rights Movement is gaining momentum, Ernest," Gram said. "The 'separate but equal' rule isn't holding water anymore."

"That Reverend Martin Luther King is a good man," Ernest said, and his face shone with pride. "He fights with words of peace. The Lord is surely on his side."

I hoped so.

Chapter 40 - The Land of Oz

L ife changed suddenly around sunset on August 24, 1956, when an unusual roar came from the north of town. It wasn't the sound of a train or even the military planes that flew over from time to time, breaking the sound barrier. Instead, it was low and ghostly, like the devil himself was coming to call.

I ran out the door behind Ernest and Gram. We leaned over the porch rail, looking for—I don't know what. The effect of the wind was what we saw first. The trees bent, and the dust swirled, crawling closer like a hand from the grave in a scary movie. Gram went back into the house, returning with an armful of blankets. Ernest ran to secure the barn doors. I followed his lead and did the same to the chicken coop without being told.

We all met at the front steps just as the Larsons' old Ford pickup flew into the yard. Willie helped Laurel climb out of the back and they hurried toward us. Mrs. Larson held blankets, too. The wind roared so loud our voices were useless, but it didn't seem like there was much to be said.

We ran like our pants were on fire to the door to nowhere— our root cellar. The Larsons didn't have one. Ernest and Mr. Larson pulled together to open the wooden door against the strength of the wind. Willie and I each held one of Laurel's hands so she didn't blow away.

It was all Gram and Mrs. Larson could do to keep themselves on the ground. The door creaked open with great protest. We tumbled into the room, rolling to the ground like loose potatoes.

Ernest and Mr. Larson braced against the inside of the door like Moses holding back the waters of the Red Sea, and maybe they were. At first, it wasn't easy to separate the new sound from the roar of the wind. We huddled together, looking toward the roof like we could see the sky, although I was glad we couldn't. Eventually, I realized the continuous beat of a hammer on an anvil was actually rain. And then, suddenly, it all ended, just as scary in its silence as the storm in its loudness.

Covered in the feeling of safety that the wool blankets gave, we didn't move—listening for something, anything. There was nothing. Minutes passed. My eyes were dry, and so was my mouth. I looked for Ernest in the gloomy darkness, and his eyes met mine, clear and strong. I knew everything would be okay.

I coughed to clear my throat, and Willie did the same. Willie cleared something else at the same time. The smell followed the sound without delay and brought us all to action. Holding the corners of the blankets over our noses, we ran for the door. Ernest yanked it open, and we filed out almost as fast as we had entered.

We stopped dead in our tracks. The world we left just a few minutes before was completely different from the one in front of us. It was like the wind had sucked the color out of the world, and now I knew how Dorothy felt.

The house and the barn stood firm, but every tree laid flat as far as the eye could see. Old Brown bellowed, turning my attention. That's when I saw it.

The others turned in a circle taking it all in, and then they saw it, too—the wide path of ground, torn open as if an enormous monster dragged his giant hoe from our yard straight toward Willie's house. We ran, following the path for a quarter-mile, seemingly into the monster's mouth.

The Larsons' house still stood.

"Thank the Lord!" Mrs. Larson cried out.

A large tree had landed on the Oldsmobile, flattening it like a cow flap. I think Mr. Larson was thankful he hadn't parked his precious '48 pickup there instead.

With the trees all lying flat, it didn't immediately occur to me at first what was missing. Then, I realized where the barn used to be, a gaping hole outlined by a stacked-stone foundation was all that was left. A few boards lay scattered around the yard. I looked to the sky.

Was the barn on top of a witch on the yellow brick road in the Land of Oz? I wondered.

Mr. Larson's knees gave out, and Ernest caught him in his arms. Sirens wailed in the distance, and high-pitched voices floated in the air like babies crying for their mothers. It was the only time I ever saw Willie completely quiet.

"Where are the horses?" Laurel asked, perfectly pronouncing each r and s, I noticed.

No one answered her.

Cars and trucks turned in the yard one after the other as they followed the line of the tornado's destruction. Sheriff Fitzpatrick led the way, followed by the ambulance and others who came to see what had just missed them.

Someone draped more blankets over our shoulders as if blankets were the answer, and they seemed to be the only answer at the moment. The clouds cleared, and the sun took one last peek before disappearing over the horizon. It didn't make things any better than blankets did.

After checking on us, the ambulance left empty, and the sheriff went home to his family. The neighbors piled back into their cars, promising to be back the next day to help. I wasn't sure what would help.

Then it was just us again, the root cellar gang. I wished we could go back there and huddle together, listening to the storm. I was even willing to live with the smell of Willie's fart if I never had to know what came after we left the cellar. But instead, we all hugged and mumbled words that made no sense. Darkness quickly covered the sight of the hole in the ground. But I could still see it in my mind.

"It could have been a lot worse," Mr. Larson said, holding his family tight in his arms.

"We're all alive, and the house is standing." Tears glistened in Mrs. Larson's eyes. "The Lord is good."

Just not with barns, I thought—*or horses.* I knew it best to keep that to myself.

"We'll be back first thing in the morning to get to work," Ernest promised.

I wasn't sure what there was to do. Would we look for the barn? Would we find the horses?

We walked home in silence. Mr. Larson came with us to get his pickup truck. He shook his head as he got in the driver's seat and drove away. Gram gathered the blankets from us and went into the house while Ernest and I checked on the animals. They were all there.

≈

Gram packed a basket of food the next day, Ernest got some tools from our barn, and we all went over to the Larsons. Others had already come, bringing lumber and food and hugs.

Laurel ran out of the house and down the steps.

"They came back!" Her face was pink and glowing. "The horses came back."

Willie was right behind her. "Damned things woke us up in the middle of the night, neighing outside the windows."

I knew Willie would not be using that language in front of his pa, but I imagined that was how Mr. Larson had said it. Maybe the horses knew where the barn had got to. I guessed it wasn't in a friendly place since they decided to come home. It didn't matter. Mr. Harlow came with a truckload of wood and nails, and everyone brought their hammers.

"It'll be a good old-fashioned barn-raising," Gram said. "Mendota is a town with values."

Everyone seemed to agree; barns were important here. Men grabbed boards and put them in place. Young and old swung hammers while the women set out tables topped with food and drinks.

Young children ran around playing tag. It was almost like a party, a barn birthday party.

By the end of the day, the barn looked good enough to put the horses in for the night. They looked pleased.

"At this rate, we will have it finished by the end of the week," Mr. Larson said. "I'm a lucky man."

"You would do the same for anyone else, Bill." Ernest shook Mr. Larson's callused hand. "Let's just hope you never have to."

After the barn building finished, the days got quieter. I went fishing with Willie and Laurel down at the creek, and that's where we found the barn. It didn't look quite the same. The cupula rested on its side in the turn of the creek, water running over and under and through it. Pieces of wood and shattered windowpanes lay scattered over the rocks and across the banks. It looked like my Lincoln Log set when I dumped it out of the round container onto the floor.

We went to fetch Mr. Larson, and he stood with his hands on his hips, looking it all over.

"Well, I think the fitting Bible verse adaption for this would be, "The Lord taketh away and the Lord giveth." Let's collect what wood we can salvage. Winter is coming, and the woodstove doesn't care what it burns."

It would be a warm winter in the Larsons' house that year.

Chapter 41 - Next Exit

The summer went by just like Superman, "faster than a speeding bullet."

"Willie, why do the summers go by faster now than when we were younger?" I asked since Willie knew everything.

"Ahh, that's just an optical illusion," Willie said, waving his arm in the air. "As you get older, you can't see every day like when you were little because you're taller."

I thought about Ernest's height and wondered how many days he had missed.

"Ernest," I said while we were weeding the garden. He was still taller than me, even when kneeling in the dirt. "What do you see from up there?"

Ernest paused and looked at me.

"Willie Larson says as you get taller, you don't see everything you did when you were little. That's why time goes by faster." I explained to him.

"Well," Ernest's eyes creased in thought. "I'd have to agree with Willie on that point."

"Really?"

"The further a man gets from the ground, he tends to lose sight of where he came from and what's important."

Ernest grabbed some dirt with his large brown hands. "That's why it's good for a man to get on his knees from time to time and give thanks."

He put the handful of dirt to his nose, closing his eyes and breathing in. So, I did the same. My nostrils burned with the smell of cow manure and decaying leaves.

"The land smells like life and death," Ernest said and opened his eyes. "It's where we begin and where we end."

I wasn't sure about that, but I wanted to know more about the speed of time. "So, how much faster do days go by for you?"

Ernest sunk both his hands into the fresh-turned dirt. "So fast sometimes I have to hang on for fear my whole life is passing me by."

I made note to remember to get on my knees more often the taller I got. I didn't think I'd tell Willie. Maybe his pa would tell him.

A cool breeze blew across my face, and clouds covered the sun. I felt a few light drops of rain on my head. Ernest looked to the sky and began to hum a tune that started slow, like rocking a baby.

He's got the whole world in His hands.

He's got the sun and the moon in His hands,

Ernest looked at me with a smile, and I joined in.

He's got the whole world in His hands.

The rain started coming down harder, and the wind picked up, yet we went on singing like the world was standing still.

He's got the wind and the rain in His hands,

Gram came out on the porch and spied us in the garden amidst the downpour. Ernest and I belted out the chorus.

He's got the whole world in His hands.

Gram hurried inside to get us a couple of towels. We laughed silly as we ran to the porch, soaking wet. The rain washed the dirt from our hands and knees. Gram handed us the towels, and we wiped our faces. She told us to get inside before we caught our death from the cold. I felt warm inside and out.

≈

After the road work finished in our area in the fall, we heard the cars zipping by on the highway at dusk when we sat out on the porch.

"We'll get used to it," Gram said. "It's like the train whistle. After a while, you won't even notice it anymore."

I didn't bother to point out we didn't hear the train whistle all that much anymore since the steam trains didn't come by as often. And I didn't enjoy the sound of the cars nearly as much. That is, until they started to get off the highway and stop at our stand.

A big green sign on Route 34 read, *Exit 72 to Mendota,* like we were important. Next, a gas station sprang up on the corner near Harlow's General Store.

"Well, I'll be darned!" Gram said. "A gas station in Mendota. I never thought I'd see it."

"Well, those tourists have to fill up their fancy cars somewhere," Ernest said, "and the Harlows are sure happy about the extra trade they're getting at the General Store."

"Next, they'll open one of those fast-food restaurants here!" Gram said with a huff.

Little Allan Harlow helped his pa put up a large wooden board on the side of the highway right next to the Mobil gas sign. They advertised soda, ice, and beer in big red letters Butch had painted by hand to match the red gas sign with the winged horse.

By harvest time, we had a wealth of bounty, as Ernest called it. He had built a roadside stand out of scrap wood while I carved and Gram knitted. Ernest made a place to put crates of vegetables and shelves to display Gram's knitted goods and my carved birds. It was a beauty, even bigger than Mrs. Larson's stand.

We asked a quarter for a dozen corn, a dime for one of Gram's handknitted washcloths, and I asked a nickel for my hand-carved bluebirds. Ernest found an old lockbox in the tack room and cut a slot in the top to put at the farmstand. Gram made the sign that told the prices, and in big letters, she wrote, "PAY ON YOUR HONOR."

The motorists filled their cars with gas at the new station, moseyed on over to the General Store for a soda and snack, and on their way back to the highway, they stopped at our stand for some corn and what Gram called country souvenirs. The tourists scooped them up.

≈

Fall was time for the Corn Festival. People came by the highway from all over to make it the biggest festival so far in Mendota. The lights on the fairway twinkled like stars in the sky at night.

Willie said, "Mendota is on the map now." I wondered if they had to print all new maps.

I never saw so much corn in one place. Booths with steamed corn and roasted corn, bowls of steaming corn chowder for sale, and stands with bags of popcorn in different flavors and colors lined the festival grounds. And corn dogs, too. Of course, they are more dogs than corn, but it didn't seem to matter at the Mendota Corn Festival; it was all about the corn. That didn't limit the number of food counters with hot dogs and hamburgers and booths with ice cream and cotton candy. You could smell the tastes in the air from a mile away.

Davey Kennedy dressed like the new singer Elvis Presley. High up on the wooden stage, he twisted his foot, leaned into the microphone, and belted out "Heartbreak Hotel" as though he knew exactly where it was. The crowd cheered and called for more. Gram and Ernest stood together in front of the stage and exchanged glances. I don't think it was to their taste in music. Davey sang "Love Me Tender" next by the same singer, but it was much slower. Ernest and Gram seemed to like that one better.

Gram and Mrs. Larson entered their pies in a contest. Mr. Larson grew a giant pumpkin for display in the farm tent. Goats and lambs wandered in a large pen for kids to feed and pet.

Even Roy Rogers showed up with his horse Trigger. I was thirteen and decided I was too old to stand in line for an autographed picture. The younger kids were all excited because Trigger signed it, too. That was one smart horse, but I didn't tell the kids he couldn't write. I believed it when I was their age, too.

The most excitement for me came from the sight of the giant Ferris wheel. Gram said Ferris wheels were a big deal in Illinois.

"The original Ferris wheel was built in Chicago in 1893 by Mr. Ferris himself," she said.

I thought the man must be a genius. When I stood at the base looking up, I felt the way an ant must feel at the bottom of an oak tree. Willie and Laurel stood beside me, our necks stretching back as though broken.

"Are you going on it?" I asked nervously.

"It's really high," Laurel said without a definite answer.

Willie, always up for a challenge, said, "Of course. It's just a wheel."

It was just a wheel—a wheel nearly one hundred feet tall.

"Yes, I want to ride it," Laurel said.

And that was all I needed to hear. "Let's go!"

We got our tickets and waited in line. My hands sweated, but thankfully Laurel couldn't see them. The lights of the Ferris Wheel sparkled in her eyes. When our turn came, we all three scrambled onto the bench seat, and the man closed the bar and locked it with force. Laurel sat in the middle with Willie and me at either end. Our seat rocked and took off with a jerk. I held back a scream while a tiny one escaped Laurel's lips. I put my hand on hers to reassure her, and Willie gave me a look, so I took it back. Laurel flashed me a sweet smile as our seat rose in the air and my heart with it.

We stopped at the tippy top, higher than the church steeple. A breeze blew Laurel's fine blonde hair across my face, and it smelled like soap and cotton candy.

I liked it even better than Ma's fancy perfume.

Both Gram and Mrs. Larson won the pie contest—Gram for her blueberry and Mrs. Larson for her apple pie. I agreed with the judge's choices. Still, I didn't think it was fair that the judges got to eat all the pies. I wondered if I could be a judge next year.

Chapter 42 - Checkmate

"It's a great year to be thirteen years old," Willie announced on our way to school. Laurel gave him a look.

Being thirteen years old myself, I was afraid to ask why. However, this didn't stop Willie from telling us.

"Thirteen-year-old Bobby Fischer is a chess prodigy."

I had no idea what a prodigy was or what it had to do with chess, or me for that matter, but Willie appeared pretty worked up about it.

"He won a match against champion Donald Byrne, a grown man!" he went on. "It's called the Chess Match of the Century!"

Laurel rolled her eyes.

I had to admit to myself that it sounded pretty impressive, but I didn't dare say it.

"Henry, that could be us!" Willie looked serious.

"Willie, we don't know how to play chess."

"That's why we have to learn."

"It sounds like an English game to me," I suggested. "Let's ask Mr. Shoemaker."

≈

"Bravo, boys, that's a great idea," Mr. Shoemaker said. "We can start an after-school chess club. I'll teach you!"

Mr. Shoemaker posted a sign-up sheet in the hall. Our new chess club met the following Friday after school. By club day,

Willie's name took the top spot on the sheet, followed by Isaac's and mine. Isaac already knew how to play a little, and his father was happy to see him interested in an after-school activity since Isaac wasn't into sports. Laurel came with us because she wasn't allowed to walk home alone.

Mr. Shoemaker provided two boards with two sets of royal-looking game pieces of kings, queens, and horse heads. He explained each piece and what they were for, then told us some basic rules.

"Would you like to play, Laurel?" he asked.

"No." Laurel had brought her homework and paid no attention to chess.

After four weeks of chess club, Willie grew tired of it. "I'm not cut out for chess," he said at our next meeting.

"It is a sport of concentration, William," Mr. Shoemaker explained. "You may come back to it when you're older. I had other interests at your age, too."

"We'll see," Willie said. "Come on, Laurel, let's go home."

"I think I'll stay," Laurel said, and Willie's mouth dropped open. "Maybe I was cut out for chess," she said.

"You're a girl." Willie's mouth twisted.

"Actually, Queen Elizabeth I was an avid chess player," Mr. Shoemaker said.

Laurel raised her chin and looked at Willie out of one eye.

"Benjamin Franklin played chess in Paris with many important women," Mr. Shoemaker continued. "And in 1950, Lyudmila Rudenko became the first female International Master. So you're in good company, Laurel."

"Henry can walk me home," Laurel said to Willie.

Willie's mouth opened and closed a couple of times, and he walked out in a huff. I didn't think I could be happier if I were Bobby Fischer.

We paired off in sets each week, with Mr. Shoemaker taking turns playing each of us. It turned out Laurel must have been paying attention as she was doing her homework. Or she was just really cut out for the game. She beat Isaac and me. Mr. Shoemaker even said she gave him a good challenge. I liked chess fine—I liked the walk home with Laurel afterward even better.

≈

On a Sunday afternoon in November, while Ernest and I ate our lunch of leftover chicken stew, Gram read the newspaper.

"The news today was worth the nickel," Gram said.

"What's the good word?" Ernest asked between spoonfuls.

"Well, the US Supreme Court declared Alabama's bus segregation illegal." She lowered the paper and looked at Ernest. "What would your ma and pa think of that?"

Ernest smiled as he answered, "My ma and pa never rode a bus. Instead, we traveled in the backs of trucks from farm to farm across the states as the picking seasons changed." He looked like he could see the road going by. "My pa probably wouldn't be as impressed with the new bus law as he would have been with Floyd Patterson, the Negro boxer who won the world heavyweight title."

"He's the youngest boxer ever to win the title, to boot!" Gram said.

She read a lot, and she seemed to like sports. Maybe that's where me and Ma got it from.

Willie and Laurel started coming to my house on Friday nights when Mr. and Mrs. Larson became interested in the new game show on television called *To Tell the Truth.*

"It's stupid," Willie said. "Three people claim to have the same job. Only one is telling the truth; the others get to lie. The celebrities have to guess who is telling the truth."

I thought Willie would make a great contestant on the show as one of the pretenders. He could convince people of anything. Even so, I thought it was best not to suggest that.

"I think the guy named Dick Van Dyke is funny," Laurel said.

"He isn't funny at all," Willie disagreed. "He's not even famous."

≈

With the money from the farmstand, it was an extra special Christmas. We didn't get a television, but with Willie and Laurel coming to my house to play games, I figured I could live without one. Besides, I didn't want Gram to start watching those soap operas and forget to make supper.

Gram and Ernest gave me a knife of my very own for carving. Gram got Ernest a small transistor radio to listen to music while working outside. At night we listened to mystery shows. Of course, it wasn't quite the same without the picture, but it was still fun. We sat in the parlor and listened to the radio on New Year's Eve. Everything seemed perfect until a month later when the military police came to call.

1957

Chapter 43 - Under Arrest

It was late January of a mild winter. Ernest and I had just returned from the root cellar with a basket of winter squash and potatoes.

Ernest was singing, *Bringing in the sheaves, bringing in the sheaves; We shall come rejoicing, bringing in the sheaves!*

I swayed to the tune and smiled up at him.

"Sowing in the sunshine, sowing in the shadows, Fearing neither clouds nor winter's chilling breeze; By and by the harvest, and the labor ended."

Ernest sang the words like the Lord speaking right to me. I joined in the chorus with gusto. *"We shall come rejoicing, bringing in the sheaves. We shall come rejoicing,"* our voices raised to high heaven.

Then I noticed it was only my voice, small and hollow. *"bringing in the sheav—"*

I turned to see a dark blue car with the emblem of the U.S. Army on the driver's door barreling down the driveway. Rocks flew from under its tires, kicking up snow that trailed behind like smoke from a brush fire. I snapped back to see Ernest's face harden like a statue. He dropped the basket of vegetables to the ground, and the winter squash rolled across the yard.

I didn't know whether to scream or cry, and I had no idea why.

Two men in tan uniforms jumped from the car, their pant legs tucked tight into neatly laced-up boots. The bands on their bulging arms had the large letters "MP" stamped on them. They pointed pistols at Ernest. He raised his hands in the air.

"Ernest L. Potts," one of the officers said in a voice that hurt my ears, "you're under arrest for crimes committed while in the service of the United States Army."

Gram had heard the car. She hurried out to take in the scene.

"Ma'am, stay back," the other soldier said with cold gray eyes. "We're taking this man in."

Gram stomped down the porch steps. "What right do you have to come on my property and arrest this man?" she demanded.

"We have the authority of the United States government, ma'am." The soldier stood stiff with his gun sights set on Ernest's head. The other returned his gun to his holster and ratcheted handcuffs on Ernest's wrists, twisting them behind him, causing Ernest to wince.

Sheriff Fitzpatrick came down the driveway in the police car in just as big a hurry. He skidded to a stop, got out of the car, and strode over to Gram, looking unsure of what to do next.

"Fred, what's the meaning of this?" Gram shouted at him.

"Marg, I don't know. I was just informed of the situation, but I'm only allowed to observe."

Observe? I didn't understand. Was this a ball game? Was he the umpire? When would the game be over? I wanted a replay.

"This man has not served in the Army near on ten years." Gram faced the soldiers and swung her arms high and wide. "Any crime you think he committed is long beyond any statute of limitations."

"No statute of limitations on murder, ma'am."

Gram's head whipped around to Ernest, her mouth open, but nothing came out.

"I tried to tell you," Ernest said. He hung his head as the soldier pushed him toward the car.

"Fred," Gram wailed, her legs failing her. "Do something!" She grabbed his blue uniform shirt with both hands. "You know Ernest didn't do it."

Sheriff Fitzpatrick shook his head with a pained look on his face. "There's nothing I can do, Marg." He looked past her. "It's military. I have no authority."

Gram's hand let loose of the sheriff's shirt. She collapsed to the ground sobbing, curled up tight as a fiddlehead in the spring.

"Take care of your Gram," Ernest said to me as the MPs jammed him into the back seat.

I searched for Ernest's eyes to meet mine, but all I could see was the top of his head through the barred window. My mouth opened in a silent scream.

The military car spun in a circle, shooting dirt and snow into my open mouth. I choked back my tears.

The sheriff helped Gram up from the ground. Putting his arm around her for support, he guided Gram up the stairs and into the house.

The yard became quiet, except for the light pecking of the chickens and the wind stirring through the trees, just like nothing had happened.

I kicked the vegetable basket and cursed. "Damned sheaves."

Chapter 44 - Long Days

Gram didn't talk much after Ernest left. It seemed like we were waiting for something to happen. Nothing did. No cars came speeding down the driveway. No police came to call. And Ernest didn't come home.

Gram kept a handkerchief in her pocket and wiped her nose often. She walked hunched over as if her back had broke, and her eyes filled with pain. I wondered if Doc had anything for her condition. I did my chores and Ernest's, too. I didn't mind the extra work, but I did miss his singing. Even the animals missed him. They were quieter than usual. Ernest Pig moped around and looked like he was losing weight. Gram certainly was. Days went by with no word about Ernest.

One day when I came home from school, Gram sat at the kitchen table with the Bible open in front of her. She held a small square of paper with a clover taped to it.

"What's that, Gram?"

"I think it's a message from the Lord," she said, carefully placing the paper between the pages.

"What does the Lord say?"

She closed the Good Book and looked at me with a sad smile. "He says, never give up, Henry." She held out her hand to me and grasped it like a lifeline. "And by God, we are not giving up."

Gram went to the Larson house next door to use their phone because they had long-distance service. She called the last place she knew Ma and Frank were living. Frank had been transferred again. The last time Gram talked to Ma, she said Frank was moving up through the ranks, which meant serving details in many places. Gram left a message with the base and prayed it would find them.

In the meantime, Gram had long-distance service added to our phone. Still, we didn't know where to call. Gram sat and stared at the phone, wishing it to ring. Finally, after a week, it rang, and she nearly fell off her chair.

"Hello," she yelled into the receiver louder than necessary. "Janie ..." she sobbed. Unable to continue, she handed the phone to me while she got a clean hankie.

"Ma," I said, "the military police took Ernest." I explained what I knew to her. Gram returned and explained the same things again. It didn't take long since neither of us knew much.

Ma was at a base in New York, and Frank was on special detail in Washington, DC, but she said he would be home the following week. "I'll tell him," she promised. "Frank will know what to do."

Gram took a deep breath for the first time since Ernest left. I hoped Ma was right. And, for the first time, I had all my hopes in Frank.

A week to the day, the phone rang again, and it was Frank. "Ma Adams," Frank said. "What's going on?"

Gram calmed a little at his authoritative voice and gave him the details.

I could hear his voice coming over the phone receiver Gram clutched in her hand.

"I'll do the best I can, Ma Adams," Frank said. "I'm getting in touch with the General. He may be able to help."

As it turned out, Frank did have a family after all. And his pa was a General. Frank called him just that, and when he said it, he sounded very official. I hoped the General was mighty powerful.

"Thank you, Frank. And thank the General, too," Gram said.

"I will, Ma Adams." Frank hesitated. "The military is a slow-moving machine. There are pluses and minuses to that," he explained. "Chances are there hasn't been a trial yet; we may still have time. But," he paused again, "nothing will happen quickly."

"That's okay," Gram's voice was the happiest I had heard since Ernest left. "As long as he comes home."

"Don't get your hopes too high, ma'am. Even if we get him home, I can't guarantee what shape he will be in." Frank's voice sank, as did Gram's shoulders.

"I'll take him, whatever his condition," she whispered.

I wondered what Frank meant by condition. Ernest was in fine condition when he left. His disease had not acted up lately. What could've changed?

≈

Frank called the next week with an update.

"We found him, and he is still awaiting trial."

"Thank the Lord." Gram clasped her hands together.

"The General says it's not an open-and-shut case. But you know how it is with people of Ernest's color," Frank said. "Facts don't always matter."

I thought about Ernest and the color of his eyes, like Old Brown, and his teeth when he smiled the color of the stars in the night sky. I thought about the color of his blood when he cut himself fixing the fence—red just like mine: many colors. But only one seemed to matter—the color of his skin.

Another week went by like molasses on toast. Frank didn't call, but Gram refused to give up hope.

"No news is good news," she said, although it didn't sound like she believed it.

When the phone finally rang, Gram grabbed it and yelled, "Frank?"

It was Ma, her voice soft and sad. "The General says it's not looking good."

"NO!" Gram shouted with the determination to stop a charging bear. "I won't accept it."

"They're still trying, but Frank wants me to prepare you. It could be bad news. I'm sorry." Ma sniffled.

Gram hung up the phone gently.

The next time the phone rang, Gram stood and stared at it. It rang five times, and she didn't make a move. I ran to grab it before the caller gave up. "Hello?"

"Henry." It was Frank. I held the receiver so Gram and I could both hear him. Gram looked like it might bite her, and I thought it could, too.

"Tell your Gram Ernest is coming home."

"Praise the Lord!" Gram cried out. She took the phone from me and cradled it like a baby. "Thank you, Frank. Thank you with all my heart!"

There were not enough hankies to wipe our tears. Tears of joy are like that.

Frank gave us a minute before he continued. "You need to know," he said, "he's not the same."

"What do you mean?" Gram's brow furrowed. "What happened to him?"

"Ma Adams," Frank said with respect. "He's been in the brig for weeks. Bad things happen to a man inside. Worse things happen to a black man in the brig."

Gram shook her head violently. "That's no matter," she said. "I nursed him to health once, and I'll do it again."

"No disrespect, ma'am, but I don't know if there is any cure for what ails him. It's more a breaking of his will."

Frank told us it would be a few more days for all the paperwork to clear and make arrangements to get Ernest back.

"Was he cleared of—of—" Gram couldn't say the word.

"Murder?" Frank asked. "Yes, well, it's complicated. But all charges disappeared." He shuffled some papers. "The incident stemmed from an altercation with an officer, which can be messy for a private of any color. The altercation escalated, and the young officer was shot dead."

Gram gasped.

"The officer was known to force his unwanted affections on military nurses," Frank went on. "He was a fourth-generation Army brat, and they can be the worst."

I thought of the General and wondered if Frank was an Army brat.

"I know the type," he continued. "And I can't say I didn't get some breaks because of who my father is, but my daddy taught me morals." Frank paused. "This incident makes me sick.

Ernest was in a field hospital in Germany after sustaining an injury. He stepped up to defend the young black nurse in question, and the officer took out a pistol."

Gram put her hand over her mouth.

"Ernest tried to wrestle the gun from his hand, and it went off, killing the officer. Many witnesses said it was self-defense, and supposedly the original records showed Ernest's prints were not on the gun trigger. He only touched the man's hands. The officer accidentally shot himself. Then the records and the gun disappeared in the ensuing years after the incident."

"How could they bring up the charges for murder against Ernest now?" Gram asked.

"After the war ended, the young officer's father became a one-star general and was eager to fight for his son's name," Frank explained. "The thing was he didn't fight fair, the charges were trumped, and the evidence coerced. The charges remained in limbo since they couldn't find Ernest without an official address."

"Until he came here to live," Gram said sadly.

"And until he registered for an ID at the Mendota town hall."

"So he wasn't a vagrant anymore."

"Yes. Then Ernest's name was back in the system. But the General has a few more stars than the other," Frank said with pride. "Now, that man not only lost his son to immoral circumstances. He will also lose his ranking as well—maybe his career."

"Ernest didn't speak of it specifically, but I know it's weighed on him all these years. He tried to tell me several times. I wouldn't let him. Maybe now that it's resolved for good, his conscience will be clear as well."

"His conscience may be clear, but his heart is still heavy. It's been a nightmare for him."

"I'll bear any burden with him."

Chapter 45 - The General

It was mid-March when I heard a car turn in the driveway. I flew out the farmhouse door like a chicken when the henhouse door was left open.

It was Ernest. Well, at least it looked like Ernest. The man in the passenger seat was big and dark-skinned like Ernest, but he didn't look the same. This man's curly hair was dull and gray. The eyes looking out at me were brown, but distant and lifeless.

A lump rose in my throat. I thought about what Gram said when Willie Larson was healing from his near-drowning ordeal. "He'll be fine. Young ones heal faster in body and soul than older people do," she had said. I wondered if Ernest would be fine. He looked mighty old right then.

The tall driver unfolded himself from behind the car's steering wheel. When he stood to full height, I saw he resembled Frank. His uniform, covered in ribbons, with four stars on either shoulder, gave me pause. He wasn't a young man, yet his eyes twinkled with mystery. His face was solemn as he walked to Gram and gently took her hand.

"I'm General Frank Wheeler Senior, ma'am. My son Frank Jr. speaks highly of you," he said. "And I'm honored to claim your lovely daughter as family."

"Thank you, sir," Gram spoke slowly with her eyes fixed on the man sitting in the passenger seat.

"I'm pleased to meet you, although I wish it was under different circumstances," the General continued. Gram glanced at him and nodded, hard-pressed to take her gaze away from Ernest. Her shoulders drooped, and her face sagged.

"Is he—?" she began. "Will he be—?" Her voice faded and cracked.

"Ma'am, I won't lie to you. In plain English, he's been through hell."

I studied every word coming out of the General's mouth. He looked like an educated man, the kind who might look down on the likes of Gram or Ernest. Yet the only looking down he was doing was from his height. He spoke from his heart. He hadn't known Ernest long in time. Still, he seemed to know him well. Ernest could do that to a person.

"I wish I could have found him sooner. The government is a bureaucracy of paperwork. The trail was long and hard to follow."

Tears flowed down Gram's face.

"I finally found him in Leavenworth. It's a hard place on the body and the mind," the General continued. "I was able to talk to him there. It wasn't an easy task to convince pig-headed prosecutors that they didn't have a case.

"I won't keep you from him any longer," the General said. "There's been enough time wasted." He paused before opening the door. "He's going to need time and a soft touch."

Gram steeled her back and lifted her chin.

"He'll get that here," she said.

The General opened Ernest's door. He helped him to get out and stand. Gram and I put our arms under him. He was thin and hunched and looked much smaller than the Ernest I remembered. General Wheeler braced his back while Ernest climbed the porch stairs one by one. His head rose when he reached the top, and he looked over at the porch chair where he used to sit and watch the sunset.

"Here." Ernest motioned weakly toward the chair, and we set him down gently. He looked out over the yard, and I got a clear look at him. Bruises of purple and yellow covered his face, and his crooked nose lay to one side. His eyes were hardly visible behind swollen slits. That old, jagged scar on his face was the least noticeable of his present features. His lips opened slightly in what could have been a smile. The sun blazed over the horizon, painting the sweeping clouds pink and purple. One cloud that looked like the wings of an angel bending to the earth caught my eye.

"You're home, Ernest," Gram whispered, placing her hands gently around his shoulders. "Home."

He nodded slowly, his voice cracked and scratchy. "Home."

Chapter 46 - TLC

Gram made chicken noodle soup for supper, and Ernest finished his bowl, although the eating looked painful. He still didn't speak much, yet he was there with us, which was all that mattered.

I helped Gram get him to her bed. She undid his shirt and told me to fetch a bowl of water she'd put on the cookstove to warm.

I heard Ernest speak as I came back into the room. "I'm sorry to be a burden."

"Don't talk silly," Gram chastised him with a catch in her voice. "I'd do this for anyone I love." She bent her head down and kissed him on his forehead, on the only spot left unbruised.

I set the water bowl on the bedside table with a clean towel I'd grabbed from the cabinet. Gram soaked the cloth and squeezed the water out slowly. "This may hurt a little," she said, holding her hands over Ernest. A slight noise escaped from his mouth that sounded like a laugh. Gram smiled sadly. "I suppose it's all relative, right?"

Their eyes met like the melting of wax on cloth. I left the room to do the supper dishes.

≈

The next day Gram called Doc. She didn't give many details over the phone. I don't think she wanted Ernest to hear her.

Doc showed up before supper, totting his black bag of needles and pills. Gram let him in and showed him to the bedroom. Doc hesitated for a moment at the sight of Ernest. But when Ernest looked over at him, he went in like he never missed a beat.

"Afternoon, Ernest," Doc greeted him, leaving off the "good" part. "Looks like you've been through quite a battle." He sat down in the chair beside him and put his bag on the bedside table.

"Yes, sir," Ernest answered in the strongest voice I'd heard him speak since coming home.

"Well, you're home now and in good hands."

Ernest nodded weakly like the speaking had taken more out of him than he expected.

"You relax, my good man. I'm just going to check you over and make sure nothing is broken. It looks like your nose has a new look to it, and there's not much we can do about that now."

"It ain't no worse than the old look," Ernest said.

I hated to disagree, so I figured the mirror would tell him another time.

Doc didn't find anything else broken beside his spirit. Unfortunately, he didn't have a pill for that.

≈

The warm spring days helped Ernest heal. By early April, he showed some improvement, although he still spent a lot of time on the porch in the rocking chair, watching the world go by. The bruises faded on his body. I knew there were others no one could see. Sometimes I heard him scream in the night, his voice more like an animal's howl than a man's. Then I'd hear Gram's softly speaking as though soothing a child. Gram tended to Ernest like a mama cat to her kittens. Willie and his pa stopped by to help with the chores from time to time. I read comic books to Ernest in the evening, and after a while, he finally laughed.

One morning in mid-April while I ate my breakfast, I noticed Gram and Ernest were extra quiet. I looked at them over my bowl of oatmeal, but I didn't see anything wrong. They didn't look mad or sad. They just weren't saying anything.

"Henry," Gram said. "Finish up your breakfast and get ready for school."

I knew what I had to do; even so, Gram seemed to find it necessary to tell me that day. She took my bowl as soon as I took my last bite. I did a quick brushing of my hair and teeth, grabbed my bookbag from the chair, and headed up the driveway.

On our way to school, Willie said, "Hey," pointing to the bus going by. "Isn't that your Gram and Ernest sitting in the back of the bus?"

I caught sight of their backs through the dirty window as the bus went by in a puff of gray smoke.

"It is," I said, swinging my bookbag. "I wonder where they're going."

"Maybe to Doc," Laurel guessed.

"Or they could be going to Harlow's General Store," Willie suggested.

"Gram usually walks there."

"Nobody walks anymore since the bus came to town," Willie said. "Except us to school!"

"We better get going, or we'll be late," I said, taking off in a run. Willie passed us since he always had to win. Laurel and I trotted along beside each other.

I wondered why Gram and Ernest didn't tell me they were going somewhere.

≈

Gram and Ernest must have gone to the General Store because we had a special evening meal. Meatloaf was Ernest's favorite, with mashed potatoes and tiny carrots from the garden. First, Gram unwrapped a big package of ground hamburger from the brown waxed paper. Then she put it in a bowl, adding an egg and breadcrumbs with some salt and pepper, mixing it all together with her hands.

As it cooked, the kitchen filled with the smell of juicy meat and spices 'til my mouth watered. I could hardly stop myself from grabbing my fork before Ernest finished saying grace. His blessing seemed exceptionally long. He did the usual thank-you for this food; then he went on to thank the Lord for home and family. My leg bounced as he continued to thank the Lord for life and happiness. I shouted out an "Amen" before he could go any further.

Then I stabbed a big chunk of meatloaf with my fork and ran it through my mashed potatoes, stuffing it into my mouth. I closed my eyes and let the taste melt into my tastebuds. "Mmmm," I said. "This meatloaf is better than ever."

Gram and Ernest smiled at each other and began to eat.

"I do believe you're right, son. Did you put something special in it today?" Ernest asked Gram.

Gram looked pleased. "Maybe a little extra TLC."

I wrinkle my forehead.

"Tender Loving Care," Gram explained.

It must have helped because there were no nightmare screams in the night, only the sound of Ernest snoring like a man who had a little extra TLC.

Chapter 47 - Evening In Paris

April 21 was Gram's birthday. That's what Ernest told me. I never knew. And I'm not sure how Ernest found out. Gram wasn't one to tell. She always said she didn't need a birthday because she was old as dirt. Of course, I didn't really think she was that old, although maybe she felt that way.

Gram actually looked younger lately, and I wasn't sure why. It could have been the smiling and the laughing. I heard somewhere that laughter was good medicine.

In any case, Ernest wanted to have a surprise birthday party for Gram. Ma and Frank wouldn't be able to come; they were overseas in Paris. Ma was probably buying French perfume and drinking champagne. I could just imagine it.

So, when Ernest asked me what he could get Gram for her birthday, I said French perfume and champagne. To my surprise, Ernest thought it was a great idea.

They didn't sell French perfume and champagne at Harlow's General Store. We could get cheap perfume at the Five and Dime. But Ernest said it wouldn't do; only the best was good enough for Gram.

Since it was her first birthday celebration I ever remembered, I figured he was right. But where were we going to get it?

"Mr. Shoemaker goes to the city sometimes," I said. "Maybe

he can get some there. I can ask him tomorrow at school."

"Make sure to tell him money is not an object."

I didn't think Ernest was fully aware of the cost of perfumes. Ma had told me some cost over twenty dollars. And I didn't think champagne was cheap, either.

I told Mr. Shoemaker what Ernest wanted and asked if he could help.

"Mr. White is the expert on perfumes." Mr. Shoemaker's eyes got misty. "But alas, he's moved back to New Orleans. He got his old job back in the hospital there."

He paused in thought, then seemed to remember I was there.

"Ah, yes. Well, some prefer the superficial appeal of city lights to the intimacy of a country sky full of stars."

I was unsure what he meant, but I wondered if Ma had similar feelings toward lights and stars.

Mr. Shoemaker seemed to brighten to the task at hand. He quickly devised a plan.

"I think I have an idea for the perfect perfume and champagne for this special celebration," he said.

I knew I had asked the right person. Still, Ernest fidgeted the whole week.

"What's wrong, Ernest?" Gram asked. "You seem like something is bothering you."

"No, no. Nothing at all."

Ernest was not good at this surprise stuff.

"Don't worry," I said when Gram wasn't around to hear. "I know we can count on Mr. Shoemaker."

And boy, was I right! Mr. Shoemaker came by the farm a few days before Gram's birthday.

"I'm looking for some fresh eggs, Mrs. Adams," Mr. Shoemaker told Gram when she came to the door. Ernest looked as nervous as my cat Mickey when Willie's hound dog was around.

"Sure," Gram said. "Let me grab a basket and get some right from the source. How many do you need."

"As many as you can spare," Mr. Shoemaker said, to Gram's surprise.

As soon as she disappeared into the henhouse, Mr. Shoemaker took a fancy little bag with a big bow from the back seat of his car along with a tall, brown paper bag. Ernest peered around to make sure that Gram wasn't looking.

We went into Ernest's old room in the barn. "What scent of perfume did you get?" Ernest asked like he was a perfume expert.

Mr. Shoemaker's eyes sparkled. "She's going to love this!" He gently removed the fancy cut-glass bottle from the pretty bag. He held it delicately between his fingers, waving his other hand around it, speaking like a television commercial.

"A feminine floral scent of violets, roses, and carnations with a pinch of powder," he said, holding it up to catch a beam of sunlight coming through the dusty window.

"The bottle is handcrafted from fine French Baccarat crystal with an elegant glass stopper, available only in upscale department stores. Every woman will love Evening In Paris."

"That's perfect!" Ernest and I said at the same time.

Mr. Shoemaker looked smug as he carefully put the bottle back in the bag. Then he pulled a bottle of champagne from the tall brown bag; no television commercial imitation was needed. The tall green bottle with gold foil at the top said Piper Brut on the label. "This is the preferred brand of Marilyn Monroe," he said with a wink.

"Whoa." *Wait until Willie hears this,* I thought. "Wait. What does all of this cost?" It occurred to me Ernest may not have enough.

Mr. Shoemaker hesitated.

"I've saved my share of money from the vegetable stand sales," Ernest said, pulling a secret stash from under his old bed.

"Ernest, you never got paid for all your school coaching. I talked to Coach, and he agreed. This is on us."

"I appreciate that. I do. But this is a gift from me, and I want to pay for it."

"I understand. And I thought you would say that. So, the perfume is twenty dollars. Will you accept the champagne as a gift for your hard work?"

Ernest agreed and gave Mr. Shoemaker the money with his sincere thanks.

We heard Gram's voice calling us, so we quickly hid the bags and went outside. Coming out of the barn, Ernest and Mr. Shoemaker appeared deep in conversation about the pros and cons of raw milk.

"I wondered where you boys got off to," Gram said, holding a full basket of eggs.

Ernest shook Mr. Shoemaker's hand while he mouthed "thank you" with his back turned to Gram.

"He certainly is a nice man, although I'm not sure why he needs so many eggs," Gram said as Mr. Shoemaker pulled out of the driveway.

"An upstanding gentleman," Ernest said, and we all agreed.

Gram went into the house, and Ernest turned to me with a new fear. "What about a cake?"

I thought a minute, "I'll ask Willie's ma. She makes a great carrot cake."

"Okay and ask them if they want to come to the party. Tell them there will be champagne."

I knew they would come without the champagne; even so, I couldn't wait to tell Willie.

On the way to school the following day, I told Willie and Laurel about the party.

"Champagne! Wow!" Willie's eyes lit up. Champagne didn't seem that exciting to Laurel, but the perfume got her attention.

"I'll tell my ma," Laurel said. "She'll be happy to make the cake. Count us in."

≈

Ernest could barely contain his excitement on the day of Gram's birthday. I thought he would ruin the surprise at breakfast, but he managed to keep quiet by stuffing his mouth.

"Ernest, I'm happy to see your appetite has improved," Gram said.

It was a Friday. I went to school like any other Friday, and I hoped Ernest could keep himself busy.

That evening after supper, Ernest jumped up to clear the dishes. "Henry and I will take care of those," he said. "You sit and relax."

"Well, isn't this nice? My two men doing dishes."

Ernest peeked out the kitchen window while he washed and I dried. The Larsons came down the driveway just as we finished.

"Look who's here," Ernest said with a big smile.

Mr. Larson carried a large sheet pan, and Mrs. Larson held a present.

I slipped out to get our gifts from the barn. I'd made something special and hid it there as well. I hurried back with the packages.

"What's all this?" Gram looked confused when she met the Larsons on the porch.

"A little bird told us it's your birthday," Mrs. Larson chirped.

"My birthday! Oh my gosh! How did you know?" Gram said, turning toward Ernest.

"I saw it on a document a couple of weeks ago," Ernest said.

Gram's face turned pink, and I wondered what document that would be.

"Well, come in!" Gram said, and the party began.

Mr. Larson set the carrot cake on the table, and Mrs. Larson handed Gram the gift.

"Open gifts first!" I said.

"Oh, my, you all shouldn't have."

The Larsons gave Gram a couple of handmade pillows filled with pine needles and spices. "For your drawers," Mrs. Larson whispered.

"I love them!" Gram passed them around for everyone to smell.

Next, she opened my gift. "Henry, how long have you been working on this? It's beautiful." I had carved a cardinal and painted it red. I remembered the Harlows used red paint for the letters on their sign. They had some leftover and were happy to give me some.

"I only started two weeks ago. I'm getting faster, especially with the new carving knife you and Ernest gave me for Christmas."

Ernest saved his gift for last. When he handed Gram the fancy bag with the big bow, you could have heard a pin drop in the old farmhouse kitchen. She looked at Ernest like he was the only one in the room.

When she slowly pulled the crystal bottle from the bag, there was a collective, "Ahh."

"Oh, Ernest, this is too much," she said and clutched the fancy bottle to her chest as if she would never let go of it.

She carefully removed the glass stopper at the top and smelled. Her eyes closed and the room filled with the smell of flowers and happiness.

The last rays of sunlight sparkled on the cut glass. Gram held it out for everyone to take a whiff. Even though we didn't need to get any closer to smell it, we all did. Mrs. Larson and

Laurel looked very impressed. Willie waited impatiently for the champagne.

Gram put the top back on the bottle and neatly placed it on the hutch where it was safe, and she could still see it.

After we each had a big piece of Mrs. Larson's delicious carrot cake, Ernest took out what Willie was waiting for.

"Champagne?" Gram put her hand to her mouth.

"It's the same kind Marylyn Monroe prefers!" I said.

"Oh well, it must be good," Mr. Larson piped up, and Mrs. Larson gave him a smart slap on the arm. They both laughed.

Ernest popped the cork, and it hit the ceiling. He started to pour the bubbly liquid into mason jar glasses.

I didn't think it was quite how Miss Monroe drank it, but it was okay for us.

There was a scary moment when Ernest asked if it was okay for the children to sample a little. Willie and I didn't move a muscle waiting for the answer.

"I don't see why not," Mr. Larson said.

"After all, what would Marilyn do?" Gram agreed.

Ernest finished filling the adults' glasses and put about a quarter of that amount in the kids'. We all lifted our mason jars and toasted. "Happy Birthday!"

"It is certainly a birthday I'll never forget. Thank you, all." She looked around the table, and her gaze came to rest on Ernest.

Laurel giggled at the bubbles tickling her nose. Willie and I just laughed at everything.

When the last drop was gone, Mr. Larson gave Mrs. Larson a silly look and said, "Ella, it's time to go home."

We could hear the whole family talking and laughing all the way up the driveway. Finally, the kitchen got quiet, and I said my goodnights before stumbling to the stairs. I heard Gram say, "It's all wonderful, Ernest, but where will I wear the perfume?"

I looked over my shoulder and saw Ernest retrieve the glass bottle from the hutch. He removed the fancy stopper and put a drop on his finger. "Wear it right here," he said, dabbing a little behind her ear.

I fell asleep in my bed to the sound of giggles,—and the sweet smell of Evening in Paris in the air.

I thought about Ma that very same night in Paris with Frank. I pictured Ma dabbing perfume behind her ears and drinking a glass of champagne from a fancy glass. And I knew for certain it wasn't as magical as the Evening in Paris right here in Mendota, Illinois.

Chapter 48 - Unconditional Love

Ma and Frank came home in September. Ma ran to Ernest and threw her arms around him. She hadn't seen him since he came home from Leavenworth. He closed his eyes and smiled the way Mr. Larson did when Laurel hugged him. It must be something about girls that did that to men. Gram looked pleased as punch while Ma chatted with her and Ernest about all the places they visited.

Frank made Major and had more pins and stripes on his chest. Not as many as the General but Willie would have been impressed. He wanted to enlist when he got old enough. Frank told me what each pin meant and how he earned them. I remembered Willie telling me the ceremony was known as blood pinning. So I asked Frank if it hurt when they pinned him.

"Not as much as the process of getting them."

I didn't think I wanted to join the military. Ernest said it was the toughest job he had ever had. Frank seemed to take to it. I think it was in his blood. When Ma finally went into the house with Gram, Frank straightened up and went to Ernest.

"It's good to see you, man," Frank said, taking Ernest's hand, he shook it firmly.

Ernest took his left hand and rested it on top of their entwined fists. "I can't thank you enough, Major. I owe you my life."

"We're family, Ernest. You call me Frank, and the only thing you owe me is a damned hug." They embraced each other like men do when they want to share emotions not easily conveyed by a handshake alone.

"Now, after I change into civilian clothes, would you give me some lessons splitting and stacking wood? We've got some wood to chop for the winter."

Ma trotted out on the porch in a red plaid shirt, a pair of slacks, and a dimple in her smile. Gram came out the door behind her with her work clothes and old boots.

"Well, I best get changed," Frank said. "I can't let the ladies get a head start!"

Frank had had some practice the first time he found the farm when he met Ma. But they had done more talking than wood-cutting then. Now, Ernest watched over Frank while he chopped. Frank said if he kept this up, he would have muscles as big as Ernest, even though we all knew Ernest's muscles weren't that big anymore. Ernest had his good days and bad. This was definitely one of his better ones, although he would say they were all good.

I helped Gram and Ma stack the wood in neat piles. After, Gram made lemonade with ice, and we all took a break on the porch.

Ma sat on the top step, wiping her brow with a paisley scarf, and I sat beside her. Frank leaned against the rail, sipping his drink, the ice cubes clinking against the sides of the orange metal cup. Gram stood behind the rocker where Ernest sat, gazing over the nicely stacked winter wood. She held her glass of lemonade in one hand and rested her other on Ernest's shoulder. He put his hand up to cover hers. I saw Ma give Frank a look, and Frank grinned over his cup.

Ernest started to sing low and slow. It was the first time I'd heard Ernest sing since he returned home.

I had wondered if he'd left his voice at Leavenworth. I was glad he didn't leave his singing voice behind in that awful brig. They didn't deserve it.

"I'm going to lay down my sword and shield,

Down by the riverside, Down by the riverside."

Gram started humming, and Ma and I joined the chorus.

"Down by the riverside. Down by the riverside."

Ernest sang the next verse a little louder.

"I ain't gonna study war no more; I ain't gonna study war no more."

Frank tapped his foot to the tune.

"I'm gonna lay my burden down," Ernest sang, and Frank joined in on the next chorus.

"Down by the riverside."

We all raised our voices.

"Down by the riverside."

Willie's old hound dog howled in the distance.

≈

With the wood chopped and stacked, the next line of business was planning a party for Ernest.

Ernest returned with more than bruises from his visit with the Army. He'd arrived home with a pile of official papers, including his birth certificate.

"This says your birthday is September 15, Ernest," I said, holding up the official document.

"Well, I'll be," Ernest said. "I really was born, after all."

"Ernest, we need to have a party to celebrate," Gram announced.

Ernest's rumbling laugh ended in a coughing jag. "Who would want to celebrate the day I was born?"

Gram thought a lot of people would. Of course, he thought it was a crazy idea, but that didn't stop Gram and Ma.

They invited nearly the whole town, then took to cooking up a storm. And I mean, you would have thought a storm rolled through Gram's kitchen by the time they finished. Everyone was supposed to bring something. So I didn't think we needed all the food they cooked, but I wasn't complaining.

Frank and I swept the porch and went to the church to borrow tables and chairs from Pastor Morgan. He was happy to share; the pastor always loved a good party.

"The Lord will provide," he said, patting his potbelly.

We began early on the day of the party, setting up tables for the food and covering them with cloths. We put out chairs, and Ma bought decorations at the Five & Dime. We all wore our best church clothes, sat on the porch, and waited.

"Is that Evening In Paris I smell?" Ma said, sniffing the air.

Gram blushed with a broad smile.

"Ernest bought it for Gram," I said.

Ma looked over at Ernest with a stunned look.

Frank gave him a wink. "Nice choice, Ernest."

We sat and watched the empty driveway in anticipation. We hadn't attended church since Ernest returned home. Gram said the sitting and kneeling were too much for him, and the Lord would understand. But maybe the townspeople didn't.

"It's a fine spread, Margarette," Ernest turned from Gram to us. "Having you all here is everything I need to make it a fine celebration."

Gram glanced again up the barren driveway.

Ma said, "Well, Frank and I would not have missed it for a trip around the world." She looked at Frank, and he affirmed it.

I saw a lone figure walking toward us. "It's Pastor Morgan," I shouted, glad to have a guest even though I knew he was one never to miss a party.

"Look!" Ma exclaimed, pointing toward the road. A line of people of different sizes and shapes, holding bowls and pans of food, were turning into the driveway and walking toward us. As they got closer, we could see the smiles on their faces. Willie and his family were in the lead, with Doc, his wife, and Mr. Shoemaker behind them.

Carloads of others followed. The Harlows got out of their pick-up, and I swear they were all smiling. Old Maid Morris brought a plate of what I guessed were her cookies from hell. More and more guests approached the porch.

They broke out in song when they got close enough to see Ernest's beaming face with his sideway nose and jagged scar. "*Happy Birthday to you!*" Everyone cheered, "*Happy Birthday, dear Ernest. Happy Birthday to you!*"

Ernest's big ole lip quivered and he clapped his hands, seemingly at a loss for words.

I knew we would sing again later when we served Gram's chocolate cake with creamy frosting. I figured Ernest had missed a few singings on his day and deserved more than one now. By the look on Gram's face, I think she would have gathered every note and kept them in a jar to listen to over and over with Ernest.

There was a flurry of activity as the women put the dishes on the tables and placed spoons and serving utensils. Pastor Morgan was right in the mix of it, taking samples. But I didn't see him take one of Old Maid Morris's cookies. I guessed a man of the Lord knows cookies from Hades when he sees them. Finally, Gram gave the go-ahead, and everyone got in line. She had already filled a plate for Ernest and brought it to him.

"This is the finest birthday I've ever had," he said, taking Gram's hand as she handed him the plate. A tic of time went by with them looking at each other like they were the only two people there.

Everyone had their fill and more. Coach took out his harmonica, and someone else had a fiddle. The music commenced, and so did the dancing. Davey Kennedy led the singing with his Elvis impression of "Blue Suede Shoes." He had everyone tapping their toes. Ernest rocked in his chair, clapping his hands to the music.

Mr. Harlow called out for a square dance, and everyone paired off to form groups of eight. Willie and I had practiced in gym class, and I was eager to join in. But instead, Willie poked me in the ribs and tipped his chin toward Sandra, standing off to the side with Laurel. Sandra wore slacks as the other girls had taken to wearing, covering her brace. However, she still walked with a cane.

Willie walked over to her, and her face lit up. My eyes met Laurel's and she grinned. I squirmed around to adjust my pants, suddenly feeling a little snugger. The four of us made our own little square, and we liked it better that way.

As the sun began to set, the music settled down to some soulful tunes, and the men assembled on the porch around Ernest smoking their cigarettes and pipes. There were stories to tell of the old days when things were good. I listened carefully, but I still didn't think they could be any better than today.

≈

Ma and Frank stayed a whole month. Ma said Frank had taken an extended family leave.

Ma and Gram cooked all kinds of delicious meals. She asked Gram to write down the recipes to keep for when they got a real home with a decent kitchen. I wondered when that would be.

After supper, we'd sit on the porch, watching the sunset and talking about happy times. I hoped someday we would sit and talk about these times.

Frank told Gram that he looked into Gramp's military papers.

"It seems Mr. Adams was of the age that he served in the First World War."

"That's right," Gram confirmed. "Henry was a good bit older than me."

"Well, I found compensation owed to him for his service." Frank handed Gram a check, and she teared up. "Now you don't have to worry about anything," Frank said.

I didn't think all Gram's concerns could be solved with money, although she thanked Frank sincerely.

The time came for them to leave, as we all knew it would but hoped it wouldn't. Gram hugged Ma like she wouldn't let her go. When she let loose, they both had tears in their eyes.

"I love you, Janie," she sniffled. "Don't you ever forget it."

"I never doubted it, Mama. No matter how hard I made it, I always knew you loved me."

Ma turned to Ernest, smiling through her tears. "You came into our lives and made us a family, Ernest." She sniffled. "A good family."

"Ah, Janie, you've made me a proud man, and I thank the Lord for you." He held his big arms out to her, and she folded into them, kissing him on the scar on his cheek.

Ma came to me and stood on her tiptoes to hug me properly.

"You're taller than me, now, Henry," she said and squeezed me. "I love you."

"I love you, too, Ma."

Frank hugged Gram with his eyes closed and a smile on his face. He shook my hand and pulled me into a warm hug. Then he embraced Ernest and patted him on the back.

They exchanged a look that I suspected held more meaning than words could tell.

Chapter 49 - Busy Hands

Ernest asked me to find him some wood for whittling. "I need to keep my hands busy."

I went to Willie's to see if Mr. Larson had any spare pieces of scrap wood from the sawmill.

Mr. Larson said, "I sure do."

I explained it was for Ernest, so he threw a pile in the back of his truck and brought it to our farm. Ernest sat in the rocking chair on the porch when we pulled in. Mr. Larson got out of the truck and went right over to Ernest.

"How are you, man?" he asked with his hand extended.

Ernest took his hand. "I'm afraid my grip isn't what it once was, Bill. Don't take my weak handshake as the measure of my gratitude."

"I take your measure by the strength of your deeds, Ernest; those are powerful, indeed."

"That's kind of you," Ernest said. "I'm hoping some carving will help strengthen my hands, and I think I have a plan for the creations."

Mr. Larson motioned toward his truck. "I brought you some nice chunks of walnut and eastern red cedar. After a run at the sawmill, we had some left, and it smelled so good I took the scraps home. I didn't know what use I'd put them to. I'm happy if you have a good plan."

"Bill, you just gave my spirit a lift." Ernest's eyes sparkled. "The dark walnut and the light cedar are perfect for what I have in mind, and the woodsy cedar smell will be a special addition."

I helped unload the wood from the truck, and we piled it on the porch.

"Thank you, kindly," Ernest said.

Mr. Larson chuckled. "I'm glad I could be of service. You take care of yourself, Ernest, you hear?"

We both gave Mr. Larson a hearty wave goodbye.

"What are you going to carve?" I asked.

"Whatever the Spirit speaks to me."

Ernest trusted the Spirit a lot. I hoped it spoke well about wood.

The weather was getting colder. So Ernest set up a chair by the cookstove in the kitchen and carved every day. He'd sweep up the sawdust with the broom and dustpan and toss it in the stove. After school, I tried to peek at his handiworks, but he kept them a surprise. He looked peaceful while he carved.

"It's good therapy for my hands and soul," he said, humming while he carved.

"You look like you're making progress on that pile of wood Bill brought you," Gram said.

"That I am. And progress on building back some strength," Ernest smiled. "Feel this grip now." He held his hand out to Gram, and she slipped hers into his.

"That's the finest hand I've ever had grip mine," she said, looking into his eyes while holding his hand for a time before letting go.

"Can I feel?"

"A firm handshake is a sign of mutual respect." Ernest grasped my hand and gave it a firm shake.

"And the sign of a good carver, too!" I said.

Ernest laughed. "Compliments will not get you a look at my carvings any sooner."

"Well, when *can* I see them?"

Ernest looked at the calendar on the wall. "In about one month."

I did some figuring. "Christmas?"

"That's right."

Ernest worked happily for the next month. I couldn't wait for Christmas.

Mr. Larson came by in December with a Christmas tree. I thought of the times Ernest and I went searching for one, but Mr. Larson did well.

"Maybe you will be able to go Christmas tree hunting again by next year," I said.

Ernest smiled. "Yes, son. Maybe next year."

"In the meantime, why don't you help me decorate this fine tree, Henry," Gram said.

We drank hot cocoa and sang Christmas songs around the tree. Maybe next year would be better, but this year was just fine. On Christmas Eve, the farmhouse filled with the smells of baking pies and cinnamon. Things seemed almost normal again.

Christmas morning, when I came downstairs, Ernest sat with his coffee in front of the woodstove, looking out the window. The scar on the side of his face sagged, no longer tight and shiny as when I first met him. His dark hair was now salted white, and his eyes dim, but his mouth drew up into a smile, and a rush of warmth filled my chest when he looked at me.

"Ernest, it's Christmas!"

"That it is, son. Praise the Lord."

Gram came out of her bedroom in her fuzzy bathrobe with messy hair. "Why didn't you wake me?" she said to Ernest. "I never sleep this late. And it's Christmas!"

Ernest looked at Gram like she was the rising sun, too bright to look at directly but too amazing to turn away. He poured her a cup of coffee, and we went to the parlor.

I wanted to open my present from Ernest in the worst way, but I wasn't a small child anymore. So, I waited. I had a special gift for Gram that Ma and Frank helped me with. When Ma was home with Frank in September, she took pictures with her new Kodak Brownie camera with the built-in flash. I wrote Ma and asked if she could send me a copy of the picture of Gram and Ernest sitting on the porch.

"Henry! It's beautiful. And a reminder of a wonderful time." She took a handkerchief from the pocket of her bathrobe and wiped her eyes.

Next, I gave Ernest another picture Ma sent without me even asking.

"This is special," Ernest said. However, I didn't know how he could see it through his misting eyes.

"It's all of us," I said excitedly. "Look! It's you, me, Gram, Ma, and Frank. We're a family."

"Yes. We are," Gram said.

Ernest nodded his head, unable to speak.

I couldn't wait any longer to open my present from Ernest. While I tore the wrapping paper, Ernest looked on with a satisfied grin. I opened the box, and inside were individual hand-carved chess pieces, each uniquely special. Ernest created each one from a block of solid wood. The light set was made from white maple and polished to glow. I unwrapped the dark set, and the smell of cedar filled the room.

"My own chess set!" I hugged Ernest, laying my head on his chest and hearing the beat of his heart.

"I'm glad you like it, son."

"I love it," I said, wondering how soon I could ask Laurel over to play.

1958

Chapter 50 - Love and Cherry Blossoms

In mid-March, Frank called. He said they were in Washington, D.C.

"Come visit us," he said to Gram. "You, Ernest, and Henry need to see the cherry blossoms in bloom. The General's home is on the Potomac River. He wants you to stay with him and meet mother."

Ernest stood beside Gram, and she glanced up at him. "Oh, we couldn't," she hesitated. "It's far, and Ernest's condition ...."

Ernest gently took the phone from her hand. "Tell the General we would be honored."

"We're going to Washington D.C.?" I asked, not believing my ears. "Wait until Willie hears this!"

Mr. Larson offered to watch over the farm and animals while we were gone. Willie said I better bring him back a souvenir. I promised I would and get Laurel one, too.

Frank knew Gram wouldn't like to fly, so he sent first-class train tickets. "First class!" Ernest said when he saw them. "My brothers from the boxcars would never believe this."

We packed suitcases Gram borrowed from Mr. Shoemaker. He traveled a lot, and he was happy to oblige. Ernest and I threw some shirts and pants into our suitcases.

Gram took forever packing her case. I think she took every piece of clothing she owned. She kept shouting reminders to Ernest and me.

"Did you pack socks and skivvies? How about dress clothes? And a jacket? It might still be chilly at night."

Ernest and I grinned at each other. We had never seen Gram so excited before.

Finally, the day arrived. The General sent a military car to drive us to Depot Station. It wasn't that far, yet he insisted we were not taking the bus.

Ernest and I were standing on the porch when the blue car with the official army emblem came down the driveway with a man in uniform behind the wheel. I could feel a shiver go through Ernest's body at the sight. But the soldier got out with a smile and held the back door open for Ernest and Gram to enter. I rode up front, wishing we could have driven by Willie's house.

We left Depot Station in Mendota aboard the Zephyr for the eight-hour trip bound for the United States Capital. First, we headed north to Chicago and across the southern tip of Lake Michigan. My eyes were glued to the window as we went through Toledo, Ohio, and around the bottom of Lake Erie. From Cleveland, we headed south toward Pittsburgh and on to the Capital.

The conductor was almost as big and nearly as dark as Ernest. They hit it right off. In between his duties, he talked to Ernest about the Civil Rights Act, the Pullman porter who helped a woman named Rosa Parks when she refused to move to the back of the bus in 1955, and that young preacher named Martin Luther King, Jr.

When our mealtime came, the conductor showed us the way to the Golden Trencher dining car. White linen tablecloths covered the tables set with fancy glass dishes and shiny silverware.

"Oh, my!" Gram put her hand to her mouth. "We can't afford this."

I reminded her that the General had paid for everything and said for us to enjoy it. I was certainly ready to oblige him. The waiter pulled out our chairs like we were royalty. Ernest looked uncomfortable, but the gentleman waiting on us put him at ease with a tip of his head and a smile.

The General himself met us at Union Station in Washington. It was a good thing, too, because we would have never found the exit door by ourselves.

The General took Gram's hand, "Ma'am, I'm pleased you accepted my invitation. Vivian looks forward to meeting you, and Janie and Frank are thrilled you are all here."

The General's house, if you can call something that big a house, had floor-to-ceiling windows overlooking the Potomac River on one side. From the other side of the house, I could see the Washington Monument piercing the sky.

Mrs. General, who said to call her Vivian, didn't look at all how I imagined. She was tall and broad with dark hair and eyes. She looked like she could wrestle a hog and in fact, she'd grown up on a farm out west, so she told us.

"I'll give you a tour of our horse barn and other animals here after you settle in," she said. "You can never take the farm out of a farm girl." Vivian gave a warm look to Gram, and Gram's shoulders relaxed.

The maid showed us to our rooms; we each got one. Mine had a high bed with four posts. I jumped on it and sank right in. I explored the drawers and large standing closet to find children's books and toys. I wondered if I was in Frank's boyhood room. There was even a picture of Roy Rogers on the wall. I knew I was going to be very comfortable.

When we all returned to the parlor, where Ma and Frank waited impatiently, Ma threw her arms around Gram and me. Ernest gave his hand to Frank; ignoring it, Frank grabbed Ernest in a bear hug.

We sat in the huge room on fancy couches while the butler served us drinks and treats. It was like being in a different world. Ernest looked around the room and said, "I have a feeling we are not in Illinois anymore." Just like Dorothy said about her Kansas home in The Wizard of Oz. We all had a good laugh.

As it turned out, Gram was right about bringing a jacket. While the days were warm, easily getting well over fifty degrees, the nights got down near freezing. None of us seemed to care when we sat in the evening on the long porch lined with rockers with blankets draped over our laps, while talking and watching the boats on the river.

The next day Frank asked Ernest if he was fit enough to walk to the monuments. He told him there were many places to sit and rest. Gram looked concerned.

"This sweet, warm air and kind company make me feel like a young man again," Ernest said. "I think I'm walking on air."

"I'll take that as a yes, young man." Frank joked with Ernest.

Frank held Ma's hand as they walked under the cherry trees with pink blossoms that looked like they were exploding from the branches. I scooped up a pile of blossoms from the ground and threw them over my head. The air filled with a sweet scent, and I felt dizzy with happiness.

Gram held onto Ernest's arm, and he put a hand over hers. They looked at each other the same way Ma and Frank did. The General and Vivian walked arm and arm beside us, pointing out the important landmarks. Near the Capitol building, we saw the young Senator John F. Kennedy. He looked full of life. The General gave him a wave, and the senator returned it with a friendly smile. The General told us rumor had it the senator would run for president of the United States in 1960.

"Kennedy told a colleague he had a dream that the Lord Himself said he would be president," the General whispered as though it was a secret. I couldn't wait to tell Willie.

Ernest said, "You can't get a better endorsement than that."

In the evening, after dinner—they have dinner in Washington, not supper—so after dinner, we sat in the big parlor. Vivian played the grand piano—and it was grand. She played a few notes, and Ernest looked up with a smile.

"Do you like this one, Ernest?" she asked, playing on.

"I do, ma'am. I sang it with my brothers while traveling in the boxcars."

Vivian's voice sounded like a morning bird. *"This land is your land."*

Ernest soft, deep voice answered, *"This land is my land."*

Each line drew another of us into the song until even the General was singing.

"This land was made for you and me."

On April 21, we celebrated Gram's birthday in the Southern Dining Room on Seventh Street.

Ernest took a big breath of the spicy air. "Hmm mmm, it smells just like my mama's cooking."

"Southern-style cooking has become popular all over the county," the General boasted, "and you will find some of the best right here." By the look on Ernest's face, he was right.

The chef, Hettie Gross, came out of the kitchen to ask if everything was to our liking.

"Ma'am, those are the best chitterlings and cornbread I've had since I left 'Bama as a young man."

Miss Gross smiled. "My mama taught me good."

We all agreed.

We stayed three weeks since Gram had got special permission for me to miss school. My teacher said I had to write a report about my trip. I had a lot to write about.

We left when the last cherry blossoms fell. It seemed like a dream. Still, I was happy when I woke up at home on the farm.

I brought Willie a souvenir coin with George Washington crossing the Potomac on one side and Mt Vernon on the other. I explained to him that it wasn't the kind of coin for spending, but Willie said he'd never spend it anyway.

I gave Laurel a water globe with a picture inside of the Reflecting Pool. When she shook it, cherry blossoms floated in the water. Laurel said a very soft thank-you. But she didn't have to say anymore.

Chapter 51 - The Fountain of Youth

After we returned from Washington, the warmth of summer came early to the farm, and Ernest said it felt good. The days were long and felt like they would never end.

When school let out, our Chess Club ended. But we didn't want to stop, so we made a summer club of our own. Laurel came by every Friday after supper. Isaac came, too. He brought his chess set and played with Ernest.

Of course, his set wasn't as nice as mine that Ernest carved by hand, but they got by. Ernest said he learned to play chess on the trains shortly after the war.

"We used an old set that belonged to one of the men during the war. A lot of the boxcar soldiers served in Germany. Chess was very popular in Europe at the time. Almost all the U.S. military hospitals had a chess set in their wards," Ernest said.

"I read a book that said chess masters were recruited in England as code breakers during World War II," Gram added. "They were known as the Gold, Cheese, and Chess Society."

That made me think we needed a name for our chess club. "How about the Mendota Chess Club," I offered.

Laurel scrunched her nose like something stunk.

Isaac agreed with her. "We need something more impressive," he said.

"What about the Society of Chess, Corn, and Champions," Gram suggested.

That suited us and we all shook hands on the name. Laurel and I held hands a little longer.

≈

I turned fifteen in July. Ma was overseas again with Frank. She sent a letter from the Ledward Barracks in Schweinfurt, Germany, saying that she and Frank were doing important work there. She forgot to say happy birthday.

The fall chill came early, and the weather seemed to give Ernest pause. We spent a lot of time inside. Ernest didn't look like the young man he felt like in Washington just a few months before. He was still Ernest, just not quite like he used to be. I wondered if he ever would be.

An early winter storm roared around the house and shook the windows. We sat at the kitchen table by the warm cookstove, eating Gram's stew. Meals always lifted Ernest's spirits. All our spirits, in fact.

"Your stew can cure what ails a man," Ernest said, wiping his roll around the edge of the bowl.

Gram smiled with sleepy eyes. "I wish it was the elixir of youth."

"I heard tell of men who searched for a lifetime for the Fountain of Youth."

"Did they ever find it?" I asked, hoping to tell Willie something he didn't know.

"No, son. They wasted away their lives trying to live forever. In the end, everyone goes home to the Lord."

Gram put her spoon down on the table. "What do you think Heaven is like, Ernest?"

"Well." He finished the last of his stew, and a glow came to his face. "It has to be a lot like this here farm."

"How's that, Ernest?" I asked.

"Overflowing with love and open to all who enter with a good heart."

Gram's eyes narrowed. "Do you think we really spend eternity with the ones we love?"

Ernest's features softened, and his brown eyes swam in little puddles of glistening moisture. "I believe it with all my heart."

I was sure glad to hear that. Still, I had to ask, "Ernest Pig, too?"

Gram and Ernest laughed. "Ernest Pig, too," they both said.

As the November chill started to set in, Ernest's blood disease worsened. Gram phoned Doc, and he came to call.

"I've got some money," Gram said. "Is there anything we can do?"

Doc agreed to take Ernest to the hospital in Joliet, but his eyes didn't look hopeful. Ernest was gone for a week, and Gram couldn't find a place in the farmhouse that suited her to sit. When the phone finally rang, Gram grabbed the receiver.

"Ernest," she said in a breath. "How are you?"

I put my ear beside hers to hear his voice. "I've been poked and prodded day and night," he said with sadness. "There's no stopping nature's course. I'm tired and hungry, and I just want to come home."

Gram burst out bawling. "I want you home."

We moved the table, and Gram set up a bed for Ernest in the kitchen. I brought his meals and read stories to him. He said the heat from the stove eased his pain. Ernest Pig liked to sleep on the floor beside him. I'm not sure which one snored louder.

Ernest listened carefully when I did my schoolwork. Once a week, I stopped at the library to pick up a book to read with him. When I spotted the one about a pig on a farm with a spider for a friend, I knew Ernest would like it. I read a chapter each night. We both agreed Ernest Pig was just as wise as Wilbur. Of course, Ernest Pig snorted in agreement, too.

The night I finished the last chapter, Ernest said, "Son, you've given me something I was sorely lacking."

"What's that, sir?"

"It's the same thing Wilbur gave Charlotte in the book."

I hated to tell Ernest, but I thought he didn't understand the story. "Wilbur didn't give Charlotte anything. It was Charlotte that did all the giving."

"That's where you're mistaken, son." Ernest rested his hand on my shoulder. "Wilbur gave Charlotte purpose. A person needs a purpose."

I thought about everything Charlotte did for Wilbur, and I realized it was me who didn't get the story. "Can a person live without purpose?"

"Yes," Ernest said. "The difference is in just living or living well."

Chapter 52 - Going Home

Before Thanksgiving, Ernest took a turn for the worse. I was thankful when Shamus came by. He had stopped a couple of times through the years when he passed through the area. I think it was fate that brought him this particular time.

He stayed a week with us. I hoped he'd brought the nectar of the gods and luck of the Irish with him. But I could tell when I looked into his eyes that neither could help this time.

Shamus sat with Ernest, telling him Irish tales, and I swear I saw sparkles dance in his eyes while he talked. If there were ever a place I would want to see beyond the farm, it would be the island of Shamus McGuire—Ireland.

"Aye, lad, I'll never forget the smell of the air while walking among the shamrocks on my álainn isle or the thrill of watching the waves crash on the Cliffs of Moher in County Clare."

Shamus mixed up more than a couple of batches of hot toddies. They helped Ernest sleep and gave the rest of us the strength to face each day. We all knew they couldn't change the future.

Before he left, Shamus sat at the side of Ernest's bed and held his hand.

"I have to be traveling on, my friend. Although it wouldn't be hard to stay here and become fat and lazy, you know."

He gave a fond look toward Gram. "The southern sun calls me to frolic in the ocean waves."

"I don't suppose I'll see you again," Ernest said.

"Hush, don't speak of it," Shamus said. "On this side or the other—you can never free yourself from an Irishman's heart."

Ernest chuckled. "You told me God has a special place in Heaven set aside for Irishmen. Will the Lord let us visit?"

"You, my good man, have a free pass," Shamus tipped his head. "I have that on high authority."

He bowed his head, closed his eyes, and clasped Ernest's hand tightly.

"I leave you with this Irish Blessing.

May the road rise to meet you,

May the wind always be at your back,

May the sun shine warm upon your face,

The rains fall soft upon your fields,

And until we meet again,

May God hold you in the palm of his hand.

"Amen," Ernest said. "Until we meet again."

Shamus hugged Gram and me and turned to leave quickly, but I saw the tears in his eyes. I think he couldn't bear to stay and see Ernest pass. I wondered how I would bear it.

Gram fell asleep in the chair beside Ernest's bed with her hand holding his every night. If I got up early, I'd see her roll out of bed beside him and pull the blanket back over him. It was a small bed to fit in the kitchen, and there was barely enough room for Ernest, but I knew he didn't mind sharing it with Gram.

Doc came by, put his stethoscope on Ernest's chest, and spoke soft words. On his way out, he took Gram's hand; with tears in his eyes, he shook his head slightly. I was old enough to know what that meant.

Each morning that week, I sat by his bed. Gram never told me to get ready for school. I was learning a lesson in life that school never teaches. School books have information on math, English, and science.

Ernest didn't use books to teach me what was truly important. Instead, he showed me in every deed he did, every word he spoke, and every word he didn't.

I wonder where I would be now if he had never been sick and come here to stay. Yet here we were, come full circle. His illness brought him here, and now it would take him away. I clenched his hand in mine as if, with sheer determination, I could hold him here.

Don't take him, Lord, my mind screamed. "Don't go," my lips whispered. But I knew it was futile. My chest ached, and a sob escaped without my consent.

Ernest's eyes fluttered, and I could see his pupils between his heavy eyelids.

"You're going to be all right, son."

But he wasn't.

And how could I or anything be all right again without him? I wanted to ask. The words stuck in my throat, but I didn't need to speak because Ernest always knew my mind.

"People come and go in life," he said. "But love is constant, son. It never dies."

Tears rolled down my cheeks unobstructed. He rested his hand on my head like he did when I was little and held it there for a long time.

I thought he wanted to tell me something else, but he just said, "You go now, son; I need to make peace with the Lord."

That was the last time I saw Ernest alive. I was sitting at the kitchen table when Gram checked on him. Her painful cry told me all I didn't want to know. My head fell to the table cradled in my cold arms; my eyes blurred and the air hummed with an energy that could only have been love.

I don't think Ernest wanted us to see him die. Nevertheless, I saw it in my nightmares a million times.

≈

The next day, I took my savings jar to the Stoneman and told him I needed a sturdy piece of rock for a good man. He looked at my jar and scratched his head. He knew Ernest, and he thought highly of him.

"I think I have something that will work," he said.

He brought me out back and showed me a flat piece of granite that wasn't exactly perfect. He said he couldn't use it for anything, and I could have it.

"I thank you kindly, sir," I said, handing him the jar. "But I want you to carve something in it, and I mean to pay you for that."

"That's mighty upstanding of you," the Stoneman said. "What would you like it to say?"

I told him the words I wanted, and I said to carve them really big. "So everyone can see them."

≈

The service was in the church, and the bell in the steeple rang loud and clear in his honor—calling the well-behaved and the wayward alike. Ernest saw the good in all.

Ma and Frank couldn't come, and Ma was real broken up about it. I heard her crying on the phone with Gram.

"It's not fair," she cried. "He was too good to die. He was the best of us."

"That he was," Gram agreed. "Life's not always fair."

Ma was overcome with grief, and Frank took the phone.

"Ma Adams, I'm sorry," he said. "The General wants me to extend his deepest sympathy, and he wants to pick up the funeral costs. He said to give Ernest the works."

"Thank him for me," Gram cried softly.

Gram and I picked out the biggest, shiniest casket the funeral parlor had. Gram said it had to be big to accommodate Ernest's size, and it had to be shiny to reflect his radiant spirit. The church filled with more people than I recalled at Old Man Larson's funeral. I didn't say that to Willie.

Pastor Morgan had tears in his eyes talking about a man he was proud to call a friend. Then he led us in Psalm 100, Ernest's favorite.

Psalm 100

Shout for joy to the Lord, all the earth.
Worship the Lord with gladness;
Come before him with joyful songs.
Know that the Lord is God.
It is he who made us, and we are his;

We are his people, the sheep of his pasture.

Enter his gates with thanksgiving

And his courts with praise;

Give thanks to him and praise his name.

For the Lord is good, and his love endures forever;

His faithfulness continues through all generations.

Mr. Larson, Coach, Mr. Shoemaker, Mr. Feinstein, Mr. Harlow, and Sheriff Fitzpatrick carried Ernest's coffin down the church aisle. I touched it as it passed and saw my reflection as though I was looking into Ernest's eyes. It was an unusually warm day in November. I stood beside Gram as they lowered Ernest into the ground. She cried, and I did, too.

1959

Chapter 53 - Together Forever

For a quiet man, he sure did leave a big empty space where there used to be sound. I missed the heavy hum of his breathing and the tunes he sang that floated in the air like the warming smoke from a campfire. I missed Gram's laughter that died with him, too. I kept busy with the animals and the farm. Gram puttered around the house. I often found her lost in thought. One time she was in the parlor holding her yarn, tears in her eyes.

"Gram, remember how pleased Ernest was with the blanket you made him?"

"I do," she said. Later that day, I saw it on her bed.

Shamus came by once and stayed a couple of days. It lifted Gram's spirits, but I could tell it was hard for him to be on the farm without Ernest. It was hard for us all.

We gathered at Ernest's grave with Shamus before he left. He kneeled and gave a gentle touch to the flat piece of granite the Stoneman placed there to remember Ernest. He read the words I had chosen and smiled. But we didn't need a stone to think of him. Ernest was with each one of us wherever we were.

≈

The year after Ernest died, I turned sixteen. And Gram passed away.

Before she left, I sat by her bed and held her hand.

"Maybe you should dust off that Bible and read me a few lines," she said.

Gram was never much for Bible reading. I wasn't sure what to read. So, I turned to a familiar psalm I once knew by heart, but I didn't know if I could recall it all.

"*The Lord is my shepherd; I shall not want,*" I read loudly so she could hear.

She stopped me. "Not that one, Henry," she said weakly.

I realized that was Gramp's psalm. I turned the pages back to Psalm 100, Ernest's psalm. I had also learned it by heart. I took a deep breath and hoped to read it without my voice cracking. Gram shook her head again with teary eyes. I thought she probably had one of her own. I was ashamed to admit I didn't know.

"Which reading is yours, Gram?" I asked. Something fell out as I leafed through the pages.

"That's the one," she said.

I held the page and bent to pick up a square slip of paper from the floor. It had a four-leaf clover taped to one side. On the back, I saw three words scrawled in print.

'*Love Always, Ernest.*'

The Bible was open to the book of 1 Corinthians. I cleared my throat and proceeded to read:

> *Love is patient, love is kind.*
>
> *It does not envy, it does not boast, it is not proud.*
>
> *It does not dishonor others, it is not self-seeking,*
>
> *It is not easily angered, it keeps no record of wrongs.*
>
> *Love does not delight in evil but rejoices with the truth.*

It always protects, always trusts, always hopes, always perseveres.

Love never fails.

But where there are prophecies, they will cease;

Where there are tongues, they will be stilled;

Where there is knowledge, it will pass away.

For we know in part, and we prophesy in part,

But when completeness comes, what is in part disappears.

When I was a child, I talked like a child, I thought like a child,

I reasoned like a child.

When I became a man, I put the ways of childhood behind me.

For now we see only a reflection as in a mirror; then we shall see face to face.

Now I know in part; then I shall know fully, even as I am fully known.

And now these three remain:

Faith, hope, and love.

But the greatest of these is love.

I gently replaced the clover in the page and closed the Bible. I'd be putting another Bible passage to memory.

"Henry," she said when I finished. "I couldn't be any more proud of you than if you were my own son."

"Well, Gram," I said. "Sometimes it ain't the ma you're born to that does the raising."

"And sometimes not the pa, either," Gram said in her weak voice.

"I had the best pa a boy could ask for." I teared up. It was the first time I had spoken the word out loud in referring to Ernest, and it weighed heavy on my tongue. "Ernest is gone, but he made me who I am, and I'm forever grateful."

Gram's eyes swelled with tears yet to fall. "He loved you dearly," she choked the words. "He was proud of you ... and he would be pleased with the man you've become." Her eyes closed for a moment, then they opened slightly. "Bury me beside him."

Those were the last words Gram spoke.

I held her hand tight as she took her last breath. It may have been the mist in my eyes, but I swear I saw her soul rise from her body in a cloud of electricity that hovered and hummed. I thought I smelled Evening In Paris in the air, although the little blue bottle sat sealed tight on Gram's dresser.

Then I felt a warm touch on my shoulder. My ears perked to a familiar tune, and a soft breeze like someone's breath rippled through my hair. I turned, half expecting to see Ernest smiling down at me. I had no doubt he was there, come to take Gram home.

Chapter 54 - Saying Goodbye

It was almost a year to the date from when Ernest passed. Ma and Frank made it home in time for Gram's services. Frank had earned his wings, so he rented a Cessna plane and flew in from Andrews Air Force Base outside of Washington, landing at the small airport in Joliet. They borrowed a car and drove the rest of the way. Ma's face was still flushed with the exhilaration of the flight when they arrived.

The church was packed, just like it had been for Ernest. I tucked the little crystal perfume bottle into the casket beside her. After the church service, we rode to the family plot behind the black hearse in a great big Cadillac with Frank at the wheel. Pastor Morgan read a passage from 1 Corinthians.

A long line of friends and townspeople told me how much they thought of Gram. They shook my hand, and some of them hugged me. The pastor was the last one.

"Your Gram was a good woman," he said. He paused and glanced back at the grave. "And Ernest was a good man. One of the best I've ever met."

I nodded my head. He pulled an envelope from his Bible, handed it to me, and said, "It was the right thing to do."

I didn't know what he meant, but I said, "Thank you, sir."

I tucked the envelope into my jacket breast pocket and forgot about it until the next day.

It was a marriage certificate for Margarette Flora and Ernest Leroy Potts, signed by Reverend Morgan, dated April 14th, 1957. It was after Ernest came back from Leavenworth. I tried to think back. It must have been that day when Willie and I saw them on the bus going into town. They snuck off and got married.

I showed it to Ma and Frank.

Ma chuckled. "He made her an honest woman, after all."

≈

Two days after we lowered Gram into the ground, Ma and Frank started to get antsy, and I knew they would be leaving soon. Ma asked me to go with them.

"There's nothing here for you now, Henry," she said.

Frank stood by Ma's side. I looked at him and weighed my options.

Frank was a good man. I didn't think he would ever be a pa. Yet he was a good husband to Ma, and Ernest would say that was the most important thing.

"I like it here, Ma."

"You belong with me. I'm your mama, son."

"That you are," I said. "And I'll always love you when you're here and pray for you when you're away."

I saw creases near her eyes I had never seen before.

"You and Frank, you got places to go," I said. "This is the only home I've ever known. I want to stay and work the farm."

Ma looked into Frank's eyes. He smiled and nodded. "Henry's right, Janie. He's old enough to know his own mind."

Frank turned to me.

"Henry, I admire you. You've grown into a fine man. If you ever need us, we're only a phone call away. We're family."

Ma's eyes sparkled through her tears.

≈

After they left, I paid another visit to the Stoneman. The flat granite stone marked Ernest's resting place. I could have done the same for Gram, but I thought they both deserved something more.

"I'm sorry for your loss, Henry. You've had more than your share these past two years."

"Thank you, sir." I pulled out my wallet. "I sold a litter of pigs, and I have money this time for a real stone," I said, laying the marriage certificate on the counter. "It's for Gram and Ernest."

"Henry, I'd trust your word if you didn't have the money. But this stone is already paid for. A man called the General sent money enough for any stone you want—for your Gram and Ernest," he said. "I think I have the perfect one."

He showed it to me, and I agreed. I gave him the rest of the dates, and he said he would get right to work on carving it.

I hesitated for a moment.

"Is there something else on your mind?" he asked.

"Well, since I have the money now, I was thinking I'd like to get a stone," I gulped, "for my gramp. His is a little worse for the wear."

The Stoneman smiled a knowing smile. "That's a great idea, Henry."

"It's the right thing to do," I said.

"I think your Gram and Ernest would agree."

"He wanted that big elaborate stone before he passed. He may see things differently from his present viewpoint," I said. "I'm thinking about a nice modest flat stone with his name and dates."

"I think you're right," the Stoneman said, "He'll be able to see it better from above."

"Do you think you can fit some words on the bottom?"

"What would you like?"

" *'He leadeth me in the paths of righteousness for his name's sake.'* "

≈

The Stoneman called to say he was bringing the stones over in the afternoon. I went to level the spot at the opposite end of the grave from Ernest's flat stone. A tune came to my lips.

"Swing low, Sweet Chariot, coming for to carry me home ...."

The sun broke through the cloud cover, filtering through like the golden fingers of God Himself. I raised my face and closed my eyes.

"Well now, if you get there before I do,

Comin' for to carry me home,

Tell all my friends that I'm a-comin', too,

Comin' for to carry me home."

I heard Ernest's voice join mine in the breeze and felt the warmth of Gram's smile. They were together, watching over me.

The Stoneman's truck banged down the driveway. Ernest Pig looked up from grazing. The Stoneman backed up to the family plot, and I helped him lower the stone with his winch. We both stood back to admire it. The granite stone in the shape of double hearts connected in the middle glistened in the sun. On the back were all the dates of coming and going. The Stoneman took his gray rag and proudly polished the front.

I read the words aloud:

Ernest L. Potts

and his wife

Margarette Adams Potts

Together Forever

The Stoneman shook out his gray cloth and wiped his eyes.

I helped him lift Gramp's stone from the truck's bed and carry it to his resting spot.

We fitted into the ground, and it settled in as though expecting it. "God bless you, Gramp," I said. We cleaned up the remains of the old, crumbled stone and put them in the back of the Stoneman's truck.

"Do you want a job, Henry?" the Stoneman asked. "I'm getting old for this work. You're young and strong, and I sure could use your help."

I thought about being a Stoneman and what it meant. This man of small stature and bulging arms reminded me of Popeye the Sailor Man. Unlike the funeral man, his business wasn't exactly death. The funeral man cleaned and dressed the dead to send them on their way in their best attire. The Stoneman dealt in memories that live on after people die. The Stoneman provided a monument to loved ones; he gave them something to look at when they couldn't gaze upon the faces of their loved ones any longer. He provided a place to go—and remember.

I wanted to be a Stoneman.

"Yes," I said. "It's a noble calling. I thank you for the offer, and I accept."

The Stoneman left me with a solid handshake and a tired smile. I looked around the family plot and thought I felt a vibration come from the ground to my feet. It was like a cat purring. All was well in heaven as it was on earth.

Chapter 55 - Life After Death

The nights were already getting chilly. I was busy preparing for the winter, and I didn't have much time to think about sad things. There was always something that needed attention on the farm. The animals had to be fed and tended. Ernest Pig worked with me. Willie came over to help, and I did the same for him. Mr. Larson was getting on in years and was glad to have an extra set of hands.

"Good people raised you," he said.

He never forgot Ernest saved his son, and he wasn't afraid to say so. We talked a lot about Ernest and Gram. Sometimes it felt like they were sitting at the table with us. Mrs. Larson always had something cooking and was determined to fatten me up. She didn't even mind when I brought Ernest Pig with me. He was slowing down with age; even so, he loved to hang around with Willie's old coon dog, his second coon dog, since dogs don't live as long as pigs. But Ernest Pig didn't seem to know the difference, or at least he didn't let on. He outweighed the dog by a good hundred pounds, but that didn't stop them from rolling around in the mud together.

And then there was Laurel. There was no hiding my feelings for her any longer. Mr. and Mrs. Larson kept a close eye on us but didn't seem to mind when they saw us holding hands on the way home from school—or talking in the dark on their porch after supper.

Willie and Sandra had been inseparable since seventh grade. She looked just like Sandra Dee, the movie star who did have a way of looking that made men want to be around her. Sandra had the same dark eyes and blonde hair. Willie was smitten with her. None of us saw her anymore for her polio leg or metal brace. We saw her as a bright and fun-loving person. Willie saw all that, and when he looked into her eyes, he saw his own Gidget with that come-hither look.

We went on double dates to the movies and stopped at the soda fountain after for shakes. Sandra became the sister Laurel and I never had. Family comes in many forms. It was true what Ernest told Ma, "Happiness is in your heart. You just have to open it up and let love in."

1960

Chapter 56 - Little White Lies

O ne day, on his travels across the country, Shamus found his way back to the farmhouse. Laurel brought over some leftover spaghetti, and we sat down to enjoy it together.

Willie knocked on the screen door and entered with Sandra as he usually did, with his hound dog trailing close behind. However, he stopped in his tracks when he spotted Shamus and started screaming.

"No, man, I'm not ready to die yet!"

We all sat stunned. Spaghetti hung from Shamus's mouth, and Willie's hound let out a yowl.

I realized the only time Willie could have seen Shamus was on his deathbed. I thought of Willie's memory of the red-headed man who brought him back from the dead with the nectar of the gods.

"Shamus, this is Willie Larson, the boy who almost drowned some years ago."

"Ah," Shamus said, sucking in the ends of his spaghetti. "I see. You're thinking I've come to take you to Heaven, are you?"

"I've been good. Can you give me some more time?"

"Willie," I put a hand on his trembling shoulder. "This is Shamus McGuire, and the only place he'd take you is to an Irish pub."

"But—but—" Willie stammered, "—he looks just like the angel that visited me in the hospital."

"Aye," Shamus winked. "That be me, but I'm no angel."

"I think we need to tell you a story, Willie."

I took the Jameson out from under the counter, and Shamus mixed up a batch of hot toddy so Willie could enjoy the mixture out of a cup instead of an eyedropper. Shamus got to mixing and boiling while he told the tale. Willie just kept shaking his head in amazement.

Sandra had never heard the story of Willie's near-death and was rightly entertained. I thought it best to leave out the part about Ernest being naked. Willie gave me a wink, and I knew he was thinking the same thought. When Shamus finished with the hot toddy tale, everyone had a good laugh.

"I can't believe you didn't tell me, Henry!" Willie punched me in the side. "You could never keep a secret, especially from me!"

"Oh, that's not exactly true," Laurel piped in. "He never told you about the time he kissed me behind the church piano when we were ten."

"Ten? Behind the church piano? You dog, you!" Willie said. "Good thing I know I can trust you with my sister and you with my life!" He shook Shamus's hand and thanked him sincerely. Shamus poured five glasses of hot toddy, and we raised them high.

"To family and friends, who are one and the same," I said, and everyone yelled, "Cheers!"

"Here's to little white lies," Laurel said with a shy smile.

"To the nectar of the Irish gods that saved my life," Willie added.

"I'll drink to that," Sandra said.

"And to the luck of the Irish," Shamus concluded.

Laurel coughed a little, and her eyes watered. I wasn't sure if it was the hot toddy or the toast.

1961

Chapter 57 - A Man of Stone

We graduated in May, and the Larsons threw a big party. Mr. Shoemaker was there, Coach, and of course, Pastor Morgan. He never missed a party.

Laurel applied to junior college. She wanted to become a nurse. I knew she would be a good one. Willie wasn't sure what direction he wanted to go, so he stayed on the farm to help his father for the time being. But his mind was on the war brewing in Vietnam.

"I'm more of a warrior than an athlete like you," Willie said.

"We're more the same than we are different." I heard the words come out of my mouth, yet they sounded like Ernest's words even to my ears. "I'm proud to be your friend."

Willie grasped my right hand in his and wrapped his left arm around my shoulder. I was glad it was in friendship because he sure had the strength of a warrior. "My brother in heart," he said, and we both looked away so as not to see each other's watery eyes.

I worked with the Stoneman, and it felt right. He was getting on in years and never had a family. He made a will naming me as the sole beneficiary of his business and all of his worldly possessions. Of course, I was honored, but I told him his wisdom and friendship were what I held dear.

I laid him to rest in my family plot when he passed away. His stone was as simple as he would have liked, and I carved the words with care.

Benjamin J. Mallett 1895-1961

Keeper of Memories and a Man of Stone

≈

I had turned seventeen, then eighteen. If it wasn't for Mrs. Larson making a birthday cake and the whole family singing happy birthday to me, I think I'd have forgotten myself.

That July, I asked Laurel to marry me. I brought her to the family plot. Not the most romantic setting, but it held everything I was made of and everyone I held dear.

I got down on my bended knee, and she smiled like the sunrise. The ring was from a fancy jewelry store in Joliet. I had saved for two years every spare dime I could. It wasn't the best they had, but it sparkled in the sun, and I hoped it would glitter on Laurel's finger. I always knew she was the one. I think I knew it the first time I saw her when I was no more than a tike.

"I love you, Laurel Larson," I said. "I love every hair on your head, every word from your mouth. I love who you are and all you've ever been. I want to spend the rest of my life with you, if you'll have me." I took a breath and closed my eyes.

"Yes."

I opened one eye and looked at her.

"Yes, Henry Adams, I will marry you," she said. "I love every hair on your head and word from your mouth. I love you today and yesterday and always. And I want to be with you for the rest of my days and yours."

I wept in her arms like a fool who had found true love.

≈

In August of 1961, Pastor Morgan married Laurel and me in the old white church with the bell ringing loud and clear.

Ma and Frank flew in from California. They looked older but happy. Sandra was Laurel's maid of honor, and Willie, my best man. I couldn't have found a better one for my wedding or my life. Pa Larson walked Laurel down the worn rug of the aisle that I had many memories of walking in good times and sad. But the sight of Laurel's smile erased any other thoughts. She clutched a bouquet of daisies in petite hands in front of her long, white eyelet dress that hugged her shapely body. Ma Larson cried into her handkerchief—tears of joy, I hoped. My eyes filled with a joy of my own. I was blessed in many ways.

Our first son Ernest, not Pig, was born in the spring of '62. The following year, we welcomed Willy with a y to give him a little distinction from Laurel's dad and brother. It was a lot of Williams, but you can never have too many. We all settled in the farmhouse and gave it new life.

Ma continued to send postcards. Frank retired from the army, but they hadn't found the perfect place yet, so they continued to search. I finally understood the look in Frank's eyes. Ma had found her perfect match. And so had I.

1965

Chapter 58 - Whiskey and War

The next time Shamus stopped, I noticed he didn't have the skip in his walk, and his red hair had flecks of gray. I thought he wasn't that different from Ma and Frank, except they had more than one change of clothes. Although, just like Ma and Frank, we never knew when Shamus would appear. He wasn't much older than them, but he traveled rougher roads, and his lifestyle took its toll. Laurel must have seen it, too.

"Shamus, do you think you'll ever give up your traveling life and settle down?" Laurel asked.

"Aye, lass, I got bit by the traveling bug long ago, don't you see, and I still have the fever."

"You know, Shamus, you always have a home here." I reached out for Laurel's hand, and she nodded her head. "You're family."

"Now, don't you be going all misty-eyed on my account. I appreciate the offer, and maybe, just maybe someday, the time will come ..." He shook his red head, rejecting the thought. "Nay. You be asking the River Shannon to stop its flow. It's against my nature, so it is."

Laurel loved cooking for Shamus, and our boys couldn't get enough of his stories. After supper, Shamus told the children how he jumped a ship from Ireland to America when he was just seventeen years old. Their eyes were big and filled with awe.

"Like a pirate?" young Willy asked.

"Aye, like a wee pirate, but I didn't get any treasure," he said. "The cook found me sleeping among the bags of potatoes. He let me stay if I started peeling." He laughed at the memory. "I must have peeled a thousand pounds of potatoes before landing in New York City."

We all laughed.

"What did you do when you got to New York?" Laurel asked.

"A wee bit of this and a wee bit of that," he said with a smirk. "Until the war. I enlisted, and they gave me citizenship for my service. Even after all I saw, I still think I got the better of that deal." Shamus's green eyes misted. "I'll always be a bloody Irishman, but I'm proud to be an American, too."

"Did you meet Ernest in the war?" I asked since I never knew.

"Ahh, well, that was the luck of the Irish, too, I'll have you know. Ernest and I ended up in the same company, and I wouldn't be sitting here now if it wasn't for him," Shamus said. "He saved my life."

"What happened?" Little Ernest asked.

"Well, I won't go into the details," he looked at Laurel and me, and we knew he didn't want to scare the children with the ravages of war. "Let's just say he found me when I was lost and couldn't find my way." He grinned. "He showed me the way home."

"Pa, is that what he did for you?" Little Ernest asked me.

"He surely did. Ernest had a way of doing that for everyone he met."

"I want to be like that," Little Ernest said, and I knew he would be. He was already kind beyond measure and wise beyond his years.

Shamus told the children a leprechaun story, and they went off to bed with dreams of rainbows and Irish treasures.

"How was it that Ernest saved your life?" I asked Shamus while Laurel settled the children off to sleep.

"Ah, well, we were part of the 96th Division, fighting in Okinawa, when I got separated from my squad." His eyes narrowed and took on a faraway look. "I couldn't find my way in the smoke and gunfire. The enemy was close at hand." A sad smile came to his lips. "I'd have been a goner, but Ernest came through the fog like a raging bull."

"I never saw Ernest angry," I said.

Shamus nodded. "Nor have I since that day." Shamus seemed hesitant to go on. "Ernest saw the Japanese soldier coming up behind me with his bayonet drawn."

"What happened?"

"He got Ernest across the face." Shamus zig zagged his finger across his cheek. "Ernest got off a fatal shot to the enemy's gut." He paused. "They trained them young in Japan back then. We were barely men ourselves—but he was just a boy. Ernest couldn't forget the look on the dead lad's face. That killing sucked the life out of Ernest, too." Shamus sighed. "Until he found the Lord." Tears welled in Shamus's eyes. "Then he found you and your Gram."

We were both wiping tears from our eyes when Laurel returned.

She didn't ask any questions and commenced making the hot toddies under Shamus's close attention.

"Not bad, lass," he said after his first sip. "But next time be a wee bit more generous with the Jamison." He gave her a wink.

We got to telling stories about Ernest until we fell silent, each in our own thoughts. Shamus raised his glass with eyes that glistened and said, "To the man!"

"To Ernest!" we shouted with tears in our eyes and a burning in our hearts more potent than Jameson whiskey.

≈

By 1965, the conflict in Vietnam had become a full-fledged war. I missed the draft, but Willie's number was called. Neither Ernest nor hot toddies could save him this time. Sandra was the love of his life, but they hadn't married yet. They had a quick ceremony before he left, just in case the unspeakable happened. And it did. I thought back to the wizard in *The Wizard of Oz* and how now I'd never see Willie with white hair and a mustache. Willie would always be the wizard of words to me.

I wrapped my arm around Laurel as we stood beside his flag-covered casket and watched the uniformed men precisely fold and present the flag to Ma Larson in exchange for her son's life. It wasn't a fair trade.

Laurel had lost half of herself, the bold half. She seemed to take it upon herself to keep that part of Willie alive. Marriage and motherhood made her confident and candid. Our strengths melded together to make us stronger than ourselves. Laurel worked part-time at the hospital while attending nursing classes. We raised the children as a team, and they were better for it, I hoped. In our actions, not our words, the boys learned we are all unique in our own way and all equal in our pursuits.

Sandra moved in with Ma and Pa Larson. She couldn't spin a tale like Willie, but she did give them a lot of comfort. She was a loving aunt to our children, a devoted sister to us, and much more. If Willie left his boldness to Laurel, he cast his curiosity to Sandra. She attended college and became a lawyer, a public defender, to be exact. She took the cases no one wanted and researched the facts. Innocent until proven guilty were not just words to her. Sandra ensured that people who couldn't afford high-priced lawyers still got high-quality defense.

Sometimes, when I looked at the sky at night, I'd see a shooting star and know it was Willie. He came like a flash of light into the world to light up the lives of everyone he knew. And just like that, he was gone. But his memory never faded.

I hoped he was with loved ones, the way Ernest believed. I imagined them all together, singing and laughing in a safe, warm place, free from human suffering and war.

1968

Chapter 59 - Ernest Lived

I never met the man who fathered me. His name was never spoken, nor was his existence ever acknowledged. But sometimes the seed that gives you life doesn't make you a man.

Wandering among the stones in the family plot on the rise above the farm, I read the names and epitaphs of those departed. I heard them speak to me like ghosts from the past—one in particular called to me. Touching the cold granite, I carefully trace the carved letters with my dry, calloused hands.

I wondered what Ernest would think of the last years since he passed from this life to the next. I hoped he would be proud of me. I strived for that each day.

It felt like the world had moved forward three steps and two steps back in the past ten years. The Civil Rights Movement was bringing positive changes, but slowly. That's how Ernest had said it would go. The '60s brought a new vision for the future with President John F. Kennedy and hope through the peaceful power of Dr. Martin Luther King, Jr. It also took both of them away.

I was relieved Ernest wasn't here to see the killing of Martin Luther King, Jr. "It was a sad day," I said aloud to him. King was like Ernest in so many ways. It was almost like losing part of Ernest all over again.

The Vietnam War would have saddened Ernest, too, and he would have mourned the loss of Willie, whose life he had saved only to have it senselessly taken away. Still, I selfishly wished Ernest was with me now to guide me with his simple words and unconditional love.

I knelt and cleared away the sod grown over the original flat piece of stone that the Stoneman gave me when Ernest died. My fingers traced the large letters I asked the Stoneman to carve. I recalled what Ernest once said. "When your days are done, and you meet the Lord, it matters not what day you were born nor the day you die. All that matters is how you lived."

"You called me son by choice, not by chance, but I never called you Pa," I said, with the stab of regret that only death can render so decisively. "I never thought I had the right." I shook my head. "But there is no excuse." I rested my hand on his stone as he had rested his hand on my head.

The sun was setting in the trees, and the sky flamed as if an artist had painted it with a palette of blues and pinks. A sweeping cloud stretched across the sky like angel wings reaching down to touch the earth, and tears escaped my eyes.

I heard the slamming of the old screen door and listened to the voices of young children, excited with the sheer breath of life. I wiped my tears on my sleeve.

"Pa! Pa!" shouted Ernest, my oldest son, seven years old, leading the way for Willy, my second son, who had just turned five, and little Daisy, born in the winter of '67 and not quite two. Running was still challenging for Daisy. As she tried to keep up with her big brothers, she stumbled. It warmed my heart to see

Ernest go back to help her. Ernest had brown eyes that held a knowing beyond his age. I could see the spirit of his namesake when he looked at me.

When they reached me, I swung Daisy into my arms. Willy threw his arms around my legs and hugged them tightly. "I missed you, Pa," he said as though he hadn't seen me in years. Willy was the dramatic one, like his uncle.

"Willy," I said and ruffled his blonde hair. He was fair like Laurel and Ma. "I just saw you at breakfast. I only went next door to Gram and Gramp Larson's to help them with the chicken coop."

"I know, Pa," Young Willy said with eager eyes. "I just didn't know if you were coming back."

"Son," I said and knelt down, wrapping my free arm around him while Ernest gathered close to Daisy and me. "You never have to worry about me leaving. There is nowhere else I want to be other than right here on this farm with my family."

Ten years had passed since Ernest had left. Sometimes it seemed like yesterday that I was working beside him, listening to his quiet voice that spoke volumes to my heart. Other times it felt like he'd been gone a lifetime. Some people come and go, like leaves in the wind on a fall day. Other people come into your life like the seven a.m. train, right on time when you need them the most. Ernest was that to me. He didn't stay long, well, not long enough for my liking, but he left me with something more important than the measure of time. His common words of wisdom helped me to grow into a good man. I'd spend the rest of my days trying to make him proud.

Laurel came up beside us and looked lovingly at the heart-shaped stone. I smiled the smile of a blessed man to see her. Ernest Pig rooted slowly around the cemetery. Little Ernest and young Willy stood by my side and noticed the flat piece of granite at my feet.

"What's it say on this stone?" Young Willy asked.

"Ernest Lived Well," Ernest slowly read the words I had asked the Stoneman to carve all those years ago.

"He surely did," I said. The words stuck in my throat a little before they let go.

"Lived Well ..." Young Willy paused in thought. "That must be *real* important, Pa, cause the letters are *so* big."

"Yes, it is, son. It's the most important thing a man can do."

THE END

A Word from the Author

I hope you enjoyed *I Never Called Him Pa*. For me, it was a labor of love that started over five years ago as a short story. The character of Henry came to me with a story to tell. I listened.

The story called for a small town setting, but it had to be near a large train hub to accommodate the history of steam engines. Northern Illinois fit the bill. Steam engines ran in that area well after being discontinued in other states.

Kari Pohar, who grew up in the area, gave me the idea of using the name of her hometown of Mendota. The original meaning of the name, crossing paths, was given by the natives of the area and fit perfectly with my theme. The name Mendota and some waterways I used are real, but all other references to businesses, buildings, or people are fictional.

When I finished the short story "Ernest Lived," it sat for a while until I finally submitted it to the Red Penguin historical fiction contest. It won first place and was awarded the anthology title.

But Henry was not finished. He had more to tell me. At one point, I wondered if I deserved to tell the important story of a black man named Ernest.

When I voiced my doubts to author Jody Crotty, she asked me, "Who are you in the story?" Without thought, I replied, "I'm Henry." She said, "Then write Henry's story." And I did.

I had no idea where the story was going. I merely followed Henry's lead. I believe good books are like that. They're not forced or engineered. They come from the heart to the mind and then to print. I hope you think so too.

I'm honored to tell this story. I hope it touches you as it has me. My wish is that we can all be a little more like Ernest.

~Diane Kane

ACKNOWLEDGMENTS

Although writers write alone, it takes a village to bring a book to publication. My village is large and filled with love and support. This novel is a lifetime dream come true for me.

Words of encouragement over fifty years ago from my high school creative writing teacher Kathleen Rogers have kept my dream alive.

I owe all my successes to a group of published women authors who took me under their collective wings. Kathy Chencharik, Sharon Harmon, and Phyllis Cochran are my mentors, friends, and Flash in the Can partners. Marsha LaCroix, you shared your secrets and guided me in creating books. Ruth McCarty, Carol Perry, Barbara Foster, Clare Green, Joan Dayton, Barbara Vosburgh, and Annette Ermini, thank you for your guidance. I'm forever grateful to Clare Kirkwood for bringing me into the fold and always making me feel like a real author. I'd be lost without all of you.

To my coconspirators at Quabbin Quills, Steve Piscitello, Garrett Zecker, and James Thibeault, I appreciate your friendship. We've accomplished amazing things together.

Every manuscript needs good Beta Readers. I had some of the best for this book. Thank you, Catherine Reed, for guidance with the details of Ernest, Kari Pohar for suggesting using her hometown of Mendota as a name for my fictional setting, Farron Dozier for sharing his knowledge of sickle cell disease, Jim Whitaker for everything farming, including the Farmall tractor.

Lynda Francoeur, thanks for having my back in bad times and good. Pete Bulloch helped me see Ernest in a new light and inspired the missing s's. Linda Bulloch, your insight was invaluable. Ursula Wong, I appreciate your professional guidance and opinion. Sue Moreines, you are a force of nature and an excellent fact-checker.

Diane Anderson, thank you for all the great feedback and for reading the entire manuscript on your phone. Kay Deans, you've helped and supported me since the first draft of the short story. Michael Young, thank you for your caring input, and Joe Lorian and Julie Hockman for your neighborly support. Jerry Caron, Vicki McCarroll, and LuAnn Thibodeau, my sincere thanks. Each one of you had a positive impact on this book.

Every author needs a great library. I have two. Athol Library with Director Jean Shaughnessy and Asst. Director Robin Shtulman, thank you for always supporting and encouraging local authors. Phinehas S. Newton Library of Royalston, MA, is a small library with a big heart guided by Director Katherine Morris.

I'm so fortunate to have the support of family and friends. Tom, my husband for over forty years, never complains about my writing obsession and gives me good advice. My daughters, Shannon and Danielle, Mark, and my grandchildren, Casey and Finn, listen attentively to all my excessive author talk. My mother-in-law Tilly told me I was an author before I was published, and my sisters-in-law who always believed in me.

My cousin Marie Drake thanks for encouraging my writing since we were kids. Thanks to my cousin Marlene and her family, who have a collection of all my books. I'm grateful to Anna Flis, my friend forever, and one of my biggest fans, Cindy Chapalonis, for years of treasured friendship; Lisa Dussault, for loving my stories before I knew what I was doing. Kelly, Marg, Abby, and all my friends at the Athol Post Office who make me feel like a rock star.

Every writer needs good editors. I'm lucky to call many my friends. Diane Hinckley, you are the best of the best. Catherine Leibowitz, thank you for your insight and enlightenment. Michael Harrison, you are an excellent newspaper editor and one of my favorite bosses. Richard Bruno, I'm fortunate for your meticulous proofreading. Marcia Gagliardi, thanks for your patience and direction in writing for Uniquely Quabbin Magazine. Each one of you made me a better writer.

This book may never have been written if it were not for my elderly dog, Milo, who needed my attention at 4 a.m. each morning. He inspired me to stay awake and write.

It was no less than fate that I found Photographer Corey Cain and the picture he captured that embodies this book to perfection. Cindy Rieth, my cover designer, has the patience of a saint with my obsessiveness. You rocked some of my other fantastic book covers, and you went above and beyond with this one.

To all the amazing people I've met on my journey and everyone who has ever read my stories and smiled, *Thank You* from the bottom of my heart. If I've forgotten to mention anyone, your name is written in my heart and will come to my mind as soon as I publish.

Many thanks to you, the readers,
for your love and support of
I Never Called Him Pa.
Please ask for it
at your local library
or bookstore.

Reviews on
Amazon or Goodreads
are greatly appreciated.

Follow me on
FACEBOOK
@INeverCalledHimPa
@Page of Possibilities
and
INSTAGRAM
@WriteofPossibilities.com
Check out my website:
http://WriteofPossibilities.com

Contact me to schedule library or book club events.

Other Books by Diane Kane:
Children's Books:
Don Gateau the Three-Legged Cat of Seborga
Brayden the Brave Goes to the Hospital
Coming soon:
Don Gateau Moves to Vallebona
Short Story Collections:
Flash in the Can Number One
Flash in the Can Number Two

ABOUT THE AUTHOR

Author Diane Kane measures her success by the friends she's made along the way.

Kane is one of the founding members of Quabbin Quill's non-profit writers' group. Q.Q. has published six anthologies to date that include works by aspiring writers and offers scholarships to writing students. Kane also teaches writing workshops and facilitates writing groups.

Her short stories appear in several Red Penguin Publications, including her award-winning short story historical fiction piece, "Ernest Lived," which was the basis for *I Never Called Him Pa*. In addition, she has multiple stories published in *Monadnock Underground* and numerous other print anthologies and online magazines.

She is the publisher and co-author of *Flash in the Can Number One and Number Two*, short stories to read wherever you go. In addition, Kane writes public interest articles for *Uniquely Quabbin* magazine and local newspapers and professional reviews for Readers' Favorite.

Kane's first children's book, *Don Gateau the Three-Legged Cat of Seborga*, published in English, Spanish, French, and Italian, won the Purple Dragonfly Awards for Best Illustrations and Caring/Making a Difference in 2020. The sequel, *Don Gateau Moves to Vallebona*, is set for release in 2023.

Her second children's book, *Brayden the Brave Goes to the Hospital*, published in April 2021, won the Purple Dragonfly awards for Best Illustrations and Health Topics. It is featured at Boston Children's Hospital and is helping children and families in children's hospitals across the country.

She lives in a small rural town in Western Massachusetts and spends her summers on the rocky shores of Maine chasing her dreams of writing. *I Never Called Him Pa* is Kane's first novel, but hopefully not her last. She sits patiently by her keyboard, awaiting new characters to talk to her.

Made in the USA
Middletown, DE
14 March 2023